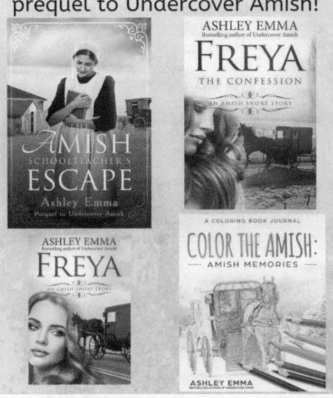

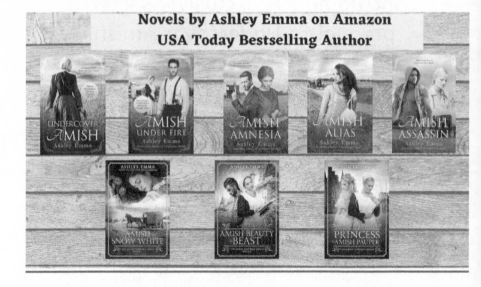

Novels by Ashley Emma on Amazon
USA Today Bestselling Author

Special thanks to:

Julie

Tonya

Kit

Gail

Tandy

Zarine

Lynn

Sara

Sami

Aurelie

There were so many readers from my email list who gave me helpful feedback on this book, so I couldn't list you all here. Thank you so much!

The characters and events in this book are the creation of the author, and any resemblance to actual persons or events are purely coincidental.

AMISH BEAUTY AND THE BEAST

Amish Beauty and the Beast

Ashley Emma

Table of Contents

Chapter One

"Belle? Where are you?" Aunt Greta called outside the barn.

Belle reluctantly closed the pages of her sci-fi novel and propped herself up on the hay. "In here." It was a cold, snowy morning in Unity, Maine, but that didn't stop Belle from curling up on a pile of hay to read a novel by her favorite author as she took a break from her chores.

Aunt Greta entered the barn, then scowled when she saw the book Belle was reading. "What is that?"

"It's the latest book in the sci-fi series I love," Belle said. "It's about time travel and secret identities and—"

"Books like that will just fill your head with nonsense." Her aunt shook her head and put her hands on her hips. "They'll distract you from your work, and some of them have inappropriate content that will corrupt your mind. It's better to avoid them completely, so you aren't tempted. You should be focusing on other things, like being baptized into the church. Have you decided yet?"

Taken aback, Belle frowned. "No, not yet. It's such a big decision. Once I'm baptized into the church, if I leave the Amish, I would be shunned, so I really want to make sure before I commit. And about my reading, in my old community in Ohio, no one ever minded that I read so many different kinds of fiction."

"Well, as you know, each Amish community has different rules."

"Is it against the rules here to read fiction?" Belle countered.

"Well..." Aunt Greta hesitated. "No. Not exactly. But it might be frowned upon, and I certainly don't approve. I'm sure your uncle won't, either. I think you should only read Bible study guides, devotionals, or books of that sort."

"My friends here read all kinds of novels. Ella Ruth, Damaris, and Adriana read clean Christian romance novels, mysteries, and other

1

types of fiction as long as they are clean and have no swearing, sexual content, violence, or anything like that. I like wholesome, clean reads, anyway. I don't read anything inappropriate. I promise."

"They don't live with me, so I don't have any say in what they read. I don't know what your parents allowed you to read while they were alive, but while you're living in my house, I expect you to follow my rules. If I see you reading them again, I might have to confiscate them. Now go do your chores and help me with breakfast." With a stomp of her foot, Aunt Greta pivoted and walked out of the barn.

Belle's heart sank to her toes as she let the book slip from her fingers and onto the hay.

There was no way she could give up reading. It was her one escape from her life, her one way to shut out the memories that haunted her, even in her dreams.

Could she keep it a secret? It would be wrong, but without her books, she knew she'd slip into a dark void.

Lifting herself from the pile of hay she'd been sitting on, she mucked out Phillip's stall and gave him fresh water and hay. After she finished, Belle hurried to the house to help her aunt with breakfast.

When she heard the voices of her aunt and uncle in the house, she paused at the door.

"I found her in the barn reading some time travel novel," Belle heard her aunt tell Uncle Josiah in the kitchen.

"Belle has good judgment," Uncle Josiah said. "I don't think she'd read anything immoral."

"Still, I don't want her filling her head with such nonsense. She should be reading only books that are biblical."

"If you think that is best," Uncle Josiah said. "She has been through so much, maybe reading fictional stories is her way of coping."

"Perhaps. I wonder what my sister let her read when she was alive. I guess we never really talked about it. Anyway, she's too old for such fictional novels. She should be more concerned with joining the Amish church and finding a husband."

"She just moved here a few months ago, Greta. Don't be in such a rush to make her join the church and then marry her off."

"She's twenty-six years old. That's far beyond old enough to get married and be baptized into the church. All our children are married and moved out, and I thought we'd finally have some time to ourselves." Aunt Greta let out a sigh, then regret tinged her voice. "It's horrible of me to say that. I miss my poor sister dearly. I miss all of them. Poor Belle. I can't even imagine what she's going through, being the only survivor."

"As I said, maybe her novels help her get her mind off of missing her parents and siblings. Yes, I know you were looking forward to us being empty-nesters, but we promised Belle's parents that if anything ever happened to them, we'd take care of their children," Uncle Josiah reminded Aunt Greta. "She's no burden. It's a joy to have her here, and she's such a help to you."

"Yes, of course. You're absolutely right. I just never imagined that all of them would be killed, leaving behind Belle as the lone survivor. The poor thing."

Belle shuddered, willing herself to not run back into the barn and hide under the pile of hay, burying her nose in her book.

They say I'm not, but maybe I really am a burden to them, Belle thought. *And they pity me, which is worst of all.*

As the firstborn in her family, she'd always had the responsibility of helping her mother care for her younger siblings. It was a duty she had loved and respected…until it had ended. Belle's heart ached. What she wouldn't give to change one more cloth diaper, to help her younger siblings with one more homework assignment, or to help her mother make soup one last time.

3

What is my life worth now? I'm useless. Maybe I should have been murdered along with the rest of them.

Her heart twisted as a tear trailed down her cheek. She knew she should walk in before she started sniffling, and then they'd know she'd been eavesdropping. Forcing herself to open the door, she wiped her eyes and pasted on a fake smile.

"Sorry I'm late. What are we making for breakfast?" she asked.

Belle helped Aunt Greta make scrambled eggs, sausage, and toast with freshly squeezed orange juice.

"I'm sorry if I was too harsh in the barn," Aunt Greta said as she grilled toast in a pan on the woodstove. "I just think it's not appropriate for Amish women to read fiction. It's my personal opinion. I'm very traditional, as you might have noticed." She gave a small chuckle. "I shouldn't have reacted like that."

"I understand. It's all right. You're just looking out for me."

"Well, I won't take your books away, but I would appreciate it if you didn't read them. Maybe that's too much to ask. Does it help you? You know, with the grief?"

"Well, yes, it does. When I'm reading, I get lost in the story, and I feel like I'm one of the characters. For a little while, it helps me forget about what happened," Belle explained, flipping local sausage in a crackling pan on the woodstove next to her aunt.

"I never read fiction much, so it's hard for me to understand."

"Oh, I can't even imagine. It's my favorite thing to do," Belle gushed.

"Well, I don't want to take it away from you, if it helps you that much, but I do ask that you read only material that is moral. No swearing or sexual content or violence."

"Of course. I only read clean books, as I mentioned."

"Well, then. I think that will be all right."

4

"Thank you," Belle said, but guilt marred her words as she remembered what her aunt had said about Belle being a burden to them. Maybe if she helped Aunt Greta enough around the house and the farm, they'd realize how much of an asset she was. She'd do her best to earn her keep.

Most of all, maybe they'd stop pitying her so much.

Belle went about the kitchen as she placed the food onto serving dishes. Aunt Greta set the table, then Belle, Aunt Greta, and Uncle Josiah sat down, ready for the first meal of the day.

"Let us pray," Uncle Josiah said. He bent his head to reveal his receding hairline. His long beard bobbed as they prayed silently.

Once they had prayed, they began to talk and pass around dishes of food as they munched on their breakfast. Belle ate quietly, mentally reviewing her routine for the day.

After breakfast, Belle had a moment to herself. Because she had recently moved here after the tragedy, she hadn't yet found a job, but she hoped to find one soon. Maybe it would help take her mind off the memories.

She went to her room and pulled a cardboard box from under her bed. Resting it on her bed, she stared fondly at it.

Belle had begun reading when she was four years old. At least that was what her mother had told her.

Thoughts of her mother brought up bittersweet memories. Belle remembered the beautiful and caring blonde woman who always had a smile and had been filled with concern for everyone who came her way. How she missed her mother!

A shudder ran through her body as she tried to push away the horrible memories. She opened the cardboard box and stared at several books in piles. This was her solace—a world away from the turmoil she really felt. Belle had read countless books of different genres. She loved adventure stories and clean Christian romances. Her favorite genres, however, were sci-fi and fantasy—her new interest and one she believed would never fade. She loved how captivating it was, from the first page to the last, leaving one wanting more.

Hallowed Ground was the book she was currently reading. It was by her favorite author, Tony Graham. She thought she'd read captivating works in the past, but Tony Graham's works blew her mind. She wanted to have just five minutes with him, during which she would find out where he got his ideas for the stories he wrote. They were incredible. It was no surprise that all his works were bestsellers and had won many awards, even if the man refused to make an appearance so that he could receive any of them in person.

"Belle? Someone is here to see you!" Aunt Greta called up the stairs.

Who could that be? Maybe one of her friends, probably Damaris or Ella Ruth. She got up and hurried down the stairs, but her stomach sank when she saw Gilbert Schwartz standing in the entryway.

Her aunt gave her a knowing smile and left the room.

At twenty-six, Gilbert was well-built with sandy brown hair and freckles scattered all over his face. Belle had spoken with him many times at social gatherings. In her opinion, he was rather boring but very persistent in getting to know her.

It was no secret in the community that he was already smitten with her.

"Hello, Belle. I'm on my way to the wood shop for work and I was wondering…Would you like to go to the Singing with me tonight? It's at the Holts' house. It would be really fun, and you'd get the chance to get to know more people."

"Oh, I don't know, Gilbert," she began, trying to think of a valid excuse. "My aunt may need my help with chores."

"No, I don't!" Aunt Greta called from the kitchen. "I don't need your help tonight, Belle."

Belle tried not to roll her eyes at her aunt's meddling.

"Come on. You'll have a good time, I promise. Did you like going to Singings in Ohio?" Gilbert asked with hopeful eyes.

"Well, yes—"

"Then come with me. Please?"

She couldn't think of a good reason not to go. Besides, she'd see her friends there. "Oh, all right then."

"I'll pick you up in my buggy just before six," Gilbert said with what he must have thought was a charming smile. "Really, it'll be fun."

She raised her eyebrows. "Sure. See you then."

***

That night, after the Singing ended, she walked out of the Holts' house with her two best friends, Ella Ruth and Damaris. They'd eaten popcorn and sung several hymns. Belle had enjoyed the night. Because of the singing, she hadn't had much of a chance to talk to Gilbert, but she knew she would when he brought her home in his buggy.

"I can't believe you're here with Gilbert Schwartz," Ella Ruth gushed. "You know every single woman in the community is after him, right?"

"*Ja,* I bet they're all so jealous of you. Why wouldn't they be?" Damaris gazed at Gilbert, who was laughing with a group of his friends. "He's so handsome and kind."

"And kind of boring." Belle laughed out loud.

Damaris scrunched up her nose, looking offended. "He is not. He's sweet, though a bit awkward sometimes, but that's only because he gets nervous."

"I'm sorry," Belle said when she realized she'd insulted Damaris, who had been friends with Gilbert since they were children. "I've gotten to talk to him enough that I know we don't have much in common. All he talks about is fishing and carpentry, and on the way here, he was so quiet."

"He's probably just nervous, as Damaris said, being out with such a beauty," Ella Ruth said with a wry smile, playfully swatting at Belle's arm.

"Oh, stop it." Belle swatted Ella Ruth back, laughing.

"So, you aren't interested in him, then?" Damaris asked, twirling a stray piece of hair that had escaped her *kapp*.

Belle kept her voice low. "No, I'm not. I see him only as a friend."

"Well, I've heard rumors that he thinks you're the one. So, you better make that clear to him before you string him along and break his heart," Damaris whispered.

Gilbert was now staring at Belle with a lopsided grin.

Ella Ruth chuckled. "I think it's too late for that."

A group of the younger teenagers was huddled together beside them, talking loudly enough to overhear.

"I've heard he's disfigured, with burn scars all over him," one of the boys said, motioning with his hands. "And he never leaves his mansion."

"Have you ever seen the manor? It's huge!" said one of the other boys.

"I've heard he only comes out at night," one of the girls added.

"And what else? That he eats children for dinner?" A boy laughed. "Come on. Really?"

"Well, he really never does leave his house. He's probably afraid of people seeing him."

"What happened to him? Was he in a fire?" one of the teenage girls asked.

"I heard he's a spy, and he was in an explosion."

"I dare you to ring his doorbell."

"No way!" shrieked one of the girls.

"What are they talking about?" Belle asked Ella Ruth and Damaris.

"There's a man who lives all alone in the manor on the hill," Ella Ruth said, a mischievous look on her face.

"Oh, yes. I can see it through my window. It's on a hill down the street, through the woods," Belle said. "And I've seen his light on late at night."

"Maybe he's nocturnal," Ella Ruth added.

"Nocturnal? Don't be ridiculous." Damaris waved her hand. "He probably just works late."

"Well, it is true that he never leaves his home. He is wealthy and has a housekeeper run all his errands and do everything for him. He doesn't even go to the grocery store."

"Sometimes kids will ring his doorbell on a dare," Ella Ruth added. "Hardly any of them actually get close enough to do it. Most of them are too afraid."

Gilbert walked over to them, smiling at Belle. "Ready to go, Belle?"

"Sure," Belle said, then turned to her friends. "I'll see you both later."

Ella Ruth and Damaris grinned, waving.

Gilbert helped Belle into his buggy, letting his hand hold hers for a moment longer than necessary. She couldn't help but pull away from his grasp.

He got in the driver's seat and clicked his tongue to get the horse moving.

"So, what did you think? Did you have fun?" he asked.

"Yes, it was fun."

"What were you and your friends talking about?"

"We heard the younger teens talking about the man who lives in the manor on the hill. Do you know anything about him? Sometimes I see his light on from my window late at night. Is it true he never goes outside?" she asked.

"I think so. That's what I've heard. You should probably stay away from there. He doesn't like visitors," Gilbert said. "He's not a nice man."

"I'll remember that," she said.

They talked about their favorite hymns that had been sung, and then the conversation lulled. The awkwardness was thick in the air, like the clay-like mud that the horse plodded through.

"What are your hopes for the future, Belle?"

She glanced at him, stunned by his surprisingly deep question. "Well, I'd like to get married and have a family, of course, but I'd also like to work."

"Work? Where?"

"There's an anti-sex slavery organization that I follow. I get updates in letters from them monthly. They rescue children from slavery all over the world, even here in Maine. I'd like to somehow work for them, even if I do it for free," she said, unable to hide the passion in her voice. Just talking about it fired her up. "Did you know that so many people aren't aware that sex slavery is happening right here in the United States, even in Maine?"

"Well, yes. We know about it well because of the girls who were abducted by traffickers here in the community. Two of them were Ella Ruth's sisters, as I'm sure you know," Gilbert said. "It was a scary time. Perhaps that line of work is too..." He paused. "I worry that type of work might be too hard on you."

Ella Ruth had indeed told Belle about how her sisters had been abducted by traffickers. Ella Ruth had actually played a huge role in their rescue by going on fake dates with a man who worked for the traffickers. This helped the police locate where the girls were being kept. Ella Ruth and her sisters had inspired Belle's desire to work for the organization. "I know it might be intense, but I want to help," Belle persisted.

"Don't you think you'll be too busy raising children and running a household to work?" he asked, giving her a sidelong glance.

She couldn't help but scoot a few inches farther away from him. "I can do both. I want to do both. There's no rule against Amish women here having a job after they get married. Why, even Aunt Greta was a schoolteacher for a few years after she got married and had children."

"Then it became too much for her, so she quit, handing the job over to a younger, single woman."

"True. But that doesn't mean I'll do that."

"When I marry, I'd want my wife to be concerned only with raising our children and running our house, not to be spending time working somewhere else," he told her.

Belle scrunched up her nose. "What if your wife wants to make extra money outside the home? Even the Millers have a bakery, and Mrs. Miller and her daughters sell their baked goods at the market. I heard that even Damaris and her mother are thinking of working for them, baking goods to sell."

Gilbert said nothing. He just stared at the road ahead.

Yes, Mrs. Miller's daughters were teenagers and Damaris' father had passed away, so they needed the income, but still.

Belle crossed her arms, annoyance welling up in her like a flame. "Even the Proverbs 31 woman worked outside the home, selling her goods in the market, trading, and buying land."

Gilbert flicked the reins, his eyebrows knit together. The silence weighed heavily upon them.

We clearly have nothing in common.

As they approached her uncle's house, Belle stepped down from the buggy before Gilbert could get around to her side. Disappointment lined his face.

"Well, I had a good time, Belle. Did you?"

"Yes, I did. Thank you for taking me," she said, trying to hide her irritation, but she knew she was failing.

"I hope I didn't offend you."

"You didn't. We can just agree to disagree."

"Right. Well, goodnight." He took her hand and kissed it in the moonlight. What was meant to be a secret yet romantic gesture just aggravated Belle, making her pull away.

"Goodnight," she said, rushing into the house, leaving Gilbert standing in the driveway. She quietly went inside, where Aunt Greta was knitting by the light of a battery-operated lantern.

"Did you have a nice time with Gilbert?"

Ugh. "Well enough. We don't have much in common, so we don't have much to talk about." She took off her jacket, scarf, and boots.

"Give him a chance. You just met him. Maybe a few more dates and you'll change your mind."

"I don't think I'll be going on another date with him."

Aunt Greta set down her knitting. "Why not?"

"I'm not interested in him. I see him only as a friend. I don't have feelings for him, and as I said, we don't have much in common."

"That could change, Belle."

"I don't think so." She shook her head vehemently.

"Well, have you given more thought to being baptized into the church?" Aunt Greta asked.

Belle heaved a sigh. This was the last thing she wanted to talk about right now, let alone think about. "Yes, but I haven't decided yet. Well, I'm really tired. I'm going to bed." Belle trudged up the stairs.

Why was her aunt pushing her so much to join the church? Yes, Belle knew she was well beyond the average age most youths joined, but in her heart, she was afraid to make such a huge commitment.

Her new home was nice, but she missed her old Amish community in Ohio. She missed her old friends. She missed her family, but she had faith in God that everything would work out for good. This was what she prayed for every night.

Lying comfortably in bed, she opened her new book. Usually, books by this author enraptured her, making her stay up well past midnight. She had to find out what happened next. However, this one was different from the others.

Using her battery-powered bedside light, she finished the last pages of the book she'd been reading, *Hallowed Ground*. She should have felt satisfied, yet she wasn't. While the other books in the series had been complex, page-turning, and full of adventure, this book had been a disappointment. She'd struggled to finish it, but had been determined to do so, as she'd read all the other books in the series.

Had the author run out of good ideas?

Maybe the next book would be better. Was it in the local bookshop yet? Maybe she'd go tomorrow.

Belle looked out her window toward the hill with the manor that the teens had talked about.

Now the manor was shrouded in darkness, showing no signs of life.

Suddenly, she saw a light flicker in one of the windows. Her eyes widened. As quickly as it appeared, it disappeared, the hill once again dark.

A draft of cold hit her and she shuddered, her heart racing with sudden fear. She quickly closed the window and pulled down the curtain, shutting out her thoughts of the reclusive and strange man who lived up the hill.

***

"I have to quit. I'm so sorry."

Cole set down his fork and looked up at his housekeeper of three years, stunned, completely forgetting about his omelet. He and his grandmother, Claire, sat at a long table in the ornate dining room filled with fine art, complete with a chandelier above them.

"Abigail, why?" Cole demanded.

"I'm sorry, Cole. Claire, I apologize to you most of all. You've become like family to me, and I've enjoyed our time together as your companion," Abigail said.

"Me too," Claire said. "This is a shock. We thought you liked working here."

"I do," Abigail said. "My mother fell and broke her hip, and I need to move back home to be with her and take care of her. Her health has been deteriorating lately, and recently it's gotten much worse. I'll miss you both, but I'm not sure how much time she has left, and I need to be with her. Family is the most important thing."

"Absolutely. I'm so sorry to hear about your mother, Abigail. We'll miss having you here," Claire said.

"You've been good to me. But to be honest, working here has been making me depressed," Abigail explained. "Cole, you're a young man who should be out in the world, meeting people and doing the things you used to do, exploring nature and rock climbing. Instead, you never leave this manor."

14

"You know why I can't go out," Cole said, gesturing to his face. "People would take one look at me and reject me. They don't call me 'the monster on the hill' for nothing."

"I think you're wrong," Abigail said. "I think most people would be kind, and you might meet some people who treat you differently. It would be a small price to pay for you to have the life you used to live."

"I've been trying to tell him that," Claire said, shaking her head. "He's too afraid."

"I am not afraid," Cole retorted, then stared down at his plate, knowing it was a lie.

"Either way, I need to go back home and take care of my mother. It all happened so suddenly," Abigail said. "So, this is my last day. I'm sorry I can't give you a week or two notice."

Cole set down his fork with a thud. Where on earth would he find a new housekeeper and companion for his grandmother? How could he find someone who wouldn't run away at the sight of him? The interview process would be a nightmare.

He stood and backed away from the table. "I've lost my appetite. I'm going to get some work done." Cole walked up to his office and shut the door, then sat at his desk and ran his hands through his hair.

What was he going to do now? Who would be a companion to his grandmother?

***

Humming happily, Belle led her uncle's horse, Phillip, out of the barn to hitch up to the family buggy. She was off to the bookstore in town and could hardly contain her excitement, hoping the next book in the series would be just as good as the other ones before *Hallowed Ground*.

"Belle?"

Consumed with her thoughts of what might happen next in the *Hallowed* series, Belle hadn't noticed Gilbert walking down the lane until he wasn't far behind her.

She groaned inwardly, resisting the urge to turn around and walk away.

How would she tell him that, after the Singing, she didn't want to go on any more dates with him?

"Where are you off to?" Gilbert asked as he approached.

"Just running some errands in town," she said, busying herself with hitching up the horse to the buggy.

"You mean…going to the bookstore?"

Belle whirled around. "How did you know that?"

"Come on." Gilbert laughed. "You think it's a big secret? I know you read a lot. In a tree, in the barn, by the pond…"

Belle felt her face heat and her temper flare. "Have you been watching me?"

Gilbert laughed. "No, of course not. Damaris told me. You're not the only one. It's okay, you know. It's not forbidden here. Many people here like to read books besides the Bible."

"I know that," Belle said, keeping her voice low. "My aunt doesn't like it. She says it fills the mind with nonsense. Although, she's not forbidding it."

Gilbert chuckled, and Belle couldn't tell if he agreed or disagreed.

"Do you read?" she asked.

"Me? No. I don't like reading. Never have." Gilbert shrugged, looking at the sky.

"Really? Why not? It's my favorite thing to do. There's a whole new world inside each and every book, just waiting to be discovered."

Gilbert laughed again. "Maybe your aunt is right. That sounds like a bunch of nonsense to me."

"Excuse me?" Belle asked and crossed her arms, not bothering to hide her offense.

"I'm sorry," Gilbert said, waving his hands. "I'm kidding. I just don't find reading interesting, that's all."

That confirmed it. She and Gilbert had nothing in common, besides the fact that they both lived here in Unity and were Amish.

"Well, I better get going," Belle said, climbing into the buggy and keeping her eyes ahead. "See you around."

"Belle, I'm sorry. I didn't mean to offend you…again," Gilbert said, coming to the side of the buggy.

"You didn't," Belle said. He'd just made it even more obvious that they shared no common interests.

Not waiting for a reply, Belle clicked her tongue. Phillip clip-clopped down the lane.

As Belle drove through town, she paid close attention to where she was going. Although she'd arrived in the community a few months ago, it still seemed strange to her. She headed to the market, where she purchased everything on her aunt's list. Then she ventured farther into town toward the bookshop and lost her way.

"Excuse me," Belle addressed two women who were walking by on the sidewalk. She leaned toward them in her seat at the front of the buggy. "Do you know which way the bookshop is?"

"Not far. It's just down there, the next block over." One of the women pointed.

"Thank you." Belle clicked her tongue and Phillip started walking.

The woman turned to her friend and muttered, "I'm surprised she even knows how to read. Did you know they go to school only until eighth grade?"

Belle felt her face grow hot, annoyance bubbling up inside her. Growing up Amish, she had heard many rude comments and had seen the stares from people on the street. While she tried to shrug it off, sometimes she just couldn't help herself. Her mother had always taught her to turn the other cheek, but Belle just couldn't suppress a retort sometimes.

Before she could think twice, Belle told them, "Yes, we go to school only until the eighth grade, but I read over a hundred books a year. Thanks again."

The women's eyes widened as they glanced at each other, but Belle turned her eyes back to the road and drove the buggy away.

O'Malley's Books was a small, quaint bookshop that didn't seem like much from the outside, but inside it was a haven of books from great writers. Belle had discovered the little bookshop a few weeks after her arrival. This was probably her third visit there, and she had to get as many books as she could, as she had no idea when her next trip would be.

The bell rang as she walked into the shop and headed for the counter. Mr. O'Malley, the shopkeeper, flashed her a kind smile. The bald old man weakly stood up as he pushed his glasses from his nose up to his eyes.

"Hello, dear. I haven't seen you in a while," he said.

Belle beamed at him. He remembered her. "Yes, I've been busy."

"How were the last reads you got?" he asked.

Belle's eyes shone with excitement. "They were all good, except the fifth book in the *Hallowed* series, *Hallowed Ground*. It just wasn't as good as the rest, but I'm hoping the next one will be better. Please tell me you have the next book in the series."

"Sadly, I don't have the next book. It probably won't be out for a long time, maybe a year or two at least."

Belle sighed with disappointment. She had been looking forward to spending the night under the covers reading the next book. "Do you have any other similar books?" she asked.

"Hmmm. I do have one of his older works, but it's in the back in the discounted section. It might take a while to find," the old man said regretfully. "It's a mess back there."

"I can find it," Belle persisted. "And if I don't find it, I'm sure I'll find something else just as intriguing."

As the old man opened his mouth to reply, the door opened and a group of school kids walked in. Belle took the opportunity to slip into the back room, which held the discounted book section.

Mr. O'Malley had been right—it was indeed a mess. Bins were overflowing with books. Some of the books were in horrible shape, with their pages ripped out. Belle shuddered at their battered state, wondering where to begin. How long would this take? She took a deep breath and began her search.

About a half-hour later, just as she was about to give up, her eyes caught a name. A wide, satisfied smile spread on her lips as she stared at an early work of Tony Graham. It was certainly worth the search.

She dusted herself off and returned to the front room, where Mr. O'Malley was still attending to the kids, who were now creating quite a ruckus.

"I found it," Belle said, waving the book.

The old man nodded with a smile. Her eyes caught another work of one of her other favorite authors on the shelf, and she grabbed it, along with a few others. Seeing that he was busy with the children, Belle placed them in a bag in front of him. He quickly looked through her books and rang up her order.

"Looks like you still found some good ones in that pile of donated books. I'll have something better for you the next time you come around!" Mr. O'Malley called as she walked out the door.

"Thanks."

She hoped so. Belle climbed into the buggy and began the trip back home, eager to find a nice spot and start reading.

However, minutes later, Belle pulled over to the side of the road. Even if it was just a page, she had to read it, to have an idea of what to expect. Her heart was racing in anticipation of what Tony Graham had in store for her. She went straight for the early publication and started reading.

As she continued turning pages in the book, she saw something else. A white envelope was tucked between the pages. Her eyebrows shot up in surprise.

What was this? Perhaps it was something that Mr. O'Malley had forgotten. She would have to return it to him the next time she went to the store.

Looking at the handwriting on the envelope, she realized it was a letter. Written in pencil, the letter was addressed to a Sergeant Hender—, but the end of the last name had been smudged off. The names and addresses on the envelope were all smudged, and she couldn't make sense of them.

The seal was still intact, so the letter hadn't been opened, but it belonged to someone. Perhaps the person had forgotten it in the book, and one way or another, it had been donated to the bookstore with the letter still inside.

Reading the letter was invading someone's privacy, which wasn't right. The best thing to do was to keep the letter safe and give it to Mr. O'Malley when she next went to the bookstore. Maybe he'd know whose it was if he remembered who had donated the book. But she had no idea when she'd get another chance to go back to the bookstore.

Belle was intrigued by this letter from a stranger that had been found in her favorite author's book.

Maybe the name of the letter's owner would be on the letter itself. Because she couldn't see the names clearly on the outside of the envelope, opening it up could be the only way to find out how to return the letter to its owner.

She struggled internally over the right thing to do. To read or not read the letter? As her curiosity took over, Belle opened the envelope and unfolded the letter, ignoring her guilt.

Dear Son,

I don't even know where to begin. I am so sorry for those hurtful things I said to you. I was so wrong. I also forgive you for everything. I do realize now that selling the logging company was the right choice.

You have the right to choose your career, and now that I've read your first book, I can see that you are remarkably talented, Son. Once I read your book, especially the part about the father and son who have a terrible argument but finally make amends, it all became clear to me.

I can see now you wrote that about us, and now I understand all the things you probably wanted to say but maybe you were afraid of how I'd react. I understand what you wanted to say now because of the story. The story pays tribute to our family history.

I understand you, and I am proud of you for serving your country, following your dream, and being a wonderful son.

I will always love you,

Dad

Tears had filled Belle's eyes by the time she finished reading the letter. Although short, it was emotional. She had no idea what the son had done, but his father's forgiveness showed his love for his son.

It reminded her of how, even after all the sins she'd committed, God continued to love and care for her. She patted her eyes dry, willing herself to not cry more. Reading the letter had thrown her into a private world of this father and son.

Perhaps she shouldn't have read the letter. But the deed had already been done. She shoved it back into the book. Next time she went to the bookstore, she would give it to Mr. O'Malley.

Belle looked around. She had been so consumed in her thoughts that not only had time flown by, ushering in the evening, but she had also lost track of where she was.

She looked around for another buggy, but the road was empty. She had taken this road before…or had she?

Belle urged the horse to walk, determined to find her way home. She soon found herself at a crossroads. She looked left and right, trying to remember which direction she had taken earlier on. Yet, she couldn't remember. Right or left?

"I think it was right," Belle mumbled to herself. "I hope this is the right way."

However, the right path seemed to take her uphill, or was it just her imagination? The earth seemed to rise. There was no doubt that this was not the direction she had taken earlier in the day. She was on the wrong path. Phillip neighed as she tried to grasp the reins to turn him around, but the road was getting narrow, and the day was getting dark, not to mention colder. Just like her, the horse was clearly alien to these parts.

"Shhh. It's okay, Phillip. We can just turn around," Belle said gently, now getting worried. The horse calmed down for a bit, yet it trudged on, refusing to listen to her instructions to turn around. The once-smooth road had given way to gravel. That fact, combined with the steep hill, meant that Phillip's hooves became unsteady. He was not used to such terrain under his hooves.

Belle tried again to get Phillip to turn, but she wasn't familiar with him yet, and maybe she was using the wrong cues. When a car flew by out of nowhere, beeping its horn, the horse suddenly took off running.

Leaves hit Belle's face as she tried to dodge them. She closed her eyes, holding on tightly to the seat of the buggy as Phillip careened into a bush. Her mouth opened into a scream as the ground seemed to give way.

Everything went dark.

Chapter Two

It was dark and quiet, calm and peaceful. All she wanted to do was stay there, gazing at the starry sky, without a worry in the world. Suddenly, a flash of pain coursed through her arm, and Belle jerked up, wincing. Her arm had been cut above her wrist. The cut was bleeding but didn't look very deep.

As she sat up on the seat of the buggy, the realization of what had happened hit her.

How long had it been since the accident? Well, long enough for the sky to be completely covered in darkness and for the horse to be gone, leaving her behind with the empty buggy.

She was on the infamous hill, the hill with the manor—the place no one went near.

Belle groaned as she managed to stand. Her body ached. It didn't feel as if anything was broken. She was not hurt, except for a few scratches and her state of abandonment. Belle grabbed her bag of books, her purse, and the supplies she'd bought.

Looking around, Belle saw trees and shrubs surrounding her. She had to find help as soon as she could. A shudder ran through Belle's body as she thought of spending the night outside without even a blanket.

As she climbed up, she realized that the accident had thrown the buggy into a ditch. There was absolutely no way she was going to get the buggy out of the ditch by herself, though she could look for the horse. By now, she guessed he was long gone, but she had to try.

Shaking her head at how her misdirection had gotten her so lost, Belle tried to navigate through the greenery. She trudged on, looking for any signs of the horse. For about an hour, she searched and called out for Phillip, but she found no sign of him. Even if he was nearby, he was not familiar with her yet, so he might not come when she called.

As Belle returned to the buggy, a cold wind blasted her, and she shivered. She chuckled without mirth as voices of the teens played in her head about the monster who lived on the mountain. What had seemed preposterous the night before didn't seem so funny anymore.

Was she going to meet the beast? Would he eat her? She rolled her eyes at her silliness. Was she really going to believe that the teens' stories were true? She was a grown woman of twenty-six and didn't believe in monsters.

Belle froze when she saw the flicker of a light. Her eyes widened. What was that? Was she so disoriented that her eyes were playing tricks on her?

The light disappeared, and she was relieved. It had been her imagination. However, the light went on again, and this time, it seemed to have spread. She emerged from the trees and realized she was in a clearing, looking up at a house.

Not a house… A manor.

It sprawled across a clearing of land surrounded by acres of forest which she'd seen from afar, its monstrosity casting a shadow even in the moonlight. A few lights were on, and it dawned on her that it was not her imagination. This was real.

The stories of the teens flooded her mind once more. This seemed like the perfect place for a beast to live. If the beast found her, no one would see her again or know what had happened to her.

Again, she chided herself for such outrageous thoughts.

Belle gulped, still consumed with fear. She hadn't believed in the children's tales before, but seeing the house out here, away from any form of life, she felt otherwise.

What if the teens had been right after all?

She turned around, away from the manor, and hissed as pain shot through her arm. She was exhausted and needed some rest. She could not be out here in the night when she had no idea where she was. A wild animal could find her. She could freeze to death. A shudder ran through her, and she knew she had no choice but to go to the manor and ask for help.

Hesitantly, Belle headed toward the manor. Her heart raced as she crossed the lawn. She found herself between two statues. Gulping, Belle began to climb the stairs leading to the front door.

God, be with me, Belle prayed, her fingers tightly interlocked as her heavy feet dragged her forward. She stood in front of a large wooden door and pressed her ear against it. She heard nothing except for silence. Surely, there ought to be some sign of life, but she didn't even hear the sound of a TV.

She knew she could remain there all night if she didn't make a move, so she slowly lifted her hand and knocked on the door with the ornate door knocker.

Belle heard the knock resonate through the night, sending a chill all over her body. She waited with a racing heart for the door to swing open.

There was no response. What did this mean? Was nobody home? This seemed like the perfect recipe for those horror books she had seen in the bookshop but never actually read.

No one knew she was here. Would they ever find her body?

Get a hold of yourself, she thought. *There's no monster here.*

She looked behind her at the forest, where the trees seemed to be waving eerily at her like spindly skeletons dancing in the moonlight.

Which direction was the community in? Disoriented, she'd never find her way home in the dark on foot. Her cut needed cleaning, too. She returned her gaze to the door.

This is totally cliché, she thought. *A weary traveler knocking on the door of a creepy manor.*

But right now, she didn't have a choice.

Belle knocked again, having no idea if she actually wanted someone to answer the door.

***

At the sound of someone knocking on the door, Cole's head shot up. Who on earth could that be? Probably some kids trying to prank him again.

He shrugged dismissively, his attention returning to his task, which was writing the next chapter of his novel.

Cole froze as the sound repeated itself. His ears were on alert, and his eyes widened in disbelief. Whoever it was, they were persistent. The infernal knocking ceased. Then, just as he was about to sigh with relief, it started up again.

Cautiously, Cole walked out of his office and into a hallway with high walls. He had a feeling he knew who was out there.

A few years ago, some of the children had been dared to come see the monster. He'd growled in their faces and they'd scattered, running off to further spread the tale of the beast who lived up in the mountain and who ate children for dinner.

It kept people away…for the most part.

He stood by the closed front door and took a deep breath, anticipating the reaction of the children. First would be the shock, which would then be replaced by fear. He opened the door and turned on the lights. What he saw stunned him. There was just one person.

A woman. A very beautiful woman.

She wore a black coat and a blue dress that reached her ankles, and her dark hair was hidden by a white bonnet-like head covering. Her lips were naturally pink, or maybe it was from the cold. Then he realized how much she was shivering, and that scratches and dirt marred her face and neck. When she lifted her hand, he noticed blood dripping down it, perhaps from a cut on her wrist or arm.

Her dark eyes searched his in desperation.

What had happened to her?

She was clearly from the nearby Amish community. What was an Amish woman doing out there all alone in the middle of the night?

He stepped out of the doorway, allowing the light to illuminate his face, to reveal who he really was. The part of him people dreaded the most—the horrid burn scars that disfigured half of his face and body. He expected her to scream and run into the night. Though her eyes widened, she stood there unafraid, as if he wasn't a beast.

Her lack of fear unnerved him. She hardly even blinked. This wasn't the reaction he had been expecting, and curiosity arose in his heart.

"What happened to you? What are you doing up here?" Cole scowled.

"I just moved here, and I got lost on my way home. My horse and buggy crashed into a ditch and my horse ran off. I don't own a cell phone, so I was wondering if I could use your phone to call our driver so I can get home."

"Your driver? I thought the Amish don't own cars," he said, perplexed.

She shook her head. "No, we don't own cars. We hire people we know to drive us in their cars sometimes, a bit like a taxi. I really need to get home. My relatives must be worried." She gestured to the blood on her hand. "I need to bandage this up, if you don't mind. I have a cut on my arm."

Normally, he would shut the door in the face of anyone who dared trespass on his property. But as she shivered in the cold and looked up at him with her big, dark eyes. With the cut on her arm, his heart softened. He found himself opening the door.

"Fine. Come in then. But just a phone call and a bandage."

As he pushed the door open, the young woman rushed in through the gap. His eyes widened in annoyance as she made her way into the house, then slowly turned around.

28

"Wow, this is amazing. It's so beautiful." She reached out to touch one of his father's sculptures.

He cleared his throat. "Let's make that phone call now." No one new had been in his house in years. Now here was this woman, touching his things like she owned the place?

As if she hadn't heard him, she rested her hand on the staircase railing.

"The phone is over here. Come on, let's go."

The woman turned to him, and he still didn't get the reaction he expected. With all the lights on, his appearance was now even more visible, yet she didn't flinch. One side of his face was the way it had always been and looked normal, while the other half was disfigured by a hideous pattern of jagged, angry scars. He had been a pretty good-looking guy before the explosion, but not anymore.

Almost everyone he had come across, including the doctors who treated him, had a hard time hiding their disgust, shock, or pity.

Except for this unfazed woman.

"What are you looking at?" Cole growled.

"You were leading me to the phone, remember?"

"This way." It wasn't his problem that the woman had gotten involved in an accident, one he had not caused. However, he looked with concealed concern at the woman, hoping she was all right.

She followed him into the living room. He grabbed his cell phone from the coffee table. "Here."

"Thanks." She took the phone and dialed a number.

The sooner she made the call, the sooner she would be gone. He didn't want a search party organized by the Amish community to be out here.

"Hello?" the woman said into the phone. She spoke to the person about what had happened and the fact that her horse was lost. "I'm at the manor on the hill. Do you know how to get here?" Belle put her hand over the phone and said to Cole, "He needs your address for his GPS. He's pretty sure he knows how to get here, but since it's dark out, it would be best if he had your address."

"Fine." Reluctantly, he gave Belle his address so she could tell it to her driver. It wouldn't be long now until someone came to pick her up.

Yet, part of him didn't want her to leave.

What was wrong with him?

The woman hung up his phone and turned to him, yet she still seemed unfazed.

"He'll be here soon. Can I get a glass of water? And that bandage?" the woman asked after a moment of silence, staring right at him with an unflinching gaze.

Cole eyed her. Would her demands never end?

"Where's the kitchen?" she asked.

He jerked a thumb in the direction of the kitchen and she walked off, headed that way. He followed her. What was she doing now?

"Mind if I have a drink of water?" she asked.

He snagged a glass from a cabinet and put it under the faucet, filling it with water. "Here." He handed it to her.

"Thank you."

As she drank it, he glared at her, but she simply ignored him, gulping the water. He guessed she must have been really thirsty because she filled up and drank two more glasses. Then she turned on the water again, lathered her hands with soap, and carefully washed the cut, wincing as she did. Finally, she took a paper towel and dried her hands and arm.

"Go back to the living room while I get my first aid kit, and please, don't touch anything," Cole said with a growl.

"Fine, Mr. Grumpy Pants," she said with a smile, walking past him back to the living room.

Wow. He raised his eyebrows, hiding a smile at her sense of humor. He was…impressed. And slightly amused. He wasn't being the most gracious host, so he knew he deserved worse.

He closed his eyes and took a deep breath. Usually, strangers annoyed him, but this woman had his heart racing. Something about her set him off, but not in a bad way, which made him all the more flustered.

Who was she? And why did he want to know more about her?

Cole heard a sound and realized he needed to return to the living room to keep an eye on the woman.

Chapter Three

Belle had survived the monster so far. She hadn't been eaten—not yet. Well, there was no monster, just a grumpy, scarred man who wanted her out of his house as soon as possible. There was no way she could wait outside in the fierce cold.

She looked around the living room. The house was incredible. It had a Victorian-era feel, complete with sculptures, tapestries, large paintings, and crystal chandeliers.

It was the most beautiful house she had ever been in—even lovelier than houses she'd cleaned in Ohio or seen in magazines she'd secretly flipped through at the bookshop. Who would have known that such a house existed here? If she didn't know that all of this was real, she would think she was in a dream.

Or was she?

The living room alone was bigger than all the bedrooms in her uncle's house combined. Sublime art lined the walls.

She wanted to trace her fingers over the paintings, but she also didn't want to upset her host any more than she already had.

So, this cranky man was the "monster" that the teens had told stories about. But he was no monster, just a man who was probably lonely living out here in this isolated place.

As he returned to the living room, Belle noticed that he was a tall man with a muscular build. His scars led down to his neck and went beyond the cover of his shirt collar. Thankfully, both of his eyes had clearly not been affected, and they looked at her curiously. The scars reached both of his arms and wrists, peeking out from underneath the long sleeves he wore, but he seemed to be able to move around without a problem.

"Have a seat. Let me help you bandage your arm," he said in a soft voice. Belle looked at him, taken aback by his unexpected kind offer, then sat on the couch. She let him take hold of her arm as he worked on it. The cut was just above her wrist, and though it stung, it wasn't deep.

As he focused on her cut, she studied him. The angry burn scars disfigured and marred one half of his face, warping and gnarling the skin in strange patterns. Yet, the other half of his face was still quite handsome. She could understand how terrified the local kids must have been at the sight of him. However, she wasn't filled with disgust at all.

What on earth had happened to him? What had he lived through?

Did she feel pity for him? No. Ever since the death of her family, she had known what pity felt like, and it didn't help her; it only victimized her, making her feel helpless. What she did feel for him was concern about how he was faring. It couldn't be easy for him living here all alone as a recluse, probably haunted by memories.

She knew all about that.

"Thank you. Your place is really big. How do you manage it all?" Belle asked. She refused to believe he did all the cleaning. He probably had help, but with the way he had reacted to her presence, he seemed to not like people.

He glared at her but she returned his look with a smile, refusing to look away or glare back at him. He rolled his eyes and her smile widened.

"I have… Rather, I *had* someone doing the cleaning," he said, settling on the couch beside her. She noticed a twinge of sadness and tiredness in his eyes.

Gently, he took her arm in his hand and began dabbing her cut with a cotton ball and hydrogen peroxide. She winced at the sting but had to admit that his hand was surprisingly warm and gentle.

As her heartbeat quickened, she blinked in confusion, flustered. "What happened to them?" she asked, trying to take her mind off whatever was happening.

"She quit this morning," the man said with a dismissive shrug. "She was a nice older woman. I'll miss having her around."

Belle could tell he was deeply affected, more than he portrayed himself to be. He was probably at a loss as to what to do now that he had no help. "Why did she leave?" Belle asked.

"She had to go home to take care of her mother. Also, she found this place depressing." He reached into his first aid kit for a bandage. "She told me I should get out more, which is just not going to happen."

Belle quirked a brow. Although the house was luxurious, it was also intensely quiet. "You know, a house is only a house, no matter how big or small or how luxurious it is. It's not about the things inside the house or how big it is. It's about the people who live inside."

Simply from looking at it, one could tell that there was no laughter in the house. Though beautiful, it was grim. The house needed light and laughter.

"Yes. Well, now I have to look for another housekeeper." He shook his head in dismay, opening the bandage. "Finding a housekeeper is going to be a difficult task for me, if you know what I mean. Not just anyone will work here. I like my privacy. I don't like meeting with the applicants. Some of them flee at the sight of me, unable to hide their disgust. It'll probably take months before I hire one who sticks around." He gave her an apologetic look. "I'm sorry. I don't know why I'm telling you this."

"It's okay. Well, since it's only you, I'm sure you'll be able to cope without a housekeeper," Belle said. She couldn't imagine him living alone in such a big house. It must have been so lonely.

"I don't live alone," he said. Carefully, he placed the bandage over her cut.

Belle tried to ignore the tender way his hand brushed hers.

"There. Done," he said, leaning back.

"Thank you," she said, taking back her hand. "Who lives here with you? Are you married?" she asked, looking at his ring finger. He wore no ring. Maybe it was because of the burned skin on his hand, or maybe he truly wasn't married.

And maybe she was asking a lot of questions but she was immensely curious about this man and couldn't help herself.

His body shook as he laughed. It was a deep rumble, and it made her feel more at ease. He caught himself laughing, and he stopped.

"No, I'm not married. My grandmother, Claire, lives with me. She's elderly and needs to be looked after. She's upstairs," he said sadly, with concern for his grandmother. "She's pretty sharp and healthy, but she needs a friend besides me. A companion. Someone to do puzzles with, go on walks with, play games with, and talk with. She likes painting, too, and reading and playing chess. Even at her age, she's still active and does what she loves."

His love for his grandmother made Belle's heart softened toward him. That said a lot about him. Suddenly, an idea occurred to her.

She shook her head. There was certainly no way. It probably had to do with her knocking her head during the accident, because she ought not to think this way.

"I…" she began.

The man looked at her, curious as to what she had to say as Belle's mouth quickly closed. Then she suddenly continued.

"I could do it. I could be your housekeeper and companion for your grandmother," Belle blurted out, unable to hold back the words. "I just moved here, and I'd love to have a job. I'm a hard worker and I'll respect your privacy. You won't be sorry."

His eyes widened in surprise and then narrowed in suspicion. Belle knew she had made a big mistake with her offer. She should have kept her mouth closed. Now she had gone and ruined the mood, whatever it had been. She got up quickly, thanking him for his hospitality.

35

Just as she got to the door, she heard him ask, "Can you cook?"

She turned around and nodded. "Yes, I can. Quite well, if I do say so myself, and I clean."

He stood. "Anyone can say that they can cook, but how well can you really cook?"

"Trust me. I'm Amish. You'd lick the plate and ask for another serving," Belle said with pride.

A smile seemed to appear on his lips but quickly vanished as he turned serious. "Do you have any cleaning experience?" he asked.

"Of course, I do. I cleaned houses for work in Ohio."

He cocked his head to the side, giving her a questioning look.

"Where I used to live, I cleaned houses. I have cleaned for a number of homes. I was the oldest of five children, so I cared for my siblings and family."

"Was?" he asked, his face full of concern. "What do you mean?"

She ignored his question, looking away. No, she wouldn't talk about what happened to her family with him.

"I could get you a list of homes I've cleaned, with their contact information. I'm sure they'll have good things to say about me," Belle said. Back at home in Ohio, when she'd first started, she'd followed her mother on her cleaning jobs, then gone on to get her own clients. That was how she'd learned the skill.

He scrunched his face in concentration. Belle would understand if he decided to not employ her. He knew her from nowhere, and he seemed wary of inviting people into his life.

"I'll need your contact details."

"I can give you the number of our community phone. As I said before, I don't have a cell phone."

"You don't even have a phone at home?"

"No, we don't have phones in our homes. Only in businesses or in the phone shanty."

"Should you even be doing this?" he asked. "I mean, will your community understand?"

"Yes, I think so," Belle said. "It's just a job."

"Okay. I want you to understand that I don't like disturbances. I like my privacy and my peace and quiet. I work all day, so I like to be left undisturbed in my office. Understand?" he asked.

Belle nodded. She understood him perfectly. He wanted her out of his sight.

"Most of what you'll be doing is cleaning, cooking, maybe some yard work in the spring, and caring for my grandmother. She's the one who needs you. You'll get the same rate as the former housekeeper," the man said, quoting her hourly wage. "And I'll pay you in cash."

Belle grinned. "Wow, that sounds great. So, am I hired?"

"One more thing. Can you play chess and do puzzles? And paint?"

Belle laughed. "Absolutely, though my painting is quite amateurish, I do admit. But I'll do it and all of those things. I also love to read. I think your grandmother and I will get along great."

He nodded. "Excellent. You're hired. Can you start tomorrow morning at nine?"

"Yes." A wide smile spread on her face at the good news. She hurried over to him and stretched out her hand for him to shake. He glanced at her waiting hand for a few seconds before slipping his hand into hers. His skin felt bumpy and rough in her hand, but she didn't pull away or react. It was a firm and brief handshake, and he quickly pulled away from her.

"I'm Belle. What's your name?" Belle asked excitedly.

"Cole," the man answered.

Just as she was about to say more, the doorbell rang. They both froze, staring at each other. Then, Belle walked to the door, knowing it had to be the driver to take her home. She looked through the peephole to make sure.

"It's my driver. Thank you. I'll see you tomorrow," she said to Cole.

He walked over to open the door for her, then quickly shut it behind her before the driver could see him.

The driver's car was parked outside, and she was surprised to see the driver holding the reins of her uncle's horse. "I saw him just over there and went to get him," he explained. "We'll have to get the buggy out of the ditch in the morning."

It was a relief to see that the horse was safe. "Thank you."

"Let's hurry. I don't like this place," the driver said.

"I'll ride the horse back. Can you drive slowly so I can follow you? It's dark and I don't know my way around yet."

"Of course," the man said, then got into his car.

Belle could only smile as she rode away, leaving the house with its mystery behind them.

***

Cole watched in admiration as Belle swung up onto the horse without a saddle and rode down the lane in the darkness, following the car. She was unlike any woman he'd ever met. That was for sure.

And he couldn't deny that he wanted to know more about her.

After making a quick evening meal in the kitchen, he placed a tray of food in front of his grandmother upstairs. Since Abigail had quit, she'd moped around all day in her room.

Claire was the only family he had left, and although she could be feisty, he loved her dearly. It was painful to see her in such a way. He tried to hold on to the early memories he had of her, when she had baked cookies with him and read bedtime stories to him whenever she was around. She had been full of life then, always smiling, teaching him how to mix the cookie batter.

Normally, Claire still had that twinkle in her eyes, but not today.

"Here's your tea, Grandma," he said, handing her a chipped tea cup which she refused to throw away.

"Thank you. And you put it in my special cup," she said, then blew on the hot liquid.

He pulled a chair close to her and removed the cover from the breakfast he'd made for her earlier that day. Claire had barely eaten any of the food, and Cole didn't blame her. Burned toast and soupy oatmeal weren't exactly the ideal breakfast of champions.

"It wasn't very good, was it?" Cole asked. "Sorry I forgot to take your breakfast dishes downstairs."

"I won't lie. Your cooking is terrible. But thank you for trying," Claire said with a smile. "The sandwiches you made for lunch weren't too bad."

Cole sighed. "Well, hopefully this dinner will be better. Sorry I'm bringing it up so late," he said. "I got a bit…distracted."

"Who was here?" his grandmother asked, looking at him with intense curiosity.

"You heard that?"

"Of course, I did. I may be old, but I'm not deaf. There was a woman here. Do you have a secret girlfriend?"

Though her health had deteriorated over the years, she still had that fierce personality.

"You'd like that, wouldn't you? No, I don't. It was just some woman who had an accident nearby and needed to make a call to get help," Cole said. "She had a minor cut and needed a bandage."

He didn't need anyone in his life to remind him of who he had become.

"Oh my!" his grandmother exclaimed. "Were you nice to her? Did you help her?"

"Yes, yes." He sighed. "She had a drink of water, called a driver, and I bandaged her up."

"Good man. I'm just glad you didn't turn her away." After eating a few bites of food, she tried to hide her disgust, but Cole saw right through her.

"I'm sorry. It's really bad, isn't it?" Cole said apologetically.

"Well, yes. It is. Nothing like Abigail's, I'm sorry to say. But you tried."

Cole sighed. His grandmother had had a great relationship with Abigail. He had no idea what the women used to talk about, but they had always been chatting and laughing, then would cease at his presence, as if he was some kind of monster. Well, he was. After all, that was what the kids around town said.

"Abigail stuck around so long only because of me," Claire said sadly, then glared at her grandson.

"What? What did I do?" Cole asked.

"Why do you push everyone away?" Claire asked. "You aren't exactly the most social person, you know."

Cole groaned. He didn't need this. Happiness was something he would never experience in his life. There was no use deceiving himself.

"Who's going to take care of you when I'm gone? I fear for what may become of you. You're so lonely, Cole. You need a woman in your life. A family. I wish—"

Holding up a hand, Cole silenced his grandmother. "I'm okay, Grandma. I'm perfectly fine. Don't worry about me," he said. "I don't need anyone."

"Everyone needs someone," Claire said wistfully. She sighed. "So how do we manage now, without a housekeeper?"

"Don't worry about that. I hired one tonight. She begins tomorrow morning."

Claire's eyes widened in surprise. "The woman who was here?"

"Yes."

"Wow. I'm shocked. Just like that?" his grandmother asked in disbelief. "You never hire someone without a long, tedious process first."

Cole shrugged. "I had a good feeling about her."

"Hmmmm…" Claire said thoughtfully and smiled wryly.

"What?" he asked, wondering what she was all about.

"Is she pretty?" Claire asked. The sound of her tinkling laughter filled the room as Cole's face turned red. He looked away. Even though he was a grown man, he could always be teased by his grandmother.

"I didn't notice," Cole said when her laughter died down. He knew he was lying, and she would know this when she saw Belle the next day.

"She must be charming. And hopefully single."

Cole laughed. "Oh, stop it, Grandma." Although she was beautiful and charming, he had no idea if she was single. He knew the Amish didn't wear wedding rings, so how would he know if she was married?

It was indeed odd how quickly he had employed Belle. Usually, he took his time hiring staff. First, he would have to do a security search on them, call their former bosses, and even do an oral interview. He had never hired staff on the spot, except for Belle, whom he knew

41

nothing about except that she was Amish. He knew that the Amish were trustworthy and good workers.

He felt like the decision had been the right one. When she'd walked out the door, he'd realized that he didn't want that to be the last time he saw her.

He couldn't help but think about Belle now and wondered if she was home safe.

"Her name is Belle," Cole said when he saw the confusion in Claire's eyes. "The woman who was in an accident. She has experience, so I employed her."

"I see. Well, I'm looking forward to seeing this Belle tomorrow. She seems…quite interesting if she got you to hire her on the spot," Claire said thoughtfully. "You're one of the most skeptical people I've ever known."

"Grandma, listen. Please don't tell her what I do for a living or our last name. Please. I don't want a repeat of what happened last time," Cole pleaded.

Claire gave him a defensive look. "What? I'm proud of your success. I want to tell people about it."

"You know what always happens once people find out. People only end up wanting something from me."

That wouldn't be the case with Belle, but he doubted she read fiction, anyway. He didn't know anything about the Amish, but didn't they read only religious books? She'd have no idea who he was, and that was for the best.

He also didn't know how good she was at keeping secrets. She said she was discreet, but what if she found out and told people?

Having people come knocking at his door asking for autographs was the last thing he wanted.

"That won't always be true." Claire sighed. "You know, I don't want you to be even more lonely when I'm gone."

"Grandma, please don't say that. I don't want you to worry about it." Opening his heart would get him hurt, as had happened in the past. He couldn't risk it a second time. "Please, just promise me you won't tell her."

Claire heaved a heavy sigh. "Fine, I won't." She paused, then gave him a sidelong glance. "Do you think you'll ever give me great-grandchildren?" she asked.

His body rumbled with laughter at the question that came out of nowhere. She glared at him. Great-grandchildren? Where on earth would he find a woman who would fall in love with him and want to have children with him?

Cole sighed. Before the explosion, the thought of having a family had certainly crossed his mind. Truth be told, he'd like to have a wife and children. Maybe three of them. Or four. He wanted daughters he could treat like princesses, and sons he could play ball with. He'd love to take them all camping and hiking and show them the wonder of the great outdoors.

But he would never have a family. No woman would ever want to marry him.

"The Cole I knew before was outgoing. He commanded a crowd," Claire said.

"That was before the bomb. That Cole is no more. He's long gone," Cole said.

At times, he liked to think about the old Cole, the happy-go-lucky Cole who seemed to have had no problem with life. He never would have thought that his life would become this. That he would be locked up in this house where he spent all of his lonely days. That he hadn't even gone hiking, camping, or mountain biking in years like he used to love doing. Even out in the middle of the forest, he was afraid someone would see him.

43

He could no longer be that Cole.

Many times, especially recently, he felt trapped in the house that he considered his sanctuary. He wanted to go out, but he was afraid of how people would react to his scarred face.

Before the bomb, he had been filled with dreams, yet all those wishes were washed away for good.

Claire smiled, her tears fading away. "Don't worry, Cole. It will all be well. I've been praying."

His eyes narrowed as he tried to understand her cryptic message. She kept smiling with a thoughtful look. It felt like she knew something he didn't. As much as he wanted to see her smile and laugh, whatever she had planned would certainly not work.

Chapter Four

"Oh, Belle!" Aunt Greta flung open the front door and ushered Belle inside the house. "What happened? Are you hurt?"

"I'm fine," Belle said. "I'm sorry to say the buggy has been damaged. I'll pay for the repairs."

"At least you're home safe," Uncle Josiah said.

"Come inside and have some tea." Aunt Greta helped Belle remove her coat.

As Aunt Greta made tea, Belle told them about the accident and how Cole had let her inside the house to make the call.

"He was very helpful. In fact…" Belle paused, glancing at her aunt, then her uncle. "Cole offered me a job as a housekeeper for the manor."

"You took a job at the manor?" Aunt Greta said, her hand flying to her heart. "No one goes near there. I've heard that man who lives there is mean."

"No, he's not. Look, he bandaged my arm." Belle showed her aunt and uncle her arm. "After I crashed, he let me inside to call for a ride, and he took care of my cut."

"I still think it's inappropriate for you to work there," Uncle Josiah huffed, sitting at the table. "Doesn't he live alone?"

"No, his grandmother lives with him. Their housekeeper just quit, and they need someone to cook and clean. Most of all, they need someone to be a companion to Claire, the elderly woman. They live there all alone, so they must be so lonely. She needs to be cared for," Belle explained with pleading eyes. "I want to save up the money so I can pay you back for the buggy repairs."

Her aunt and uncle looked at each other.

"If anything happens that makes me uncomfortable, I'll quit immediately." Belle placed her hands on the table.

"Well, I suppose that's all right. But if he does anything inappropriate or is cruel or unkind, then I do expect you to keep your word and quit," Uncle Josiah said with finality. Aunt Greta still looked unsure, but Belle was satisfied.

"Thank you. I will."

***

The next morning, Belle hummed excitedly as she left the house holding a basket of pastries covered with a white cloth napkin. It wasn't a long walk from her uncle's house if she took the shortcut through the woods. She didn't mind the walk, even in the cold of winter. Though the buggy was fit to use, she wouldn't want to take it away from her relatives every day. Uncle Josiah and some of the other men had pulled it from the ditch early that morning.

"Belle!" a cheerful voice called down the dirt lane. Before she turned around, Belle knew it was Damaris.

"Good morning, Damaris," Belle said as her best friend barreled down the lane toward her, blue skirt flying.

"Good morning. I heard you got into an accident with the buggy. Are you hurt?" Damaris asked, out of breath.

"No, I'm fine."

Before Belle could tell her about how Cole had helped her, Damaris went on. "I heard you crashed in front of the manor, and you got a job there too. What's he like? I'm sure by now you've heard what people say about him around town. You know we try not to gossip, but..." Damaris looked around to see if anyone was around. "What does he look like? Is he truly covered in scars? The poor man. I've also heard he's mean. I can't believe you went inside the manor."

"Well, he does have scars on one side of his face and on his arms, but he certainly isn't mean. The manor is beautiful inside. He wasn't very

46

social, but he was kind enough to let me inside to use his phone and bandage a cut on my arm."

Damaris took hold of Belle's arm. "Oh, does it hurt?"

"It's better today. Cole isn't what I expected. I think he's really lonely."

"I can't believe you'll be working there. What will you be doing?"

"Cleaning and cooking, and I'll also be a companion to his grandmother."

Damaris' eyes were wide. "Wow. It sounds exciting. I hope to hear more about how it's going on Sunday."

"Of course. How are Coco and the puppies?" Belle asked. Damaris' dog Coco had had a litter of puppies a few months ago.

"Oh, they're doing well, but you know how puppies are. They're always running around and getting into things. Will you come by and see them soon? They're much bigger now than when you last saw them, I'm sure."

"Of course. I'll be by soon."

"See you later," Damaris said, turning to go.

"Bye." Belle turned and continued down the lane.

As she walked up to the manor, she took a deep breath. This was it. Her first day of work, and she was early.

Belle walked to the door. She climbed the three steps of the porch, then rapped on the door. There was no answer. She knocked a second time, and it went unanswered. Just as she was about to knock a third time, the door opened and she was staring at an elderly woman.

Claire was a tall, thin woman with a pale complexion. Her hair was completely white, and her face was covered with lines of age. She

47

smiled broadly at Belle, who still looked surprised to see her instead of Cole.

"Hello. You must be Belle," said the woman, grinning.

Belle nodded. "Yes, I am. You must be Claire, Mr. Cole's grandmother."

Claire laughed. "Mr. Cole? Just call him Cole. I bet he'd tell you the same. Come in, come in," Claire said, welcoming her inside.

Claire turned and walked in, then sat on the couch. Belle followed the older woman inside, and they sat adjacent to each other. She could feel the woman's gaze on her, and although it wasn't uncomfortable, it was curious.

"You have such a lovely house, Mrs.—"

"Just call me Claire. Thank you for the compliment. This house used to belong to Cole's father, but after he died, Cole inherited it," Claire supplied.

"Oh, I'm sorry about that. I don't mean the inheriting part. I mean…I mean…"

Claire burst into a laugh, shaking her head. "I think I'm going to like you. You're a breath of fresh air. Abigail, the other housekeeper, was great company, but I think you'll be better than—"

"Grandma. What are you doing here? You should be resting," Cole demanded as he entered the living room. His hair was wet, as if he'd just showered. He turned to Belle. "I'm sorry, I didn't hear you knock. You're early."

Conversation between the women ceased, and they both turned around to Cole.

Claire glared at her grandson. "Why should I be in bed? I'm not a baby. You may be a grown man, but I'm still your grandmother. Understand?"

Belle watched, amused, as Cole's countenance changed from angry to apologetic. "I'm sorry, Grandma," Cole said. "I just don't want you to wear yourself out."

"Well, I was just introducing myself to Belle. Besides, how could I not answer the door?" Claire said. "I didn't want to keep her waiting outside in the cold."

A look passed between grandson and grandmother, then Claire turned to Belle. "I'll see you later, dear." Then, humming, she walked off, leaving Cole and Belle alone.

"I'm sorry, I didn't know your grandmother wasn't supposed to be down here," Belle said, uncomfortable with the silence that followed.

Cole shrugged. "You heard her. No one is the boss of her. I just try to make sure she gets enough rest. You're early."

"I had to walk here and I wasn't sure how long it would take," Belle said. "I wanted to make sure I had enough time to get here. Besides, I like being early. It gives us enough time to go over my responsibilities."

"What's that?" Cole asked with a nod at the basket that sat on the floor beside her.

"Pastries, muffins, Amish friendship bread—"

"Really? You bake?" Cole asked excitedly, his eyes lighting up like a little boy's.

Belle smiled at his enthusiasm. "Yes, I do. I hope you like them."

"Thank you," Cole said quietly as he recoiled back into his shell. "I've never tried Amish friendship bread. I've heard it's good."

"It is. So, would you like me to make you breakfast, or did you already eat?" Belle asked.

"Well, I tried to make breakfast yesterday, but it was a disaster. So, yes, breakfast would be great," Cole said. Then, mumbling that he

49

would be out when it was ready, he hurried off, leaving her alone. She let out the breath she had been holding in.

That hadn't been bad. All she had to do now was impress her bosses with her fine cleaning skills and a tasty breakfast. She had a feeling that was under control as well. Everything was going to be just fine.

Belle headed to the kitchen, remembering its location from the night before. In her state yesterday, she hadn't had time to admire it. She looked around the wide kitchen and sighed with pleasure. It was a cook's dream. The appliances were sleek and modern. The white cabinets glistened above black marble countertops. She opened the oven and peeked inside. Yes, she could tell she would enjoy baking lots of treats in there.

She opened the cabinets and closets, looking for ingredients she could use to plan breakfast. Opening a door, she found herself in the large pantry, which was well stocked. Pancakes would make for a lovely breakfast, with scrambled eggs. She guessed tea for Claire and a pot of coffee for Cole.

She placed the ingredients she needed on the island, then looked at them anxiously. This was her first opportunity to impress them, and she had to do it right. It was just a simple meal, but it could determine a lot. Taking a deep breath, she became more confident. She could do it. She had cooked for her family over the years, and they had sung her praises.

A few minutes later, a scintillating aroma filled the kitchen. Humming, Belle placed the last of the scrambled eggs onto a plate, next to another plate filled with pancakes. She placed the pancakes, eggs, some fruit, tea, and a pot of steaming coffee onto a trolley.

Belle rolled the trolley into the dining room. It had a long table with sixteen chairs. With just two people in the house, it seemed like a waste, but perhaps there had been a time when more than sixteen people had occupied it.

As she placed the plates on the table, Claire walked in. "Hmmm… It smells so nice," Claire remarked as she took her place at the table.

"Thank you." Belle smiled. She hoped the older woman would be pleased with the meal. "I wasn't sure if you take tea or coffee. I should have asked."

"Don't worry about that. I love tea. Later, we'll talk about what I do like to eat. He likes me to have oatmeal and fruits when all I want is pastries for breakfast."

"Grandma," Cole scolded, hearing the end of her speech as he walked in.

Claire flashed him a smile. "What? I'm only telling her that I have a sweet tooth, no matter how much you try to suppress it."

"Well, I happen to have brought some pastries I made," Belle said, setting the basket on the table.

"Oh, my! These look lovely, Belle. Thank you." Claire smiled.

"You're welcome." Belle set a tea cup on the table for Claire and was about to pour the tea when she noticed something. "Claire, this cup is chipped. Would you like me to throw it out? It could cut someone." Belle reached for it.

"No, no," Claire said, gently placing a hand on Belle's arm. "That cup is special to me. Cole broke it when he was a boy. He was so ashamed that he tried to hide it, but eventually he told me the truth. He was always such a sweet boy." Claire smiled at Cole. "I told him I'd love him no matter what, and he didn't have to hide anything from me. Isn't that right, Cole?"

Cole looked at Claire as they shared the memory. Was that a hint of a smile on his face? No, it couldn't be, could it?

"That's right, Grandma. You always took the best care of me." He nodded slowly.

"You bet I did," Claire said. "So, Belle, this cup is very nostalgic and special to me. Broken with some sharp edges, but still good. Like some people I know." Claire gave Cole another glance. He looked away, an annoyed expression on his face, but it seemed as though he was still trying to hide a smile.

"Well, then. I certainly won't be throwing it away. Just be careful to not cut yourself." Belle poured the tea, and Claire added a lump of sugar and some milk.

"I hope you enjoy your meal. Do you need anything else?" Belle asked.

Claire stopped her before she could walk away. "You must join us."

"Is that appropriate?" Belle asked timidly.

"Grandma's right. You should eat with us. Besides, we need to talk about the things you'll be doing," Cole said. "Did you have breakfast yet?"

"Well, no. I was too excited to eat." After blurting that out, she blushed. "Let me grab an extra plate," Belle said, hurrying off.

After she sat down, they dished out the food onto their plates. Belle put food on her own plate and Claire's, but Cole served himself.

Belle bent her head for a silent prayer.

"Would you like to pray for our meal, Cole?" Claire asked Cole when she saw Belle about to pray. Belle looked up.

"I normally pray silently, but I'd love it if you said the blessing, sir," Belle said with a nod.

Cole shook his head briefly. "No thank you. I haven't prayed out loud in ages."

Belle drew her brows together. Was Cole not a believer?

"Well, then, I'll do it," Claire said, giving him a look. She bowed her head. "Dear Lord, thank You for this wonderful food Belle has made for us. Thank You for bringing her to us exactly when we needed her. Thank You for our warm home in this cold winter and for bringing life to this house again. In Your name, amen."

Belle looked up and smiled at the older woman. Then they began to eat. Conversation at the table started slowly before Cole dove in.

"Look, Belle, I know this manor is too large for one person to manage perfectly. I don't expect every room to be perfect, mainly just the main living areas—the living room, entryway, kitchen, Claire's room, and the hallways, etcetera. Of course, the grocery shopping and cooking will need to be done. I will clean my own room and office, which are in the west wing. I do like my privacy, so the west wing is off-limits."

Why was it off-limits? Though curious, she nodded. "I understand."

After that, Cole barely said anything. Claire did most of the talking with Belle, while Cole merely listened to them, more interested in his food. Belle could see the annoyance in Claire's eyes at his silence, but the woman let him be, turning her attention to Belle.

"I've never had a housekeeper as young as you. Are you married?" Claire asked.

"Are you?" Cole asked, rather too loudly, both women's eyes turning to him. "I wouldn't want your husband to create a ruckus with you working here."

"No, I'm not married. I live with my family in the community," Belle said. She felt no need to tell them that the family she lived with were her relatives, not her immediate family. The loss of her family was a topic she preferred to not talk about with anyone.

"Any man would be lucky to have a beautiful woman like you, who is an amazing cook," Claire said. "This is delicious."

Belle smiled, her cheeks burning. "Thank you."

The rest of the meal went on with small talk. Cole barely participated. When it was over, he thanked her for the meal and vanished, leaving her with Claire.

"I apologize for my grandson being so antisocial. He wasn't always this way. I hope one day he'll break out of his shell again. Why don't you do the dishes and when you're done, find me in the greenhouse?

We have a lot to discuss regarding your duties. I'll be waiting." Claire stood and ambled away.

After clearing the table and putting all the dishes in the sink, Belle took a few minutes to figure out how the dishwasher worked. It was a strange feeling to load up the contraption with the dirty dishes and let it do the washing for her, but she might as well get used to using the modern appliances here. After all, she didn't own them and they weren't in her home, so it wasn't against her community's rules. She was so used to hand washing dishes every day that she had to admit this was a nice change.

After finishing the dishes, Belle wiped her hands dry with a napkin. Breakfast had gone well, just as she had wanted it to. She knew she had impressed them with her cooking.

Belle walked to the back door and stepped out into the greenhouse. It had surely seen better days. What had once been a well-structured garden was now disorganized with dead plants, climbing vines, and weeds. It seemed more like an overgrown jungle. The vegetation had begun to grow with a will of its own. While some plants were still growing, many had died. The greenhouse was in dire need of a landscaper to trim the plants that had survived, plant new flowers, and put everything back in order. Clearly, Cole didn't care about how this greenhouse was faring.

Belle passed a water fountain with dead petals and leaves floating in it.

A potted rosebush sat in the middle of the greenhouse. A few petals and leaves were scattered on the floor, leaving behind woody stems. It looked as though it was dying along with many of the other plants.

"Over here."

Belle looked up to see Claire on a marbled bench next to a small pond. She went over to the older woman and sat beside her.

Claire gestured to the rosebush. "I've been trying to take care of it, but the petals keep falling. Maybe it's running out of time." She sighed and looked around. "This place was once a beauty. It still is in its own way, but back then, it was perfect. My son, Cole's father, was the gardener. He spent whatever free time he had tending to his babies, as he loved to call the plants. But Cole has no interest in flowers. Abigail couldn't keep a plant alive at all, though she tried. I'm the only one who still cares for the garden," Claire said with a hint of sadness. "I've somehow managed to keep that rosebush alive, though it doesn't look it, with the petals falling off. At least, I think it's still alive."

Claire stood and walked over to the rosebush, grabbing a pair of pruning shears on a nearby table. She cut off one of the lower branches of the rosebush, slicing at an angle. She held up the branch to Belle.

"See? It's still green. That means there's hope that we can revive it. I read it online. We'll need to prune off all the dead stuff and water it every day. It looks dead, but with you helping me, maybe we can make it bloom again."

Belle nodded. "Of course, I'll help you."

"I wish I had done more to take care of this bush and this whole greenhouse. I certainly don't have a green thumb, and Cole wouldn't be happy if he knew I was out here watering the plants, so I have to be sneaky about it," Claire said with a forlorn look.

Belle had no idea what to say. She could tell the woman was awfully lonely.

Claire sighed and returned to her seat beside Belle. "Anyway, that's why I keep the thermostat around sixty degrees during the day and I lower it to around forty degrees at night. I don't know much about it, and what I do know is what I've looked up online and read about in books. I'm trying to keep these plants alive, if I can. The other flowers are mostly tropical plants. As you can see, it's too big of a job for only me to take care of this place."

"I'll certainly try," Belle said. "I'm sorry to say I don't know much about gardening. I should know more. My mother was a gardener, but she grew mostly vegetables. I never liked gardening. Now I wish I would have spent more time doing that with her. I should have made more of an effort." Belle shuddered at the guilt that crept over her. "I'd like to learn more about it. Maybe I could help you with this." She made a sweeping motion with her hand, gesturing to the plants surrounding them.

"Cole doesn't want this place to look beautiful again," Claire said, slowly shaking her head.

"Why not?"

"It reminds him of the past."

Belle nodded, filled with confusion. She wanted to ask so many questions but she also didn't want to pry. Something terrible must have happened for Cole to not want this greenhouse taken care of. With proper care, it could be wonderful. But it wasn't her place. If Cole wanted this greenhouse left alone, she'd have to do as he wished.

"So, there's nothing much around here to do," Claire said, changing the topic. "Our meals are the main duty, I believe. We love to eat, Cole and I. Abigail could cook, but not anything like you." Claire winked at Belle. "I know there will be no issues with that since your food tastes divine. There are clothes to be washed, and the cleaning. Aside from that and going shopping, the major duty you have is caring for me. I'm quite an old woman, with a grandson who's a recluse, and nothing I say will change his mind. He prefers to spend his days locked up in his office, working. While he may be lonely, I need company. I hope you don't mind spending your time with an old woman like me."

Belle laughed. "No, I don't at all, Claire. I believe you will make great company."

"I believe the same as well. So, I'm guessing you don't have a car," Claire said. "How will you do the grocery shopping? Would you want to take your buggy?"

"Well, I might be able to take the family buggy, but my aunt and uncle might need it."

"Pish posh. We can't have that. We'll have a driver take you then, if that's all right with you."

"Sure. Actually, the people in my community have a few drivers we hire to take us places. If you don't mind, I could have them take me, since I'm familiar with them," Belle said.

"Of course, dear. Whatever you're comfortable with. I'm sure Cole won't mind." Claire smiled. "Now, let me give you a tour of the house. I know you must be excited to see it."

"Yes, I am."

Claire laughed. "Indeed, you'll make great company. Cole, are you coming along?"

Belle was surprised to see Cole standing in the doorway, listening to their conversation. How had Claire known he was there?

He glanced at Belle. "Careful. She has the ears of a bat."

Belle chuckled, then offered to hold Claire's arm, but the older woman turned her down. "Thank you, dear. I may be as old as the hills, but thankfully, I can still get up on my own."

Belle knew already they'd be great friends.

"And please, don't bother to fix up this garden. It's been like this for a long time. I ask that you leave it alone," Cole said, turning and walking out with finality.

Belle gave Claire a questioning glance.

"Don't mind him. As I said, he's a grump. He lets the past haunt him, and this garden only reminds him of his parents, especially his father. I do wish he'd let us make it beautiful again."

"Maybe if we did and surprised him, he'd end up loving it," Belle said softly. "How could he not?"

"You may be right," Claire said, holding a wrinkled finger to her chin as she thought. "I do like that idea. Let's talk about it later. I guess he's not coming with us, so let's get going."

Side by side, they walked back into the house. Belle already knew the kitchen, so they went to the laundry room, which was downstairs. She was used to hand-washing clothes in a non-electric Maytag wringer washer. Normally, she'd manually wring out the water, then air-dry the clothes on the clothesline.

Now, she stared at the washing machine, dryer, and ironing board.

"I know you're used to your own ways, but this isn't difficult to use, and it does save time. However, if you're not comfortable with the machines, you can always do what works for you as long as the end result is achieved: clean, nice-smelling clothes," Claire said.

"I could give it a try," Belle said. "I don't have a problem using them. We just aren't allowed to own them. I think I could learn how. After all, I figured out the dishwasher this morning."

Claire chuckled. "There's a first time for everything, I suppose."

They moved on to the music room. In it was a baby grand piano, and Belle looked at it in awe. What would it be like to know how to play such a glorious instrument?

"My son used to play the piano. Cole and I don't play. Like the greenhouse, it's a reminder of the past." Claire turned to her, eyes hopeful. "Do you play?"

"Me? No." Belle shook her head. "The Amish don't play instruments."

"Not at all? Why not? Isn't playing musical instruments also a form of worshipping God?"

"We believe it draws too much attention to the person playing."

"I'd love to hear someone play it again. I was never good at reading music and now my eyesight isn't what it used to be. Cole hasn't played in years, and I never learned how to play more than a few songs."

58

Belle could sense that there was more to the story, but she said nothing. If Claire felt it was right, she would tell her.

"Would you like to try it? I do remember one simple song. I could teach you," Claire offered.

"Me? Oh, no, I couldn't," Belle said, taking a step back. It was such a beautiful instrument, she was almost afraid to touch it.

"You can't tell me there isn't one small part of you that is curious to know what it feels like to play an instrument," Claire said with a wink. "Come on, I won't tell anyone."

"Are you sure?" Belle asked. "And yes, I am a bit curious."

"Of course." Claire sat on the bench and patted the spot next to her. "Here, let me teach you. This is A, B, middle C, D, E, F, and G."

Claire showed Belle where to place her fingers to play a simple tune. Claire played the song slowly as she said the notes, then Belle copied her.

"That's it. You've got it," Claire said, beaming. They went on for a few more minutes. Belle's heart was filled with joy, not only from her first experience of playing an instrument but also how happy it was making Claire. The woman was grinning ear to ear as she encouraged Belle to keep playing.

Suddenly, loud footsteps resounded in the hallway. The smile fell from Claire's face as she stopped playing.

"What's wrong?" Belle asked her.

Cole burst into the room and glared at them. "What are you doing?" he demanded, his deep voice echoing off the walls.

"Cole, this was my idea. I offered to teach her a song—" Claire began.

"No. I don't want anyone playing this piano!" Cole boomed. His eyes fell directly on Belle. She suppressed a shudder.

"It's not her fault," Claire persisted, but Cole whirled around and stormed out.

Claire heaved a sigh and gave Belle an apologetic look. "Sorry. I didn't think he'd get so worked up about it. You know, he's a wonderful pianist. His father taught him."

"Oh," Belle said, still stunned by what had just happened. "I should have known better, though." She shot up as if the bench were hot.

"No, you were just humoring an old woman." Claire shook her head. "Did you like it?"

Belle nodded. "Yes, actually. I've always wondered what it would be like to play an instrument. Thank you. I may never get the chance again."

Claire gave her a sad look but didn't pry. "Well, let me show you the rest of the house."

They climbed the wide stairs. Belle marveled at the artwork that lined the walls. Though beautiful, each piece was painted in dark colors in a distinctive style, presenting a message of pain and sadness.

"The bedrooms are all here, except for one downstairs. My room is close to the staircase, while Cole's is down the hall. He loves his privacy. You must know that by now," Claire said.

Cole came out of one of the rooms.

"Yes, I do like my privacy. In fact, it's one of the things most important to me." He closed the door behind him before Belle could see inside it. "This is the west wing, and as I said before, it's strictly off-limits. I'll clean it myself."

There were three doors. Belle craned her neck, not caring if she was being too bold. "What's behind the third door?"

"As I said, this wing is off-limits. Understand?" Cole stared at her intently until she nodded, then he went back inside the room he had just left.

Claire continued the tour. The other rooms in the house were neat, but they were unoccupied. They had been for years. Claire said that she doubted they would be occupied anytime soon.

"It's rather lonely here, as we don't have guests around. It's just Cole and me all year round," Claire said with a shake of her head. "Come. Let me show you the rest of the house."

Belle wondered what Claire wanted to say, but she let it slide, following her out of the room.

"My grandson can be an ogre, but deep down, he has a good heart. Just be patient with him," Claire said.

Belle nodded. Maybe she was right. After all, Cole had been so helpful to her last night after she'd shown up at his door in the cold. There had to be more kindness like that inside of him.

After they toured the top floor, they returned downstairs and Belle sat with Claire, who told her more about the house. She also filled her in on details of their likes and dislikes regarding food and other aspects she hadn't discussed with Cole.

"You have Saturdays and Sundays off. On Fridays, you will make enough meals to last us for the weekend," Claire said.

Belle nodded. The instructions were simple and straightforward. Claire reached for her hand and held it in hers.

"I'm really glad you're here. I just hope you'll be patient with my grandson, like I said before. If he annoys you, just tell me and I'll yell at him or pull at his ear," Claire said.

Belle laughed. She doubted there would be any need for that. He didn't seem that bad, and she would try to stay out of his way if he became rude and annoying.

"I have a good feeling about you." Claire smiled.

61

Chapter Five

It was a beautiful Sunday morning, and the church service was over. Unlike many Amish communities, the Amish of Unity had built their own church building instead of hosting services in alternating homes.

Outside the church building, which doubled as the Amish school, people milled about while others got into their buggies. Belle walked up to Damaris, Ella Ruth, Adriana, Liz, Leah, Charlotte, and Maria— a group of lovely women who had befriended Belle upon her arrival in the community.

Damaris told the group, "Belle got a new job."

Belle smiled at Damaris. Her friend was kind, but could often be quite nosy.

"I heard you got a job," Liz said, her eyes wide. "Where is it?"

Belle took in a deep breath, wondering what they would say. "I'm working at the manor on the hill. I clean and cook, and I'm a companion to the elderly woman there."

"Wait, I thought only a man lived there," Leah said. "An elderly woman lives there too?"

"Yes. She's Cole's grandmother."

"His name is Cole?" Charlotte asked.

"What? Wait a minute. Hold on. Back up. You're working at the manor? How on earth did you get that job?" Maria asked, holding her young daughter, Rebecca, on her hip.

"I'm still new to town, but I've heard everyone is afraid to go near there. I'm surprised he didn't turn you away at the door. Everyone knows he doesn't go out or talk to anyone," remarked Adriana, who had recently joined their community.

Belle explained how her horse and buggy had fallen into the ditch, then how Cole had helped her. "He doesn't have great social skills, and he's a bit grumpy, but he was kind to me. You can tell he doesn't get out. He let me use his phone and have a drink of water, and he bandaged the cut on my arm." Belle held up her arm. "It wasn't bad at all, but he took care of it for me. It's all better now."

"That is so romantic," Leah said with a sigh, clasping her hands together.

Charlotte laughed at her sister. "Oh, Leah. You would think that's romantic."

Leah elbowed her sister, smiling.

"So, how's it going? Do you like it?" Ella Ruth asked.

Belle nodded. "It's going well," she said.

"Just that? Come on, tell me all about your boss. What does he look like?" Liz whispered. "Is he scary?"

Belle laughed. "Don't tell me you think he's a monster like all the children say. He's just a man."

They all looked at her skeptically.

Belle continued, "Okay, well, he has scars covering his arms and one side of his face. I think he was in a fire. But really, I don't know why the children say he's a beast. I think he's lonely and that something terrible happened to him. I think if people got to know him, they'd like him. It's sad, really. All he has is his grandmother, and he adores her, though he tries to hide it. I think that, past his tough exterior, he has a kind heart. That's what his grandmother says."

They all stared at her, then looked at each other.

"Is he single?" Adriana asked.

"Well..."

"Oh, wow. Belle, are you falling for him?" Maria asked, giggling. "To me, it sounds like you like him."

"No. That's not appropriate. He's not Amish, and he's my boss," Belle said, but she could already feel her cheeks burning.

"Shh. Look. Gilbert is coming this way," Liz said. "Probably to talk to Belle."

"I told you all that I'm not interested in him," Belle whispered.

"Why on earth not?" Damaris said. "He's so handsome. Anyone can see that."

"Damaris!" Maria scolded, then laughed. "We aren't supposed to comment on outward appearances."

"What? I have eyes." Damaris shrugged. "And I'm not married."

"Why don't you date him, then?" Belle said.

"Oh, come on. We're just friends, and we have been since we were toddlers. He clearly is head over heels for you," Damaris said.

It was no secret that Gilbert had been trying to court Belle ever since she'd arrived, and it seemed like all the single young women were after him except her. Out of all her friends, Belle was the only unmarried woman left besides Ella Ruth and Damaris. Sometimes she felt out of place, but she knew her friends did their best to make her feel like she belonged.

All of them turned around as he approached.

"Good morning, ladies," Gilbert greeted them all.

"Good morning," Belle said, then turned to see her friends smiling at her and walking off casually, waving.

Why were they leaving her stuck talking to Gilbert?

"I hope you enjoyed the service," Gilbert continued.

Yes, Belle had. It had been all about forgiveness and the ability to move past those who had hurt you, just as Christ had forgiven our sins and died on the cross for all mankind.

"How are you doing, Belle? You look beautiful this morning, but then you always do," Gilbert said, the stain of a blush appearing on his face. "I'm sorry. I know we aren't supposed to compliment outward appearances. I can't help it."

Trying to change the subject, Belle ignored what he'd just said. "How is your family?" she asked as they began walking toward the path in the woods.

"My parents are fine, and my younger siblings are still pests, as they always are," Gilbert said, then grimaced as he saw a shadow cross her face. "I'm sorry. I shouldn't have said that...because of what happened."

Belle shook her head, knowing he was referring to her own family. "Don't feel bad, please. I like hearing about your family." She didn't want people to feel like they had to watch what they said around her.

"How is your work at the manor? I heard about it from your aunt, and I was surprised. Is it safe?" he asked with concern.

"It's very safe. My boss is a nice man," Belle said. "I work for him and his grandmother."

"Oh. So... Is it true that he looks like a beast?"

Belle sighed as they walked through the trees. She didn't want to hear one more word about the beast. Cole was not a beast. "There's no beast, Gilbert," Belle advised. "I keep telling everyone the same thing. He's just a man."

"My cousin saw him once, and he told me that he looks like a monster," Gilbert said confidently. "That his face is all disfigured."

"He has burn scars, but everyone here knows that outward appearances don't matter. Right?" she asked, feeling her blood begin to boil. "Why are people so quick to vilify one of God's creatures just because he has been disfigured? Something terrible must have happened to him, but it's no one's business."

"Well, I mean…" Gilbert ran a hand through his hair. "Yes, but does he treat you well?"

"I love working there, and they are really nice to me."

"I'm sorry. I just want to make sure you're safe. Belle, I'd like to ask you a question. Don't give me an answer now," Gilbert started.

Belle sighed, inwardly groaning. They were far enough into the trees that they were out of earshot of the church. "Gilbert, if this is about—"

"Please, Belle, don't give me a decision now. I know I've asked you before, but I'm asking you again, and I want you to give it a lot of thought. I care for you very much, Belle. I'd like to marry you, if you'll have me."

Belle's stomach lurched, then sank to her toes. She felt the blood drain from her face. Was he seriously asking her to marry him already?

"I know we don't know each other that well, but I already know in my heart I want to marry you. It would make your aunt and uncle so happy. Please think about it," Gilbert pleaded.

Belle took a step back, too shocked to speak. "I…I have to go now," she stammered, hurrying off to join her relatives for the ride home, eager to get away as quickly as she could.

Why did I say that? Belle thought. *I already know the answer is no. I should have been upfront with him.*

She should have told Gilbert outright that she couldn't marry him, but she hadn't wanted to hurt his feelings.

After lunch, Belle's aunt and uncle called her to the living room. She looked worriedly at them, wondering why they had to talk to her in private.

"How's work?" Uncle Josiah asked.

"Work is good," Belle said. "What's this about?"

Her uncle smiled. "We'd like to discuss something with you. What do you think of Gilbert Schwartz?"

Belle froze, her blood turning cold. "Well…he's nice and a good friend. Why?"

Had he already asked their permission?

"He told us that he'd like to marry you, and he asked for our blessing," Aunt Greta said, clasping her hands over her heart. "Isn't that wonderful?"

A sick feeling filled Belle's stomach, and she sat on the couch to steady herself.

"Gilbert is a good man and a hard worker. He'd make a fine husband. We've known him his whole life," Uncle Josiah said.

Belle shook her head with more force than necessary, and a few dark, stray hairs escaped her *kapp*. "He already asked me today, but my answer will be no. I don't love him," Belle explained. "I see him as a friend and nothing more. There's no way I could marry him."

"I just want you to remember that you're not getting any younger, and neither are we." Aunt Greta leaned forward and patted Belle's hand. "Do you want a family of your own?"

"Of course. But only when I fall in love with the right man," Belle countered. She wouldn't marry just anyone.

"And what about joining the church? I know you've been through a lot, but don't you think it's time to either be baptized into the church or…" She let her voice trail off, not saying out loud that the alternative would be to leave the Amish. "You know, you're well past the age when many young people decide to join the church."

"Greta, maybe she needs some time after everything that has happened," Uncle Josiah said.

"I know I'm plenty old enough to join the church, but Uncle Josiah is right. I do need some time, but I'll decide soon enough. I know you want the best for me. But Gilbert isn't the man for me. I'm sure of it. I'll wait for the right one."

Belle began to turn away.

"How do you know he isn't right for you?" Aunt Greta said. "Why don't you give him a chance?"

"Greta," Uncle Josiah said in a low voice. "Don't pressure her." He turned to Belle. "Belle, all of this is your decision. These are big, life-changing choices that should not be taken lightly, so take your time."

"Thank you." She nodded to her uncle, and then looked at her aunt, trying not to glare. "This is my decision, and my decision is no. If you don't want me to live here anymore, I can find somewhere else to stay, but I will not marry a man I don't love just so I can have a place to live. I'm capable of finding a place to stay on my own, if that's what needs to be done."

With that, she walked off to her room, where she plopped on her bed, a mixture of anger and guilt rising in her chest. Maybe she truly was a burden to her aunt and uncle, but why was her aunt pressuring her so much? Belle did her best to help her aunt around the house and with the farm, so she thought by now they'd see her as helpful. She didn't have enough money saved up for a place of her own, on top of paying for the buggy repairs.

When she heard hushed voices downstairs, she slowly opened her door and crept to the top of the stairs to listen to her relatives talking in the kitchen.

"You're too pushy with her," Uncle Josiah said. "As I said before, she isn't a burden to us. Why are you trying to get her out of here so quickly?"

"I'm sorry," Aunt Greta said with remorse. "I just want what's best for her, and she deserves a nice husband and a family of her own. I think if she waits for someone better to come along, that may never happen, and she may live alone in regret. We aren't getting any younger, and I want to make sure she'll be well taken care of after we're gone. We promised her parents we'd look after her."

"That doesn't mean forcing her to marry someone she barely knows and doesn't love, Greta," Uncle Josiah said. "Her parents wouldn't want that. Your sister wouldn't want that."

Aunt Greta heaved a heavy sigh. "You're right. But you know I have only good intentions."

"Of course. But you need to let her make her own decisions. This isn't up to you."

Belle retreated to her room and sank onto the bench near the window.

Her aunt and uncle were caring and kind, but they were getting on in years. Of course, they wanted to keep their promise to her parents to make sure she was always taken care of, but this was not the way.

"God will bring the right man for me," Belle whispered to the ceiling. "If He has one for me."

***

Cole's fingers hesitated above his computer keyboard. Then he slammed his hands on his desk and pushed back his chair.

The distant sound of laughter infuriated him. It was a beautiful sound, but that only irked him more. What was so funny?

Cole walked down the stairs. The women seated on the couch ceased talking when he walked in, the laughter coming to an end. It should please him to see Grandma so happy, and he found himself wanting to hear the sound again.

What was so amusing?

"I see you've decided to honor us with your presence," Claire said dryly.

He ignored her. Now was not the time for her to complain that he worked too much, spending hours bent over his computer. He had a deadline to meet.

The women continued talking, acting as if he weren't there. He watched Belle as she talked and laughed with his grandmother. Cole could tell that she was an interesting person. It had been only a week since she'd started working in the house, and he found himself taking breaks more than usual. He would come downstairs to find them talking, and he would join them without contributing a thing. A few minutes later, he would return upstairs to continue with his writing.

He would like to find fault in Belle's duties, but so far, he couldn't. She arrived early and left when she was supposed to. She did her duties diligently and remarkably. Her meals were the best he had ever tasted, and he always shyly asked for seconds and desserts. The clothes were well washed and ironed, and the rooms were clean. There was certainly nothing he could fault her with, but something about her niggled at him.

Perhaps it was how happy she seemed to be—so full of life while he was so dead inside. Clearly, nothing bad had ever happened to her. She was the epitome of innocence while his mere memories would frighten her.

Was that what was irking him?

"So… What's for lunch?" Cole asked.

Both women glared at him at the interruption in their conversation, and he resisted grinning.

"Cole, leave us alone or I'll box your ears," Claire threatened.

It was an empty threat, considering she'd never done anything like that to him, even when he'd been mischievous as a child. She just acted rough and tough. Inside, she was a softie.

Rolling his eyes, he got up and returned to his office, leaving the women to continue with their conversation. He sat on his chair, his hands on the keyboard, but he couldn't get anything to flow. Why did he want to return to the living room and join their conversation?

He looked around his office, which had a dark interior, including the tiles on the floor. The curtains were drawn to hide the light from outside. A huge light overhead supplied all the illumination he needed.

The office was always lonely. It was always beyond the reach of everyone else, including his grandma. It was his sanctuary. Sometimes, he would remain here all day, writing.

His phone rang, and he reached for it. It was Simeon Blake, his literary agent.

Simeon was a lanky man who was always full of life. When Cole had met him, he had been a young writer brimming with ideas. Simeon had read his first work and had been hooked, telling him he knew that Cole would become a successful author.

Cole sighed as he looked at the screen. Was he ready for Simeon today? Not with his mood. He allowed the phone to ring several times. With a groan, he pressed the answer button, then lifted the phone to his ear.

"Simeon," Cole said flatly.

"Tony Graham, my favorite client. You didn't want to pick up the phone, did you?" Simeon teased.

Cole rolled his eyes. Tony Graham was the pen name he used. It allowed him to keep his identity a secret from the world, to keep his life private. He'd never imagined his career would be so successful, so he was glad he'd decided to not use his real name. "What do you want, Simeon?"

Simeon was used to Cole's moodiness. "In a bad mood, are you, Cole? But when are you not? How is everything over there?" Simeon inquired.

"Fine," Cole said.

"And Claire? I should pay her a visit one of these days, but there's a troll living with her who would probably shut the door in my face," Simeon went on.

"What do you want, Simeon?" Cole repeated. He knew he was being rude, but he didn't care. He just wanted to be left alone, and he needed others to respect his decision.

"The publisher is asking questions. How is the progress with the new Tony Graham book?" Simeon asked.

"Slow," Cole said, staring at the screen. His new book was supposed to have a word count of 85,000, but he was still at around 5,000. Yes, it was that pathetic, especially for the best-selling Tony Graham. Even what he had written so far made no sense to him. He'd probably have to delete it and start all over again.

"That sounds bad. You sure you don't have writer's block?"

"No," Cole retorted instantly. It wasn't writer's block. It was just a phase.

"You could take a trip somewhere to get some inspiration, like to New York City. In a few months, there will be an authors' conference there. It's going to be huge. Many writers will be there, and lots of your fans. I want you to be there, Cole. I want you to be the featured speaker. Right now, all the authors have photos, but yours is one big mystery, and everyone is dying to know Tony Graham's true identity. It would be great publicity if you reveal who you are."

Now Cole knew why Simeon had called. This was not the first time Simeon had suggested that Cole make a big public appearance, revealing himself as Tony Graham. Every time, the idea was ridiculous. "You know that's not possible, and I wonder why you keep trying," Cole said. "I write under a pen name so people don't know who I am."

"Come on, Cole, nothing is impossible. Your latest book blew up the bestsellers' list. Imagine if you come out right now. It will be an unbreakable record. I know your reservations, Cole, but wouldn't it be great to use this momentum to sell even more books?"

"Simeon, I appreciate your concerns, but it's still a no. I'm not going to make a public appearance, and I never will. Please, don't mention this again," Cole warned.

Simeon sighed. "Just think about it. You've put in a lot of work over the years. You have a strong fan base, and they won't care what you look like. They really want to see you. You read your fans' letters, don't you? These people are passionate about you," Simeon pushed.

"Yeah," Cole said dryly. His email inbox was flooded with thousands of emails from fans. For the most part, he ignored them.

It had been this way for years. He didn't read them, because he was sure they were all the same. Some of them praised his writing, telling him they were impressed. Some had suggestions for what he should write about and which characters he should kill off or improve.

Then there were the ones who wanted to meet him. Some were ready to do anything to do that. He was sure if he told them he was based in Antarctica, they would still come to meet him. It was indeed a crazy world out there, and he was glad that he lived far away from all the mess.

While he appreciated his fans, he wasn't going to get out of his comfort zone to meet with them. He would continue to write, but revealing himself as Tony Graham would never be an option.

"Can you honestly tell me that there's no part of you that wants to get out, meet new people, and do fun things like you used to? Don't you miss hiking and mountain biking or just going out with friends?" Simeon pressed.

"Well…" Cole hesitated. Of course, he missed it. All of it.

"I know you miss it, and I know you want to live a normal life like you used to. What's holding you back?"

Fear, Cole admitted to himself. *What will people say or do when they see me?*

"My grandmother and my former housekeeper have encouraged me to get out again, and I admit I do want to, but... Simeon, you don't understand what it's like. The last time I went out, people were shocked at the sight of me, staring. I don't want to go through that again." He shuddered at the memories. "I know they want what's best for me, but that's not why I wish I could do it. I want to do it for myself, but I'm just too scared, to be honest."

"That was a long time ago, right? I bet your scars have healed more since then."

"They're still hideous."

"What's the worst that could happen? A few little kids or rude people point at you? So what? You've fought off terrorists in the desert. Why are you so afraid of this?"

Cole pondered his words silently.

"Besides," Simeon continued, "You might be surprised. I think people are much more accepting than you think."

"I can't, Simeon."

"Come on, Cole, don't do this to me. Please," Simeon said. "The publisher is really pushing for this."

"I'm not doing it."

Simeon sighed. "The publisher won't be happy about this."

There was a knock on the door, and Cole froze.

It must be Belle.

"Yes?" he called, placing a hand over the phone.

"It's Belle. Lunch is ready," she said from the other side of the door.

"I'll be down in a few minutes," Cole said. He waited for her footsteps to move away before he returned to his call.

"You have a woman in your house? Who is that?" Simeon demanded. "That wasn't Abigail."

He rolled his eyes at Simeon's enthusiasm. Could he be more annoying? "Calm down, Simeon. She's just the housekeeper, nothing else."

"What happened to Abigail?"

"She quit. Her mother is sick. I had to employ another housekeeper," Cole explained.

"This one sounds pretty," Simeon said mischievously.

Cole wasn't going to confirm his statement. "Look, Simeon, I need to go."

"Okay. Think over what we discussed."

Cole hung up, taking delight in the silence once Simeon's voice was gone.

He stared at the screen of the laptop, then deleted everything he had written in the past few weeks. None of it made sense to him. He had to start afresh. Words failed him at the moment. He would give himself a few days off. Hopefully, when he returned to the keyboard, the words would flow effortlessly.

He got up, and as he did, his stomach rumbled in hunger. Lunch was waiting for him downstairs, and he wondered what Belle had made. Whatever she'd made, he was sure it would taste amazing. She had also been doing the grocery shopping and making new recipes that he and Claire had never had before, mostly Amish dishes.

He had no idea the Amish made such good food.

Claire and Belle were at the table. He sat at the head of it.

As usual, Belle bowed her head for silent prayer. Claire followed suit, while Cole watched them. This was their new routine. Apparently, in Unity, the Amish usually prayed silently at meals, and Claire wanted to make Belle feel comfortable.

Yes, Cole believed in God. But it had been so long since he'd prayed, he'd almost forgotten how. Now, he was relieved they were praying silently.

Belle looked up. Before she could begin to serve him, he lifted a hand, stopping her.

"Thank you, Belle. But as I've told you before, you don't need to get it for me," Cole said, scooping the taco casserole she'd made onto his plate. "Is this an Amish dish?"

"Yes. My Aunt Greta makes it quite often. Maybe it's a family recipe of hers."

"Hmm. I wouldn't expect taco casserole to be a typical Amish food."

"I don't know if other Amish communities make it often, but we do. Back at home, growing up, my mother didn't make it. But my aunt loves to make it, and I learned the recipe from her," Belle explained.

"Back at home? Where did you live before?" Cole asked.

Belle looked down at her plate. "Ohio."

"So…" Cole hesitated, a bit confused. "Does your mother also live with you? And your father? I've heard you mention only your aunt and uncle."

"Just my aunt and uncle." Belle dodged his question by asking, "So, what do you do stuck in your office all day? Or is it that you just want to avoid talking to us?"

Claire raised her eyebrows, then poked at her food. She looked like she wanted to tell Belle about what Cole really did for a living, but Cole had begged her not to.

Still wondering why she'd avoided his question, Cole didn't even think to answer Belle. Why wouldn't she speak about her parents?

Were they gone, like his own parents? What had happened to them? What about her siblings?

"He—" Claire started, but Cole stopped her with a look, trying to silently remind her of the conversation they'd had about not telling Belle what he did for a living.

"I work in my office," he said.

"Yes. So, what is it you do?" Belle asked.

"Business," Cole mumbled, taking a bite of the casserole, which was delicious.

Couldn't she just let things be and move on?

"There are lots of types of businesses. Are you an investor? Accountant?"

Cole's lips turned up in a smile, then he frowned as he caught Claire watching him. Investor? Accountant? Definitely not. He had never been good with numbers.

"Are you an artist? A graphic designer? Undercover spy?"

"You have quite an active imagination." He chuckled, then reached for his glass of water and took a drink. "I write books you wouldn't be interested in, under a pen name you've never heard of."

Not daunted, she leaned forward. "I read a lot. What's your pen name? Maybe I've heard of you."

His eyebrows shot up. Maybe she had. Still, he lied, "I seriously doubt that."

Claire said, "What do you like to read, Belle?"

"All kinds of novels. I like thrillers and mysteries, but my favorite is sci-fi and fantasy," Belle said.

Almost choking on his water, Cole coughed hard. The Tony Graham books were all sci-fi and fantasy. Was it possible that she'd read any of his books?

"Are you okay, Cole?" Claire asked.

"Yes. It just went down the wrong pipe," Cole said, tapping his chest. "Anyway, I'm surprised, Belle. I figured the Amish didn't read novels."

Belle looked down at the table. "Some Amish communities have no problem with us reading those types of fiction. There aren't any official rules about it here, but it's frowned upon by some people, like my aunt and uncle. I like to visit the bookstore in town secretly."

Cole ignored the amused smile his grandma wore.

Perhaps, if he grew to trust Belle, which he doubted, he'd let her know more about what he did.

Perhaps.

* * *

After the meal, Cole took a walk to the greenhouse before returning to his work.

If he had his way, the greenhouse would be cleared out, and a pool or something else would be put there. But his grandmother cherished it and refused to let him do otherwise with it. It was a mess. A dead, overgrown, tangled, pathetic mess that only reminded him of the past.

He knew his grandmother kept it heated and was watering the plants, but he pretended not to notice. Cole didn't have the heart to tell her it was a hopeless cause, just like he was.

He walked into the greenhouse, past the grimy water fountain.

It looked peaceful, even with the brown and dried-up branches. Calm. There was a nice tingle in the air, and it soothed him. He sighed.

He really wanted to hate this place.

Cole sat on a marble bench by a small man-made pool that had long ago turned green. Another wilted rose petal from the rosebush disdainfully floated to the floor. How much longer would that plant last before it completely shriveled up?

"It's calm out here, isn't it?"

He jerked at the sound of Belle's voice. She stood behind him.

Without an invitation, she joined him on the bench.

"Your grandma says you hate it here," Belle said.

"My grandma talks too much," Cole mumbled.

"She's just worried about you. That's what families do. They worry and want the best for you," Belle said.

Not all families. He knew that from experience. His mother had certainly not cared about him.

To break the silence, he told her, "You know, I thought that rosebush would survive, at least. Abigail might have watered it, or maybe Grandma was doing it, because it lived all this time, but it's dead now." He gestured to the bush in front of them. "I know Grandma keeps the heat in here and tries to take care of the plants. I just don't have the heart to tell her that rosebush is already dead and this place won't ever be like it used to be."

"Actually, it's not dead. There is still green in the stems. If it's taken care of properly, it can be revived especially if the heat stays on and someone keeps watering it faithfully." She gave him a sidelong glance, wondering what his response would be.

"Are you sure? Look at that thing. So many of the petals have fallen off."

"Claire looked it up online. As long as the stems still have green in them, there's a good chance we can help it bloom again," Belle explained.

"I have a feeling Grandma thinks that if it really does die, that if all the petals eventually fall to the ground, all hope will be lost for me," Cole said with a sigh. "So she's trying to keep something alive that just won't survive in the end. It's truly hopeless."

Belle turned to him, determination in her eyes. "It really could survive. If it's taken care of, it has a fighting chance. How could you blame her? She's trying to do what she thinks is right, trying to keep some form of life alive in this manor. There's hope for you, too, Cole. You just can't see it. The night is darkest just before the morning, you know."

"Still. She can keep watering it I suppose, but I don't want you both to try to revive this greenhouse. Just leave it alone. It's a lost cause and I don't want to get her hopes up. Understand?"

Belle looked down at her lap, looking disappointed. "Yes."

Cole sighed, guilt gripping him. "I owe you an apology for how I reacted when I found you and my grandmother playing the piano. I'm sorry I got so upset."

After a silent moment, Belle said, "I overstepped."

"No, it's not your fault. I know how persistent my grandmother can be. I'm sure she talked you into it. I don't blame her." He looked out over the dying, overgrown garden. "That piano hasn't been played in years. The only reason why it's not full of dust is that Abigail cleaned it."

"Claire said your father taught you how to play," Belle said softly.

"See? She does talk too much," Cole said to lighten the mood. That got Belle to smile a bit. "Yes, he did. He was a very skilled pianist."

"She says you play very well too. Why did you stop?"

Cole sighed heavily. How many secrets had Claire told Belle?

Would she really keep his most important secret of all?

"I used to play before my father died. After he died... I just haven't been able to bring myself to play. I guess it reminds me of him," he said, staring at his scarred hands.

"That's not a bad thing if it reminds you of him, is it? Yes, it hurts, but would he have wanted you to stop playing?" Belle persisted.

Cole paused. "No. He wouldn't." He let out a heavy sigh at the realization.

"Well, I would love to hear you play sometime," Belle said with a smile.

He couldn't help but smile back. "Maybe one of these days."

They sat in silence for a moment, but it wasn't awkward. In fact, he felt perfectly comfortable just sitting there with her.

"You said before that you live with your aunt and uncle. But what about your parents?" he asked, changing the topic from him to her.

Belle was quiet, as if she hadn't heard his question. He was about to ask her again when she spoke. "My parents are dead."

So, they did have something in common.

"Oh..." He was instantly filled with concern for her. He reached over and placed his hand over hers, just for a moment, then pulled away. "I'm sorry for your loss. I know how difficult it is to lose a parent," Cole said. His mother's loss had hurt him a lot, but worst of all was losing his father. This had driven him over the edge. It was the one thing he would never be able to recover from, even after everything he'd been through overseas.

"It is the worst thing that can ever happen. Everything stops for you, but life still goes on. You're wounded, you can't breathe, you just want to wake up from the horrible dream, yet you're trapped in it. You try to control the pain, you try to move on, but you never can. You can just never let go of those painful feelings," she said. "So, I understand how you feel a little bit."

Her words struck him. They were so heavy with emotion, and he wanted to hug her and tell her that everything would be all right, that it got easier with time. But how could he do so when he was still fighting his own demons? He watched her as she stared straight ahead.

Cole now saw her in a new light. He could tell that something had happened to her, something that gave her pain that she tried so much to hide. He never would have guessed. She had always come off as a joyful person, but she carried her pain with her. He'd always assumed she'd had a perfect life without anything painful ever happening to her, without ever facing loss.

"Actually," she added, "it's not just my parents. My whole immediate family is dead. My siblings too."

"Your whole family?" Cole echoed, his eyes wide. It took everything in him to not ask more questions. He wondered what had happened to her family. Had they been ill? An accident or something? He was curious, but he would rather not invade her privacy. She would tell him when she was ready.

Most of all, how could she be so cheerful with her family dead?

Belle said, "My aunt and uncle have always been nice to me. They treat me as their child. I should be grateful, you know, that I have a roof over my head. That I have people who care for me. Some aren't that lucky. Some go through worse, and they have no one to stand by their side. Being alive, we should be grateful. It means there's hope, and that we're capable of achieving anything."

He wished he was as positive as she was. But he had seen enough in his life to know that he was going to continue living miserably. He was

82

used to it and wasn't complaining. It was better to have his life figured out than to hold on to delusions.

"I'm so sorry, Belle."

She shrugged. "I don't want to talk about it. Tell me about your parents."

When it became clear that she really didn't want to tell him anything more, he broke the silence. "You know, I loved this place so much. It was my quiet place where I could hide when we had guests over. I wasn't a fan of the fancy parties my parents hosted, so when I saw the vehicles arriving at the front, I would hurry out of my room and come here. I would sit here, hidden away from the guests, and cook up stories of adventure." He had no idea why he was telling her this. He usually didn't share his childhood with people, but there was something about her that made him comfortable talking to her. "When I was a child and my parents fought, I came here to cry my eyes out. Here, I couldn't hear them yelling at each other. I couldn't hear my mother threaten to leave. There were times when I even slept on this very bench, only to wake up in my room after being carried in by my father."

He had fond memories of his father kneeling in this very garden, digging into the soil as he pulled out weeds. His father had not been a professional gardener, but he had been born with a green thumb. His grandfather had planted the garden, but his father had nurtured it and made it flourish. Cole's father had spent his free time here, making it beautiful, especially after Mom had left. It had been such a breathtaking sight.

"My mother loved this garden. I don't like to be reminded of her," Cole said. "She loved flowers so much. She's the reason my father picked up gardening. He wanted to create a world of flowers for her." He laughed bitterly. "Dad tried to give my mother the world. He tried to make her happy, but nothing he did pleased her. Nothing he did could make her stay in the end. She left us. She didn't care about the repercussions of her actions, that her leaving would ruin the lives of those she left behind. I located her and tried to contact her, but she would hang up on me whenever I called."

"I'm so sorry, Cole. Your dad seemed like a really great man and your mother was—"

"Cold, selfish. She didn't deserve my father. She toyed with him, knowing he had a weakness for her. When she left him, he was devastated. He would take care of the plants every day, especially that rosebush. That was his favorite." Cole gestured to the bush. "He acted as if his wife hadn't just left, caring for the garden like it was his baby. I think he thought that if he made it beautiful enough, she'd come back. I'd always seen him as a strong man, but for the first time, here in this garden, I saw him cry."

The memory was still fresh in Cole's mind. It had made him realize that his father wasn't so tough after all and that he was hurting badly.

"One day, when I was a child, I was looking for my father. When I came out to the greenhouse, I saw him on his knees near that bush, tears rolling down his face. There was so much pain in his eyes. He was so broken, yet he pretended to be strong for me. The man I loved so much had crumbled, and it was all because of my mother. I promised myself that day to never be like my father. I told myself that I would never put myself in such a vulnerable state where I would be hurt by a woman," Cole said.

Placing her hand over his, Belle said, "I know you were hurt a lot by your mother, but not every woman is like her. There are good women out there who love without holding back. There's a woman out there for you."

He laughed at her kind words. "What woman would want to be with a monster like me? Have you taken a look at me lately? I'm not capable of being loved by any woman."

"No, Cole. Some women don't care about outward appearances. They care only about the heart."

"The only woman who loves me is Claire. You know what other women will do? Treat me with disgust. Sure, there would be women out there who would pretend to love me, perhaps because of my wealth. They probably wouldn't care about how horrible I look. All that would matter to them would be the money, and eventually, they would treat me with scorn. Sometimes I feel like my looks are a blessing in disguise. In a way, they give me the safety I want from being hurt," Cole admitted. It hurt knowing he would never have a wife and children. It was a hard truth to accept, but it was one that he couldn't change.

"There you are. I've been looking for you two," Claire said, approaching them.

Cole instantly stood up, a blush spreading over his face when he realized how close he'd been sitting to Belle. His grandmother stood in front of them, a knowing smile playing on her lips.

"I thought you had both run off," Claire teased.

He shot her a warning look, and she laughed. She clearly was enjoying this. Since he had been a teenager, she had found every opportunity to tease him when it came to the opposite sex.

"We were just talking…about life," Belle said.

And death, he added inwardly.

Claire rolled her eyes. "Why don't we do something fun? Like a game of cards? Monopoly? Oh, yes. Or Scrabble."

"Grandma, not a game," Cole groaned. When it came to games, his grandmother was very competitive. She could turn from a loving old woman to a woman on a mission in a matter of seconds.

"Yes, we will play a game. I call Scrabble," Claire said, ignoring him. She hurried back into the house excitedly, surprisingly spry for a woman her age.

Cole turned to Belle. When he saw the sad look on her face, he froze. "What's wrong?"

"Oh, nothing. I'm fine. It's just…" She wrapped her arms around herself. "I don't really like board games."

85

"Why not? Are you not allowed to play them?"

"It's not that. We Amish play board games often. It's just..." She looked away. "It's something my family liked to do. It reminds me of them. Actually, it was the last thing they did before they..."

When her voice trailed off, he tried to lighten the mood. "We don't have to do what she says all the time, you know."

"She is the boss, though." Belle gave a weak smile.

"I thought I was the boss," Cole said, pretending to be offended.

"No, she's right. I am the boss!" Claire shouted from inside the house.

"That woman has the ears of an owl," Cole whispered to Belle, shaking his head

"I wish!" Claire called, sticking her head out the doorway.

Belle burst into laughter. "And the energy of a ten-year-old kid."

"She'll outlive us all," Cole said as they meandered into the house. "Really, if you don't want to play—"

A look of determination came over Belle. "You know what? I want to. My family wouldn't want me to stop doing fun things just because it reminds me of them."

"Exactly. They'd want you to enjoy life, Belle."

"Just like how your father would want you to keep playing the piano."

He raised his eyebrows, unable to think of an argument. She was right.

She nodded, smiling at her small victory over him. "Let's go, then."

Cole said, "Just know that she's a sore loser and very competitive. She likes to win at all costs."

A fierce smile appeared on Belle's lips. "Oh, I guess she has met her match then. I grew up playing board games."

Why did he feel like this was going to be the toughest game he had ever played?

The women started a brutal war of words.

He watched, amused, as they tried to win with declarations that each other's words weren't right. It was absurd to see both women create nonexistent words as well as their meanings. Claire and Belle used a big dictionary to check the credibility of the words.

"This game has to end," Cole declared, as the women reached a tie for what seemed to be the hundredth time.

"No, we still haven't gotten a winner," Claire said thoughtfully as she eyed her letters.

"Yes, the game is still on," Belle agreed.

Not for him. If they could have their way, they would play all day. This game should have ended long ago, but for their stubbornness to back down. With one swift move, Cole leaned over and scattered the letters on the board.

The women looked at him in surprise, then pounced on him with their words.

"Why did you do that?" Belle demanded.

"You're such a cruel child," Claire said, glaring at him.

Laughter erupted from him. It felt so strange to laugh, but he loved the feeling, enjoying the shock on the women's faces.

"Now the game is over," Cole pronounced.

"For now. There will be a rematch," Claire said, giving Belle a nod.

"There has to be," Belle agreed.

"Not on my watch," Cole said. Hopefully, he would be locked in his office, as there was no way he would be stuck again playing a game with these women. They were game monsters. He had thought Claire was bad enough, but with Belle, it was a complete disaster.

He felt much better when he returned to his office. It felt so strange to admit it, but he had surely had fun with those women downstairs. They had made him laugh. They had made him happy. It was the most activity he'd had in days, and he wanted more of it.

Belle was a kind, beautiful woman, but that didn't mean she would want him. Besides, she was Amish. From what he knew about them, they couldn't be with outsiders. He liked her more than he let on, but he couldn't complicate things. She deserved a life of freedom.

This was something he would never be able to give her.

***

As Belle got ready to leave that evening, Cole walked up to her.

"Belle, have you been walking here every day?" he asked.

"Well, yes, but I don't mind. My aunt and uncle sometimes use their buggy during the day, so I didn't want to prevent them from doing that. Really, it's not that long of a walk when I take the shortcut through the woods. I don't mind."

Cole bit his lip. Maybe, but in the evenings she must be tired. "Tell me, does your community allow bicycles?"

"Oh, yes. Some communities ban them, but ours allows them. Some of my friends ride them around town. For short distances, it's easier than hitching up the horse and buggy. In fact, one of the families owns a bike repair shop near where I live. Why?"

"Do you know how to ride a bike?"

Belle laughed. "I haven't ridden one in a long time, but yes, I do know how."

Cole nodded, his mind working. "Thanks. I was just wondering."

Belle got her things and left. He stared out the window, watching as Belle walked down the lane toward her home.

She'd been doing such a wonderful job that he wanted to do something nice for her to show his appreciation. He knew just the thing.

Dropping the curtain, he returned to his seat, where he had been making no progress all day. He searched online for a bicycle. After a while, he chose one and ordered it.

Now it was time to get back to work.

As much as he hated to admit that Simeon was right, he was. Cole had writer's block, and it irritated him. He had deleted sentences several times because they made no sense. He couldn't even come up with a decent plot. Everything he wrote seemed to be a flop.

There had been a time when every word he wrote meant a lot to him. But now he felt like a machine, churning out one book after the other to keep up with the demands of his publisher, writing what they wanted to sell.

His passion and inspiration were fading.

Cole went downstairs to see Claire. Right away, she read his expression.

"Simeon asked you to go to the conference again, didn't he?" Claire asked, joining him on the couch. "Why won't you go?"

"Grandma, I know where you're going with this. Just as I told Simeon, I'm not going to the conference. He needs to shelve that idea," Cole said.

"Why not? Your fans would love to know who you are."

He sighed. He really didn't need this. "Grandma, I can't go. Why are you acting like you don't see what I look like? Look how horrible I am," he said, his voice rising as he pointed to the disfigured, burned half of his face. "One look at me and they'll run screaming. Think of the whispers and the looks of disgust I'll get. After they see the real me, no one will purchase my book again. My career will be over. No one wants to associate with a monster."

"In my eyes, you are handsome, and I am sure your fans will think so too." Grandma leaned forward and touched his face lovingly. "Now, is that all?"

"I'm afraid, Grandma." He looked away, not wanting to see the tears in her eyes.

Softly, she said, "You're not a monster, Cole. You're a kind-hearted man, though ornery at times, and you've refused to see the good in yourself. You've let your sadness get the best of you. Anyone who looks at you with disgust is an idiot and isn't deserving of you. You are braver than this, and your military awards prove it. I'm sure you've faced much worse than the worst possible scenario that could come from this."

He chuckled humorlessly.

"There's so much in store for you in life," Claire said. "You just have to be willing to accept it and open your heart. Be the brave man I know you are."

Chapter Six

Belle woke up quite later than she usually did, but it was Saturday, and she had the weekends off. She turned and tossed in bed before finally getting up. Kneeling, she said her prayers, then made her bed.

Ever since she'd begun working at the manor, she cherished her weekends more. It was the time she had all to herself. Well, aside from the work at home. However, her work here had been reduced to give her enough time to rest.

Aunt Greta was sitting at the kitchen table, and Belle joined her.

"So, how is work?" Aunt Greta asked, as she often did.

"It's good, really," Belle said. "I enjoy it."

The only issue she had with Cole was his grumpiness and his secrecy. She couldn't help but wonder what he was doing in there.

"And the grandmother?"

"Oh. Claire is a darling." Belle smiled. "She makes working at the manor a joy."

Belle had been surprised to discover that the older woman had once been a ballerina. Claire had shown Belle a few elegant moves, which she had tried and failed at.

"This is harder than it looks," Belle had cried, laughing as she toppled over.

With Claire, she could talk about almost everything. It was like a breath of fresh air. While Belle loved her aunt and uncle, she felt as though she couldn't open up to them about her hopes and dreams. However, Belle and Claire discussed a huge variety of topics.

"I just want to make sure you're safe working there," her aunt said, bringing her back to the here and now. "I don't really like the idea of you working for a man alone."

91

"Claire is there. I'm not alone. Really, they're very nice to me. I love working there."

"I'm sorry. I just worry about you. I promised your mother years ago that if anything ever happened…" Aunt Greta looked away, sadness filling her eyes. "I still miss my sister. I can't even imagine what it's like for you."

"I miss my family every minute of every day," Belle said, reaching for her aunt's hand. "They would appreciate everything you've done for me. Thank you." Belle hugged her aunt. She knew they were concerned about her.

Some days, Belle felt like the world was over. Other times, she just kept pushing, holding on to rainbows. No matter what, she'd survive and remain joyful.

That afternoon, Belle drove the buggy to Damaris' house to see how the puppies were doing.

"Hi, Belle!" Damaris called as she came out of the house, wiping her hands on her apron. "I'm so glad you're here."

"I did promise to come by soon to see the puppies."

"They're in the barn. Let's go," Damaris said. A few of her six siblings came out of the house, following them.

Dean, Damaris' younger brother, sneezed as they came into the barn. He smiled sheepishly. "I'm allergic to hay."

Danny, who was older than Dean, crossed his arms. "You're allergic to everything."

"Aren't they so cute?" Daisy squealed, flouncing toward the puppies to pick one up.

Delphine stood in the corner shyly, just smiling as she watched silently. Desmond, the youngest, giggled as he chased the puppies.

"They're adorable," Belle said, gasping when she saw the sweet German shepherd puppies toddling around. "What are you going to do with them all?"

"We could give them to the neighbors if they're interested," Dean suggested.

"They're old enough now," Damaris said.

"That's a good idea," Belle agreed. She smiled at the little puppies, which had the same tan and black coat as their mother, with black pointed ears. The smallest, the quiet one of the litter, came up to her and licked Belle's shoes. She bent down to pick him up and lifted him to her chest. He cuddled against her, and love warmed in her heart. She instantly felt a connection to the puppy.

Suddenly, a crazy idea occurred to her. She'd been trying to think of a good Christmas gift for Cole. Now that she was holding this sweet puppy, he seemed like a perfect companion for her lonely boss. He was all alone in that big house all the time, so wouldn't he like a dog to keep him company?

"We named that one Beast," Daisy said.

"Daisy and Dean named him. It started as a joke because he's the runt of the litter," Damaris said with a smile and a shrug. "It stuck."

"Beast," Belle said, then giggled when the puppy licked her face. An idea popped into her head, and even though she wasn't sure if it would work, she knew she had to try. "I think I know someone who would want him. Can I come to get him on Christmas Eve?"

"Sure," Damaris said. "Who do you think would want him?"

Belle leaned toward her friend and said quietly, "Cole."

Damaris' eyes grew wide. "Really?"

Belle's face heated. "You know, for a Christmas gift. I just figured, because he's so lonely—"

"I think it's a great idea. Beast is a very sweet puppy. He'd make a great companion for anyone." Damaris grinned. "You can come by and get him when you're ready. I think by then many of the other puppies will be getting new homes too."

"Thank you."

After leaving her friend's house, Belle took the buggy into town to run errands for Aunt Greta. When she was done, she stopped by the bookstore.

"Hello, dear," Mr. O'Malley said as she walked in.

"Hello." Belle smiled. This was the first time she'd been to the bookstore since she'd been hired. She had been too busy to come around, and she sure had missed it.

"I was beginning to think you were never going to return," Mr. O'Malley said.

"Oh, I've been busy with work," Belle said. "I like my new job."

"That's good to hear. Did you enjoy the book you got last time?" he asked.

"Actually, Mr. O'Malley, do you remember that book I got last time? It was by Tony Graham," Belle said, remembering the book in which she'd found the letter. "It was called *Hidden Treasures*."

He nodded. For his age, he had an impeccable memory. "I think it was donated here years ago along with several other books by the same author. I can't remember when. I think you bought some of the other ones before."

"Someone donated several books by the same author? Can you remember who donated them?" If she could find the person, perhaps she could reach out to them and return the letter, hopefully giving them some closure.

"Oh, no, dear. It was a long time ago. Why, is something wrong?" he asked.

94

"No, I was just curious," Belle said. As much as she wanted to know who owned the letter, she didn't want to share it with anyone except the rightful owner. Belle looked through the newest books on the shelves. "Nothing new from him yet?" she asked.

She didn't have to mention his name for Mr. O'Malley to know who it was.

"No. I did hear that he's working on something new, but these things take time. It could take a year or two for that book to be released, or even longer, especially because his last one was recently released."

"Oh." This was sad news to Belle. She was greatly looking forward to the next installment in the series. However, no matter how long it took, she would be waiting.

"Mr. O'Malley, do you have any books on gardening?" Belle asked.

"Why, of course. Right this way."

Belle smiled. Claire would be so pleased.

***

Chapter Seven

Cole waited by the door for Belle to arrive, excited to give her the gift he'd bought for her to show his appreciation for a job well done so far. When she walked up the lane, he opened the door before she could knock.

"Good morning," he said with enthusiasm.

"Wow. Good morning to you too," Belle said, her eyes wide. "What has put you in such a lively mood?"

"I have something for you," Cole said, stepping out onto the doorstep next to her. She took a small step back. He wondered whether he had been standing too close. Had he made her uncomfortable?

"Follow me." He hurried to the side of the house where he'd hidden the bike, which was propped against the manor. It was complete with a helmet and a big red bow.

"Consider this an early Christmas gift. It's to show my appreciation for a job well done. I see how happy you make my grandmother and how thorough of a job you've done with maintaining the house. Also, we love your cooking. We're both very happy with your work, and I know you've been walking here every day. I just hope this will make your life a bit easier," he said, gesturing to the bike. He tried to read her expression, which was a mixture of surprise and contemplation.

"It's beautiful. But I... I can't accept this. It's too much, Cole," she said, a hand on her chest.

Had he crossed a line?

"Why not? It's not too much. I knew you'd probably want something not fancy at all, so I got the plainest one I could find. I didn't want you to get in trouble with your church."

"Thank you. I do appreciate it. But..." She hesitated. "Is it appropriate for you to give this to me?"

Oh. That's why she was hesitating. After the heart-to-hearts they'd been sharing lately, did she think this was a romantic gift?

"It's not like that," he stammered, feeling his face heat. Well, he couldn't deny that he did have feelings for her, but he certainly couldn't let her know that. That *would* be inappropriate. He was her boss. "I just don't want you to have to walk to work every day in the cold. I figured this would get you home faster. I wanted to show my appreciation for a job well done. That's all. Honestly."

"Well then..." She bit her lip as she stared at the bike, then smiled. "Thank you, Cole. I love it."

"Go on, try it out," he urged. She walked to the bike, bringing it to the driveway. She put on the helmet and got on the bike, minding her skirt, obviously trying to keep it away from the chain and pedals, but it didn't seem to be an issue. She started pedaling, laughing harder and harder the farther she went.

"I haven't done this in years!" she cried.

He couldn't help but laugh himself. Then he heard another laugh. He looked up to see Claire in the window upstairs, watching them with a wistful smile on her face. She winked at him.

Oh, Grandma.

After a few more laps around the driveway, Belle came back and got off the bike, her face pink from the cold and exertion.

"So? How do you like it?" he asked.

"It's great. Thanks so much, Cole. I'll get around so much quicker on this."

Her eyebrows were knit together in what looked like confusion that she was trying to hide. She smiled at him, but her eyes didn't twinkle like they normally did when she grinned.

What was going through her mind? Did she misread his intentions?

97

"I'm so glad you like it. Let's get back inside before we freeze," he said, trying to break the awkward moment. She put her bike near the door, and they hurried inside.

***

Belle walked up the stairs to Claire's room, completely confused.

At first, she'd misread Cole's gift. After the deep talks they'd had recently, she thought maybe, just maybe, he felt something for her much beyond a boss and employee relationship.

She'd thought at first that the bicycle was a gesture to show his feelings for her, but then she'd realized how ridiculous that had been when he'd assured her otherwise. So, she'd been wrong. Why would a wealthy man like him be interested in a woman like her, his housekeeper?

Belle shook her head, feeling utterly foolish. Apparently, she'd been very wrong, and now she'd embarrassed herself.

She knocked on Claire's door and entered when Claire called for her to come in.

"Good morning, Claire," Belle said.

"Good morning, dear." Claire smiled, standing near her window. "I saw you riding your bike. You sure looked like you were having fun."

"It was fun. It's been a long time. It was very nice of Cole to get it for me." Belle busied herself with making Claire's bed, trying to hide her feelings of bewilderment.

Claire took a step toward her. "Are you all right, dear?"

"Of course," Belle said.

"You know, Cole thinks very highly of you."

"I know. He's so kind. You've both been so kind to me." Belle fluffed the pillows and straightened out the blankets.

Claire came forward and touched Belle's hand. "Belle, you don't understand. He thinks the world of you. I see how happy he is when he's around you. You've brought the light back into his life."

Belle could feel her heart swell. "Truly?"

"Do I look like I'm lying?" Claire retorted. "Of course, he does."

"Well." Belle resumed making the bed. "I do appreciate the bike."

"You know, Cole has a way with words on paper, but in real life, he has a hard time expressing his feelings." She shook her head. "He's like that even with me. Anyway, what's the plan for today?"

Belle turned to Claire, grabbing her hands. "With Cole giving me the bike this morning, I completely forgot to tell you that I got some books about gardening at the bookstore. They're in my bag downstairs."

"Wonderful," Claire chirped. "And with those supplies we ordered online, we can now fix up the greenhouse and surprise Cole."

"Oh, yes. I hid them in the greenhouse once they arrived. He has no idea," Belle said.

"Once he sees it looking beautiful like it used to be, I know he'll fall in love with it again."

"I hope so."

"Let's get to work," Claire said, turning and walking toward the door.

Belle smiled, shaking her head. The woman truly did have the energetic spirit of a child.

***

Cole couldn't focus.

As his hands hovered above his keyboard, he let out an exasperated sigh. Maybe he needed a break.

99

He wandered down to the kitchen to get a drink, then stopped when he heard laughter. Smiling, he followed the lovely sound. Belle sure had made his grandmother happy, and that alone made him glad he'd hired her.

Cole continued following the sound, realizing it was leading him to the greenhouse. What were they doing in there? It wasn't that pleasant of a place to spend time in, with its dead branches, overgrown plants, and shriveled-up blooms that had once made the place beautiful.

He got to the doorway of the greenhouse and stopped cold when he saw Belle and his grandmother planting flowers and other greenery. They'd already planted several from the looks of it and were now putting seeds into a large pot on the left side of the room, laughing and talking jovially as they worked.

Claire was grinning, and Cole had to admit, he hadn't seen his grandmother look so joyful in a long time. But that was beside the point.

His eyebrows knit together in annoyance.

They were disobeying his direct orders. Claire knew Cole was completely against replanting this garden, and he had told Belle to leave it alone, that he didn't want it fixed.

They finished with the pot, then looked as if they were going to tend to the rosebush in the middle of the greenhouse.

Annoyance turned to anger that boiled inside him. He could feel it surging up his chest as his fists clenched and his veins ignited with fire. Cole knew he wouldn't be able to contain it much longer.

"What do you think you're doing?" he roared as they approached the rosebush with a watering can and pruning shears.

Belle jumped, the small ceramic pot in her hand falling to the floor and shattering.

"Cole!" Claire snapped. "You scared us half to death. What does it look like we're doing? We're making this old, dead garden beautiful again."

"I specifically asked you to leave this alone," he said, setting his eyes on Belle. "I told both of you to leave it alone."

Belle paled, then bent to pick up the shards on the floor.

"Oh, Cole, stop being such a bear. It's not her fault. I talked her into it." Claire turned to Belle. "Dear, be careful. You might cut yourself," she warned.

"How dare you both defy me like this?" Cole continued, stepping closer to them. "There's a reason why I don't want this garden fixed up. You both know why. I know you've been out here, Grandma, secretly watering my father's rosebush, and I haven't stopped you, but this has gone too far."

"I know this greenhouse reminds you of your parents," Claire said, holding up her hands. "Especially your father. We just thought that if we made it beautiful that—"

"That what? I'd suddenly love it again?" Cole retorted.

"Yes," Claire said, hands on her hips. "But you're too stubborn to even let us try or to even consider the notion."

"I'm sorry, Cole," Belle murmured as she continued to pick up pieces of the pot. Then she gasped. She held up her hand, blood trickling down it from a small cut.

"Both of you, get out!" Cole ordered, pointing to the door. "And please, don't come here anymore."

"Cole, how can you do this? Can't you see Belle is hurt?" Claire pleaded, gesturing to Belle.

Blinded by his rage, Cole had hardly noticed her injury. Guilt sent a pang through him. "I'm sorry, I—"

"I should go," Belle said, her voice cracking. She held her hand to her chest and bolted out the greenhouse door, skirting around Cole.

"Wait. Belle, are you all right?" Cole asked, but she was already out of sight.

Cole glanced at his grandmother.

"That is about one of the coldest things I've ever seen you do," his grandmother said, slowly shaking her head.

"I'm sorry, Grandma, I—"

"Forget about me. I'm used to your stubbornness. Go after her," Claire said with surprising force.

Cole nodded and darted out the door.

"Belle, wait!" he shouted, then heard the front door slam.

She was already gone. He rushed to the door, yanking it open, and saw her pedaling down the driveway on her bicycle. She looked as if she was struggling to grip the handlebar. The bicycle wavered, careened, then tipped, and she fell to the ground.

Cole was already running, calling Belle's name. He was by her side in a moment, helping her sit up.

"Belle? Are you okay? Are you hurt?" he asked, looking her over. Her hand was still bleeding, but she looked otherwise uninjured.

"I'm fine," she whispered hoarsely. "I think I just bruised my knee and elbow. The blood on my hand made the handlebar slippery, and I couldn't hold on."

"Come inside so I can bandage your hand," he said, helping her stand. He led her slowly toward the house, letting her lean on him. If he hadn't been so wracked with guilt at the beastly way he'd just reacted, he would have savored the feeling of her closeness.

They came in through the front door, where Claire was waiting.

"Are you hurt, Belle?" she asked.

"Just minor injuries," Belle insisted. "The cut on my hand is small. Really, I'll be fine."

"Sit here," Cole said, helping Belle onto the sofa. He went to get the first aid kit and returned, sitting beside her.

"This is getting too familiar," Belle said with a humorless laugh.

"I was thinking the same thing," Cole said, then turned serious. "I'm so sorry. This is all my fault. I shouldn't have gotten so angry in the greenhouse. You were just trying to make the place beautiful again. I'm so sorry I overreacted."

Cole noticed Claire slipping out of the room, giving him a knowing smile.

"Thank you," Belle said. He wasn't sure if she was referring to his apology or the bandage he was wrapping around her hand. "I forgive you, Cole."

Cole looked up from her hand to her eyes. How could she forgive him, just like that? "I was an utter jerk. I have no excuse."

"Yes, you were." A small smile lifted one corner of her lovely lips. "I do forgive you. I'm sorry for going against your wishes and fixing up the garden with Claire. We just thought it would make you happy, and she was so excited to do it. You know it's impossible to say no to her. But truly, I wanted to do it."

"It did make her happy. I saw how you were both laughing and how happy she looked. You make her happy, Belle. I don't remember the last time I saw her smile and laugh like that. Thank you. I'm so sorry I messed up everything."

Belle smiled shyly, watching as he tenderly wrapped the bandage around the cut on her palm from the pot that he'd caused her to drop. This cut truly was his fault.

"I still feel so terrible. If I hadn't startled you, you wouldn't have dropped the pot and cut your hand, and you wouldn't have rushed out and fallen on your bike." He shook his head slowly, feeling like the most terrible person in the world.

Belle rested her good hand on Cole's arm, making him stop what he was doing. He gazed into her eyes, his heart stumbling at the way she was looking at him. Her touch sent a spark up his arm, shooting warmth through his entire body, thawing his heart, which had been frozen for far too long.

"Cole, I told you. I forgive you. God calls us to forgive. I understand that the greenhouse is special to you and brings up painful memories. You made a mistake. We're all human. Let's move on, okay?" She gave him a merciful smile that turned his heart to melted wax.

"Belle, you are…" Though he was a writer, he couldn't find the words to describe her. At least, not ones that he could say out loud without embarrassing both of them.

Beautiful. Kind. Thoughtful. Too good for him.

And her dark eyes were now staring into his, melting his soul.

"I think you should finish the greenhouse," he blurted before he could change his mind.

What was happening to him? Why was he saying these things, telling her to do the thing he had just ordered her not to do? Why did she have this effect on him?

"Really? Oh, Claire will be so excited," Belle said, grinning in a childlike way.

"Oh, yes," Cole agreed. "I think it would be good for all of us."

"I can't wait to tell her."

"Finished," Cole said, reluctantly letting go of her hand. He had a strong urge to kiss her injured palm, but again, it was impossible. It would make things extremely awkward, then she'd quit for sure. "Thanks for not giving up on me."

Belle shook her head, giving him a small smile. "Oh, Cole. I could never give up on you."

He stared at her intently, wondering what she meant. Did she mean in a professional way? In a friendly way?

Or something more?

The way she was looking at him made him feel like he could do anything, even go to that conference in New York and reveal himself to his fans. Maybe if she was by his side, he could.

"So," Cole said, trying to change the subject to break the tension. "I know you like to read, but what else do you like to do? Do you have dreams, maybe a certain career you want to do?"

"Well, yes. Before I moved here, several of the young Amish women were abducted by sex traffickers, including some of my friends. I went to the library and did some research online, and I found an organization that rescues children from sex slavery. They also provide aftercare for them, where they get medical care and counseling. I want to work for them. I saw on their website that they're looking for people to do fundraising and marketing for them. I just have this burning desire in my heart to help. More than anything, I want to raise awareness for them because so many people have no idea slavery is still such a huge problem in the world. If I don't, I think I'll regret it for the rest of my life."

"So why don't you work for them? Why not apply for the job?"

"I can't. It would require me to do a lot of work online and to travel, asking churches and businesses to support the organization. There's no way I'd be able to do that and remain Amish. There's no way it'll ever happen." Belle shook her head, dismay in her eyes.

Cole frowned. "I mean, I know you're not allowed to use the internet, but why not travel at least?"

"I'm just an Amish woman. I admit that I want so much more out of life, but I'm restricted by rules. If I wanted to do this job, I'd have to get a computer and use the internet, and leave the community long-term. I'd have to fly on an airplane, most likely. That's all against the rules." A shiver ran through her at the idea. For as long as she could remember, she had always loved the Amish life, surrounded by friends and family. Could she give it up to pursue her passion of helping victimized children? "I don't know if I could do it. I want to do it so much, but would I be willing to give up my entire life for it?"

"You'd never know unless you tried. Who knows? You might be giving up something good for something truly incredible."

"If I did leave, I'd be out there alone without any family. If I failed, I could always return to the community, repent, and rejoin the Amish. But then I'd have to admit to myself that I was a failure."

"No. If you gave it your best, then you wouldn't be a failure. I think you'd be perfect for that job. Belle, don't underestimate yourself," Cole advised. "In the future, you may have a family and everything else you want, but unfulfilled dreams can leave you empty. When you're old and gray, do you want to look back and regret not ever doing what you really wanted? Will you regret not helping rescue children from sex slavery?"

His words hit her directly in the heart, lodging there like a thorn.

Cole was speaking from experience. He had always loved writing, ever since he was a kid. It had been a solace, a respite from all that was happening in his life. Even though his life had gone awry, he still wrote. Many times, he had shuddered to think of his life without writing. He would have been so miserable. Claire and his writing were the only things that really mattered to him.

"Thank you, Cole. I really needed to hear you say those words," Belle said brokenly. "I guess I'm just scared. It's risky. Either way, I could have regrets."

"Of course, it's risky. But if it's what you want to do, then you should do it. It might be hard, but that doesn't mean you shouldn't try."

"Well, kids. Have you worked things out?" Claire asked, sauntering into the room.

"Cole says we should finish the greenhouse," Belle said, standing up carefully. "What do you say?"

Claire hurried over to her grandson and hugged his neck. "Oh, thank you. I promise, you won't regret this, my dear."

At the sight of the two women hurrying away, giggling like schoolgirls, Cole chuckled.

"I hope not."

Chapter Eight

On Christmas Eve morning, Belle left early with Beast, excited as she walked the energetic puppy on a leash. Cole had told her she didn't have to work that day, but she wanted to so that she could give him his gift and make some cinnamon rolls for Claire.

She unlocked the back door and hurried to the kitchen with the puppy. She found a cardboard box and set Beast inside it with some things to play with so he wouldn't get into mischief as she cooked.

Now it was time to make a magnificent holiday breakfast. She began cooking eggs, sausage, and pancakes.

"Merry Christmas," Claire said, joining her in the kitchen.

"Merry Christmas, Claire."

"It smells amazing in here. What kind of feast are you making? We're only three people." Claire laughed, then her eyes narrowed as Beast made a move in the carton. "What is that?" she asked cautiously, edging toward the door.

"My friend's dog had puppies a few months ago, and I thought one of them would make a nice gift for Cole."

Claire stared at her intensely, and Belle felt uncomfortable. Her gaze was scrutinizing, as if she was trying to see something.

"What? Was it a bad idea?"

"You got Cole a puppy?" Claire asked.

Belle laughed nervously. "I thought he'd make a nice gift for Cole. Maybe I should have asked first. I just thought you'd both like the companionship."

Claire looked at the puppy thoughtfully for several long moments, a forlorn look on her face, then turned to Belle. "You know what? I'm sure Cole will love his gift," she said, smiling broadly.

"And this is for you," Belle said, handing Claire a small gift.

"For me? Oh, dear, you didn't have to give me anything," Claire said, carefully opening the package. Inside was an autographed, early edition of a novel by one of her favorite authors. "Where did you find this?" Claire asked, her eyes glassy.

"I found it at my favorite bookstore in town," Belle said. "I remembered how much you said you loved that author, and when I realized it was autographed, I knew I had to get it. Many of the books there are donated."

"This is so special, Belle. Thank you." Claire gave Belle a hug.

Beast whined in the box, disrupting their hug. Belle eyed the puppy nervously. "Are you sure about me giving the puppy to Cole? I could just take Beast back home…"

"Belle, don't start getting cold feet. You'll know if he likes the puppy only if you give it to him," Claire said.

She'd been so excited, she hadn't thought this through. What if he didn't like Beast? What if he hated dogs? What if he was allergic?

"Stop stressing yourself, Belle. Just go give him to Cole and—"

"What do you want to give to me?" Cole asked, suddenly appearing in the doorway.

The women froze in surprise. Belle gulped. She turned to Claire, who nodded her head, giving her the go-ahead.

But Belle couldn't find the words.

"Is anyone going to say anything?" Cole asked.

"Well…" Belle stammered.

The box rattled as Beast tried to climb out. Cole jumped, then walked closer to it. "What was that?"

Two soft ears peeked out from the top of the box.

"Is that a puppy?" Cole asked, his eyes wide in surprise as he looked from Claire to Belle.

"Well, yes. My friend's dog had puppies a few months ago and she's been trying to find homes for them. I thought you'd like one of them. If you don't want Beast, I can always take him home. I just thought…" Belle knew she was rambling, but she had suddenly become nervous.

Why wasn't he saying anything? Cole approached the box. He peered into it, his hands clenched into fists. He stared at Beast, his jaw set firmly. His hands were shaking.

"His name is Beast?" Cole uttered in a low voice.

"Well, yes, but I didn't name him. My friend's younger siblings did. Please, don't think—"

"Were they making fun of me by naming him that?" he demanded.

"No! They just thought it was a cute name for him because he's the runt of the litter, but he has so much spirit."

Yes, this was definitely a mistake, Belle thought.

When Cole finally turned around, a tear crept down his cheek.

"Cole, what's wrong? I'm so sorry if I overstepped—" Belle began, heat rising in her face. What was happening?

"Get that dog out of here," Cole said with a sorrowful demeanor Belle had never seen in him before, as if he was about to weep. "I never want to see it again."

With that, he stalked out of the room. A moment later, somewhere in the manor, a door slammed.

Belle winced, then turned slowly to Claire. "What… What on earth just happened? Why was he so upset? Is he that offended by Beast's name? Does he hate dogs?"

110

"No, no. It's not that. At least, I don't think he's actually upset about Beast's name. It's something else. I'm sorry, Belle. I thought maybe this puppy would make him happy, but I was wrong. He had a dog before. Well, technically, it wasn't his." Claire threw her hands up. "It's complicated, and it's not my story to tell. You should go talk to him."

"Now?" Belle asked, placing her hands on the counter to steady herself. What had she done?

"Well, in a minute. This is all very emotional for him, clearly. I should have known. I'm sorry." Claire looked sadly at the puppy, sighing. "What a sweetie. It's too bad."

"I'm not even sure if I should finish making breakfast," Belle said, looking dejectedly at the cinnamon rolls she'd been preparing.

"There, there. It'll be fine. He's probably in the greenhouse. Go on, talk to him," Claire said, making a shooing motion with her hands.

Feeling incredibly uncomfortable, Belle darted out of the kitchen and headed toward the greenhouse. As she approached the doorway, she hesitated.

"I can hear you, Belle," Cole muttered. "Come in."

Cautiously, she approached, stopping a few feet from where he sat on the bench in the middle of the greenhouse, which was now improving, as Claire and Belle were fixing it up. Yet, Cole held a dead rose in his hands—one that had dried up long ago.

"I'm so sorry, Cole. I really should have asked before bringing Beast here. I just thought he'd be a good gift for you, since you're here all the time. I'm sorry if you were offended by his name. I promise, my friend's younger siblings didn't mean any harm at all when they named him that. They're sweet kids," Belle said.

Cole grunted. "People around here call me the beast, as I'm sure you've heard. I thought they were making fun of me."

"They weren't. Not these kids."

111

"If you say so."

"I do say so. I promise. They said it started as a joke, but the name stuck. They weren't referring to what people call you at all." She took another step closer to him.

Cole looked up at her. "Are you sure?"

"Of course. You know, dogs are wonderful companions." Belle stopped abruptly, remembering what Claire had said. "But you already know that, don't you?"

"How much did my grandmother tell you?" Cole asked, frowning.

"She just said you had a dog once, but it wasn't technically yours."

"That's right."

Belle took another step closer. "Want to tell me about it?"

Cole sighed.

She took another step and sat beside him on the bench, looking at him expectantly. His eyes were red from crying. Was that why he'd run off? Because he didn't want her to see him cry?

"You did nothing wrong, Belle. I'm sorry for how I reacted. I'm not angry." He plucked a wilted, dried petal from the dead rose. "Just...sad."

"What happened?" she pressed. "You know, they say it helps to talk about what's bothering you."

"People say a lot of nonsense."

Belle cocked her head at him, scowling.

"I'm sorry," Cole said, taking a deep breath. "I... have been doing some thinking. Lots of thinking. I apologize for being a jerk to you when you first arrived. I'm not so good at meeting new people."

"I forgive you, Cole." She understood where he'd been coming from. He was called a monster by people who had seen him, and he had thought she would find him repulsive.

"I wasn't always this grumpy or shy. I wasn't this person. Once upon a time, I was a happy man and thought I could change the world," Cole said, with a faraway look.

"And what happened to that young man?" Belle asked.

"He changed. I left home when I was eighteen. I was done with high school, and I felt I had to travel the world to see what was in store for me. There were many things I could do. Join the family business. Go to college. But I wanted none of that. I wanted some adventure. Something to add value to my life. So, I joined the Marines." He nodded as he continued. "I hadn't expected fun in the Marines, but it was so much harder than I expected. There were times I felt like giving up, but I wanted to serve my country. Over time, I came to love being a Marine. I had new friends whom I considered brothers and sisters. I became good at what I did, and I thought it would only get better."

"And then the scars happened?" Belle couldn't help but guess.

A sad look covered his face. "Yes."

"You don't have to tell me," Belle said, placing her hand over his. She didn't want him to relive the horrible experience.

"No, I have to. I served in Afghanistan twice. At the end of my second tour, everyone was excited as we neared the end of our time there. But only a few days before we were scheduled to come home, there was a kidnapping in a remote village. Some rebels were holding women and children hostage. My team and I went on the mission, along with my partner."

"He must have been an amazing friend," Belle said, noticing the tenderness that filled his eyes.

Cole chuckled. "She was a dog."

Belle's dark eyebrows shot up.

"Her name was Echo, and she was assigned to me. I never knew I could love an animal that much. But from the moment I set my eyes on that brown dog with her black ears, I knew she was mine. Military dogs are trained to track, detect explosives, attack, and do search and rescue. Echo's specialties were search and rescue and tracking."

Belle wanted to ask so many questions but remained silent.

"I was friends with everyone on my team, but Echo was more. She would cuddle up beside me. She followed me everywhere. It was just supposed to be a simple rescue mission, but it turned out to be more. We walked into a trap. The tunnel we passed through had been rigged with explosives, and…"

Tears welled in his eyes, and she felt her eyes stinging with tears as well. Belle wished she could take away his pain.

"I was far enough away, in the back, that I was only knocked off my feet and I got all this," Cole gestured to the scars on his face and arms. "I survived because of Echo. I tried to pull out as many of my comrades as I could, but when I passed out, Echo pulled me away from the flames to safety. She went back for one of the men, but the movement triggered another bomb." Cole let his face fall in his hands. "By the time I woke up, it was too late. She was gone, and many of my team members didn't survive. I should have saved them. I should have protected her like she'd protected me so many times. So many men and women on my team died. My brothers and sisters in arms. Friends whom I called family. I failed them. If only I hadn't been knocked unconscious…"

Belle wanted to reach out and touch his arm, but she didn't know where exactly the scars were located under his sleeve or if they still hurt, so she pulled back her hand. "There was nothing you could have done, Cole. It's not your fault that you were knocked unconscious."

Cole shook his head. She saw the hardness in his eyes, but beyond that, there was grief and regret. Was the gruff exterior just a façade that he used to hide what he was really feeling?

"I'm so sorry, Cole," she said. "I'm so sorry for all you've lost. But none of this is your fault. Echo was loyal to you. She cared for you. Think of the good times you spent together. She wouldn't want you to be sad. I miss my family every single day, and I wish they could come back. I feel guilty for being the only one alive, but then I think about how happy we were. I think about what they would have wanted for me. They would have wanted me to be happy. They would want me to face life with happiness instead of remorse. My family would want me to live my life, and your comrades would want you to live your life, too."

Cole sighed, knowing she was right. "Echo would want me to live. She always loved to play fetch. She was so amazing, you know. She was playful, but when it was time for work, she would have this..." Cole chuckled as he relived memories of his lost dog. "She would have this focused, serious look until we were done with work. Then she would become so playful. You're right, she would have wanted me to be happy."

She waited for him to open up more. She knew there was a lot more he had to say, and she was grateful that he trusted her.

"I woke up three days after the explosion. I was in so much pain. I saw Claire, and there was so much sadness and worry in her eyes. I was told that I had been brought to the States. I broke down when they told me about Echo. She had been buried, and I had never gotten the opportunity to say goodbye. They told me a lot of damage had been done to me during the explosion. When I looked into the mirror for the first time, my face covered with bandages, I broke down again. I was stunned by how I looked. The doctors told me the scars would never go away. I would never look normal again. I had lost everything. My friends, my dog, my career, my happiness. Even my father had died while I was gone, and I didn't even find out until I was in the hospital. It was the lowest point of my life. I didn't even want to live anymore. I lost everything, Belle."

"No," Belle retorted. "You didn't lose everything. You have yourself, Claire, me, and Beast, and this beautiful manor. You still have your life. I know you hurt badly, but you're alive, and you need to appreciate this. How do you think Claire would have been if she had lost you? Do you know the pain your team's friends and families still go through with the loss? You're blessed to be alive, Cole. You haven't lost your freedom. You haven't lost your will to live."

Cole was quiet for a while. "You're right. I never thought about how devastated Claire would have been if she had lost me. She would be so alone. I've been so selfish. Yes, I'm blessed to be alive."

She was glad he was seeing things that way. He shouldn't guilt-trip himself over being the only survivor. He was blessed and didn't even realize it.

"The reason why I reacted the way I did to Beast is that he looks so much like a small version of Echo. She was also a German shepherd," Cole explained. "It brought everything back. I didn't mean to make you feel like you did something wrong."

"Maybe Beast is your second chance, Cole. It's okay to have another dog in remembrance of Echo. It's okay to move on," Belle said. "I think Echo would want you to forgive yourself."

"Dogs are very perceptive...and loyal." Cole nodded slowly.

"Of course. I think Beast will make you so happy," Belle said. "If you give him the chance. If it's too painful, I understand. I can take him back home with me."

"No. You're right, Belle." Cole stood so suddenly that Belle jumped. "In remembrance of Echo." Then he hurried out of the greenhouse.

Belle stared after him, eyes wide.

When she reached the kitchen, Cole was already standing over the box. He hesitated as he stooped. Then, gently, he removed the puppy from the box and cuddled him to his side. "You're such a cute puppy, aren't you?" Cole asked, in the gentlest voice Belle had ever heard. Beast barked in reply and Cole laughed. It was a sweet sound, making tears well in her eyes. She wanted him to laugh more.

Claire was also grinning, her own eyes wet with tears. She smiled at Belle, then leaned over and squeezed her hand. "Thank you," Claire whispered.

Belle smiled, then turned to Cole. "So, you want Beast?"

He nodded. "Yes, I do. Thank you so much, Belle. This is the best Christmas gift I've ever received."

Belle beamed, a hand on her heart.

"I hope you don't mind going into town to get some supplies for Beast?" he asked.

"It would be a pleasure."

He headed to the kitchen door and turned around. "Thank you very much for this. Thank you, Belle. It really means a lot to me," Cole said. With that, he turned around, humming as he walked away.

"That wasn't too bad," Belle admitted.

"He loves the puppy," Claire said, patting her eyes. "I haven't seen him like that in so long."

"Are you okay?" Belle asked, walking over to Claire and placing an arm around her.

"Oh, yes. These are tears of joy, dear. I love seeing him so happy. Did he tell you about Echo? About how he got his scars?"

Belle nodded.

"It's been a long time since I've seen him happy. His eyes lit up with excitement. He looked so much like the little boy I once knew, like the young man I once knew. Thank you for doing this, Belle. You have no idea how much this means to us both. Thank you."

Belle smiled with tears as Claire hugged her. It was a long hug. Moments later, Claire pulled away from her. Belle had had no idea how much happiness a puppy could bring into the home. It was certainly worth the joy on their faces.

"I almost forgot," Cole said, bursting into the kitchen. "I was so enamored with Beast that I forgot to give you your Christmas gift, Belle."

Her eyebrows shot up. She hadn't been expecting anything. He'd already given her a bicycle.

"Here, Grandma. Do you mind holding Beast for a bit?" Cole asked, holding the puppy out to Claire.

"Not at all," Claire said with a grin, taking the puppy.

"This way," Cole said with a mischievous smile.

He led her down a few halls, toward his office.

"Are we going to your office?" Belle asked.

"No. Don't get too excited. I have something much more interesting to show you than my boring old office."

Belle raised one eyebrow, convinced there had to be something interesting in his office.

"I know I always tell you to not come to this area of the house, the west wing. In this hallway, you are now allowed to go into this room but only this room. I still don't want you in my office or bedroom. Understand?"

Belle nodded eagerly.

"Your Christmas present, Belle," Cole said, opening two large wooden doors.

Belle gasped as she walked into the library. When the doors had opened, they revealed magnificent rows of shelves that covered each wall of the room, traveling two stories high.

It was gorgeous, she thought, and she wasn't referring to the beautiful dark mahogany wood of the shelves and other furniture. No, she was referring to the rows and rows of books that filled the room.

On the shelves were hundreds—possibly thousands—of books.

Belle stepped inside and walked in a circle several times, in awe of the towers of books surrounding her.

This was bliss.

"My father was a book lover, and he collected several original works, which are preserved here," Cole said. "It's been unused for a long time. I'd like to see someone enjoy it."

"I love books so much. To me, books are everything. I haven't seen so many books in one place before. I mean, I go to the small bookstore downtown and the town library, but they're certainly nothing like this." Belle knew she was babbling, but she was so overwhelmed. She had never expected to find such a massive library in the house. This was an abundant blessing. "Can I...touch them?"

He laughed. "Of course."

"Thank you," Belle said breathlessly. She walked along the shelves, reading the titles and pausing occasionally to pull down a book to look at it. She had read a few of the titles, but there were so many she hadn't read. She was looking forward to coming here in the future.

"This is incredible," Belle said as she turned to her boss.

Cole smiled. "It's quite pleasing to see someone appreciate this."

"This is like a dream come true!" she cried, her eyes stinging with tears again. "I've never seen so many books in my whole life. Have you read any of these?"

"Well, most of them." Cole shrugged.

"Really?"

"I do love to read," Cole said. "And I know you do too."

"So, I get to come here whenever I want?" Belle walked to a shelf and read several of the titles.

"Actually, all of this is your gift. All of these books are for you to keep."

Belle whirled around. Had she heard him right? "You mean, all these books are mine now?"

Cole crossed his arms and laughed. "Yes, that's what I mean."

"There are so many! What will I do with all of them?"

"Read them, hopefully."

"I mean, you know…" Belle looked at the floor. "If I ever leave here, how will I take them with me?"

Cole looked away from her. "Let's not worry about that right now. Right now, just know that all of these books are yours."

Belle ran to him, then threw her arms around him. Yes, she was raised to not show such bold physical affection, but at that moment, she didn't care. She was so happy, her joy overflowed into that hug.

At first, Cole stiffened, then he relaxed and wrapped his arms around her. Belle smiled, savoring how nice it felt to be held in his solid arms.

"Thank you for telling me about Echo and how you got your scars," Belle said quietly into his ear.

He released her, then looked away again. "Well, now you know how I came to look like this and why people call me the beast who lives in the manor. You know, I was quite beautiful before." He played off the word *beautiful* as a joke, but Belle could see beyond the lighthearted comment.

"But you *are* beautiful, inside and out," she blurted. Then her face flamed with embarrassment at her corny and completely humiliating choice of words.

Why did I say that? she wondered. *To my boss, of all people.*

Cole turned to her slowly, a look of tenderness on his face. It was obvious to anyone that with the one side of his face unscarred, Cole must have been a very handsome man before the explosion. In Belle's eyes, he still was.

His scars were part of what made him beautiful.

"I'm sorry," Belle said, her face still hot. "I shouldn't have said that. But it's the truth. You can fire me if you want."

Cole reached forward and took Belle's hand in his, his bumpy, scarred skin enveloping her fingers. Her heart tripped at the surprisingly pleasant feeling of his warm hand on hers. He said nothing, but there were so many emotions in his eyes, Belle got lost in that moment, trying to read them.

Her heart sped up even more. Why was he having such an effect on her?

Did he feel the same?

"Belle, you can say anything to me. I like that you're honest and speak your mind. You don't ever have to apologize to me for that," he finally said, almost in a whisper. He squeezed her hand lightly, then let go.

"Thank you for all of this," Belle said, looking around the library again. "This is the best Christmas gift *I* have ever received."

Beast barked from a distance, then the sound grew closer as small paws clambered down the hallway toward them. The puppy appeared in the doorway, then ran up to Cole, pawing at his leg.

Cole laughed, bending down to pick him up.

Claire came hobbling in. "He can't get enough of you, I guess," she said with a laugh. "He was squirming on my lap so I finally let him go to find you. I hope we didn't interrupt anything. Also, I wanted to give you this, Belle." Claire handed Belle a box wrapped with a bow. "Merry Christmas."

"Oh, thank you, Claire," Belle said, opening it. It was a game of Scrabble. She smiled.

"I remember you said you didn't have one of your own since you moved here," Claire said. "You're so good at it, you should have one of your own."

"Thank you so much," Belle said. "I'm going to see if my friend Damaris would like to play with me. She likes other types of board games. Then I'll get in some practice so I can win next time you and I play."

"Ha! Never," Claire scoffed. "Did you hear that, Cole? She thinks she can beat me."

Cole barely heard his grandmother. He was now holding Beast, scratching his ears and playing with him. Belle laughed, filled with joy at the tender sight of Cole talking sweetly to the puppy. It was a side of him she'd never seen before, but she knew she wanted to see a lot more of it.

***

After Belle finished cooking, they shared a wonderful Christmas Eve breakfast. Cole remained quiet, but there was a gleam in his eyes. Beast sat at his feet, and Cole kept giving him bits of breakfast to eat. He was enamored with the puppy. Belle was sure he would spoil Beast rotten. She had found the perfect home for the runt of the litter.

"So, I did some research and drew up a list of what Beast needs. He needs a food bowl, water bowl, some treats, and a chewing toy," Cole listed out. "Not to mention dog food. He should also have a collar and a leash."

"What about clothes?" Belle teased.

He realized what she was saying and his eyebrows shot up, making the women laugh. He smiled.

"Okay, okay. I want him to have the best. If you don't mind, you can go shopping next week," Cole said. "I'll call your driver and have him take you to the store to get the supplies. I'll pay you for your time, of course."

"I don't mind going today," Belle said. It would be a delight to go shopping for Beast. "He especially needs his dog food right away."

"But the stores will be packed."

"I don't mind, really. Let me at least get him some dog food."

"Thank you," Cole said. Then, lowering himself to Beast, she heard him say in a sweet, low voice, "Who's my Beast? Who?"

She exchanged a look with Claire, who was fighting a laugh. It was so incredible to see Cole act in such a way. If Belle had known that a puppy would make him as excited as a playful child, she would have brought him one a long time ago.

After breakfast, Cole went up with Beast to his office. She envied Beast, who was new to the house, yet had the opportunity to go into Cole's office and see what Cole did all day for work.

Would she ever find out?

***

Cole woke up to a tiny, warm body pressed beside him. He was stunned for a moment, then his training made him jerk awake, his hands in combat mode. He stared at the small puppy curled up beside him, sleeping peacefully.

A grin spread on Cole's face, and he chuckled. It was only Beast. He knew the puppy should be sleeping in his own bed, which Belle had brought home for him, but Beast had shown him those soulful big eyes

123

of his, and Cole had given in. He could already tell that he was going to be jelly around Beast.

If this was a dream, he certainly didn't want to wake up from it.

"Dear God, I know I haven't prayed in a long time, but I thank You for bringing Belle and Beast into my life. I think I might be lost without them," Cole prayed quietly. "Please, help me be kind and good to Belle. Please thaw my frozen heart."

He could see now that something had been missing in his life. While the puppy filled a void inside of Cole that he hadn't even known existed, Cole knew what was really missing was his relationship with God, which had deteriorated. Belle had shown him that.

After the explosion, everything changed. Now he knew he had to rebuild his relationship with God.

Cole scratched Beast behind his ears, and the puppy rubbed against him.

It was so thoughtful of Belle to give Cole this precious gift. Beast was a gift that Cole truly cherished and would always be grateful for.

Chapter Nine

"So, what do you think of my grandson?"

The question came out of the blue. After Christmas, the two women continued working in the greenhouse, planting new flowers and taking care of the ones that had survived.

"Well, he's nice," Belle answered.

Claire rolled her eyes. "Only sometimes. What else?"

"Um…" Belle hesitated. What could she say? That he'd been coarse and cold before, but now she saw the gentle and caring, even fun side of him?

That he was the most intriguing person she'd ever met?

Claire groaned, rolling her eyes. "You children are just unbelievable."

Belle wondered what Claire wanted her to say. That she really liked seeing him smile? That she thought he was an amazing person even though he tried to hide it? She knew he was kind by the way he treated his grandmother and Beast. She also knew he was hurting.

"You're hardworking, Belle, and you're an amazing person. It's a surprise no man has won your heart."

Perhaps, that was because Belle never allowed them to do so. She'd turned down every young man who'd ever been interested in her.

"Is it that you're scared of getting married? Because I know some youngsters feel that way nowadays."

"No, I'm not scared of getting married. I loved seeing my parents being affectionate toward each other. They were very happy. I'd like to get married someday. I'd like to be a mother and have children," Belle admitted.

"How many?" Claire asked, amused.

"Lots of them."

The women laughed, but Belle was serious. She had grown up with several siblings, and she wanted the same for her children. "I know I'll make a great mom, and that I'll shower them with love and care."

"Then I was wrong about you being scared of marriage. However, why haven't you gotten married? I wasn't joking when I said any man would be lucky to have you as a wife. You're a catch," Claire said.

Belle blushed at the older woman's praise. It was something she wasn't used to. She lingered on Claire's question. "I haven't met the right person yet. I've never been in love. When the time is right, the Lord will reveal the right person to me. In the meantime, I'll continue to live my life."

The sound of a piano being played suddenly filled the house.

"What is that?" Belle asked.

"That is my grandson playing the piano again," Claire said slowly, her eyes wide. "He hasn't played in years."

The notes fumbled at first, as if he couldn't remember how the song went, but after a few moments, the song flowed as if years hadn't passed since Cole had last played.

"It's beautiful." Belle smiled, standing up eagerly. "Come on, let's get closer and listen."

Claire nodded, and they went to the piano room. As they approached, they slowed down. Would Cole stop if they went in?

As if reading her thoughts, Claire touched her arm. "Let's listen here. He's rather shy about it."

The song carried on, and the notes surrounded Belle. She'd never heard anything more exquisite. She closed her eyes, letting the notes melt and pour over her like warm caramel. What she wouldn't give to learn how to play the piano like that, but she knew it was impossible. Her community was strongly against the Amish playing musical instruments.

The music slowly ended, and Claire stepped into the doorway. "Oh, Cole. That was wonderful!" She clapped enthusiastically.

Belle followed Claire, her eyes locking onto Cole's. "It was beautiful. Claire said you could play well, but I had no idea."

Cole's face reddened as he scrambled to stand up and close the music book. "It's been a while. I'm a bit rusty."

"Please, will you play another?" Belle asked. "I've never heard the piano being played before. It's almost...magical." She smiled sheepishly.

"Yes, Cole. Please play more." Claire plopped down on the sofa in the corner, and Belle joined her.

"Well, fine. If you insist. But as I said, it's been a long time. I'll make many mistakes." Cole reluctantly sat back down on the bench.

Claire waved her hand, dismissing his worries. "Pish posh. Mistakes are what make us learn. They make life beautiful."

Cole smiled, then turned to the keys and began to play. He played several songs for them, and at the end of each one, Belle and Claire applauded energetically. Belle enjoyed every moment, watching Cole's fingers move swiftly over the keys as he was clearly lost in the music. It was a side of him she'd never seen before—a tender yet serious and focused side that she admired.

After the next song ended, Belle sighed. "I wish I could learn to play like that."

"I could teach you, Belle." Cole turned on the bench to face her. "I'd be happy to."

Belle shook her head. "I can't. If anyone at home found out, I'd get in trouble with the church. In my community, we are forbidden from playing any musical instruments."

"Why?" Cole looked aghast.

"We believe the person playing might draw too much attention to themselves or become prideful." Her face burned. "I don't think that of you, though. In fact, I've never really agreed with that rule."

"In the Bible, many people praised God with instruments. What about David? He wrote songs for God and played instruments while praising Him," Cole argued.

"You're right. That's part of why I never understood why we aren't allowed to play instruments."

Cole shook his head. "I don't understand some of your rules."

Belle chuckled. "That makes two of us. I've followed them all my life, but sometimes I wish some things were different."

Cole gave her a sympathetic look.

"Don't worry. I'm happy, and it's worth it to me," Belle assured him. "It's what I've known all my life."

"Of course," Cole said, nodding awkwardly. "If you want to learn to play the piano, I could still teach you in secret. No one else would have to know except the three of us. You wouldn't get in trouble."

"I'd better go make lunch," Belle said, standing up and hurrying out of the room.

As she walked down the hall, questions raced through her mind. Could she secretly learn to play the piano? It would be wrong, wouldn't it?

But she couldn't deny that she wanted to do it.

She shook her head, chiding herself. No. It was against the rules, and no matter how badly she wanted to, she couldn't give in to her temptation.

***

"I'm leaving the house tomorrow," Claire announced.

Belle and Cole both looked at her in surprise. Belle's eyes narrowed. It felt like something was going on with Claire that she wasn't telling either of them.

"Why? Where are you going?" Belle asked.

Claire laughed. "You do realize I'm not a prisoner in this house, unlike some people," Claire said, her gaze resting on Cole, who scowled at her.

"My grandmother tends to leave the house once in a while. The last time she left was over a year ago. I think she's long overdue," Cole informed Belle.

"Oh, do you have someone you visit?" Belle asked.

"I mostly just stay in a hotel, just to get away from him," Claire said with a playful smile.

"I'm not that bad," Cole grumbled.

"Of course not, dear. Really, I just like to go out, see friends, stay somewhere nice, go shopping, and go out to eat. Maybe play some bingo. Don't worry, Cole, I won't go clubbing."

"I wouldn't put it past her," Cole whispered to Belle with a chuckle. "She'd show up everyone on the dance floor, I bet."

Belle laughed. "How long will you be away, Claire?"

"A week or two," was Claire's answer.

"A week or two! You haven't been away for that long before," Cole said, aghast.

"What? You have Beast and Belle to keep you company. You don't need an old woman like me around."

"I'll always need you," Cole said, hugging his grandmother affectionately.

It was a kind gesture, and it brought tears to Belle's eyes. She loved seeing him fawn over his grandmother. They had a great relationship; at times, they were like the best of buddies, while at other times they were like siblings—and then, of course, like grandmother and grandson.

"I hope it won't be a bother to you, Belle," Claire said.

"Of course not."

It was going to be strange having just Cole around, but he'd probably be in his office all day, anyway.

"Well, let me go pack my things," Claire said. She lifted a hand to stop Belle, who was standing up to help. "Don't worry, dear, I can do it myself."

Claire left the room.

"You could take the rest of the week off until Claire returns. A paid vacation, if you want," Cole suggested to Belle.

"Why? You don't want me around?" Belle asked with a smile.

"No, it's not that," Cole stammered, blushing. "I don't think I need to be looked after. Well... I do love your cooking and your pastries. Beast does too."

"Don't worry about me, Cole. I'll come around so I can see Beast," Belle said. "And also take the chance to read in the library."

It wasn't the whole truth. She was so used to coming over to the manor that it had become a part of her. It was better than being at her aunt and uncle's house, where she felt so out of place most of the time. Though her aunt had told her she wouldn't forbid her from reading novels, Belle still felt like she had to hide her reading from her aunt to avoid upsetting her.

She didn't want to be away from the manor just because Claire was going on a trip.

Who else would take care of the house? Who else would make sure Cole didn't retreat back into his shell?

Chapter Ten

That morning, a taxi came to pick up Claire for her trip.

"Please take care, Grandma." Cole hugged her tightly.

"You too. Please, please reconsider going to the conference. I truly think it would be good for you."

"Grandma—"

Claire held up a finger. "That's my one request while I'm away. You know why. I don't want you here all alone forever. It's time you get back out into the world. Hasn't Belle made you want to get out and live again?"

"Well…" He tried to deny it, but he couldn't. "I do admit she inspires me to be a better person, to be brave again. She makes me feel like maybe it would be possible to go out and meet new people again, to see people again…" He trailed off and sighed.

Claire gently patted his arm. "All I see is a handsome, talented, successful young man. They will too. And if they don't, then who cares about what they think?" Claire clicked her tongue and walked to the door. "Don't have too much fun without me. No parties, please."

Cole laughed. "I'll try."

As his grandmother drove away, Cole instantly missed her. An ache in his heart grew. At least Belle would be coming over later that day to fill the house with life again.

***

It was going to be strange not having Claire around—at least Belle thought so.

When she got to the manor, it was oddly quiet for a few minutes, then Beast came down the stairs. He ran around excitedly in circles.

Smiling, Belle crouched beside him. "Hello, Beast. You seem happy today. Where's Cole?" she asked.

"I'm here."

She looked up, and her heart leaped at the sight of Cole. He looked no different than he usually did, so she had no idea why she was so excited. Perhaps it was just the idea of them being alone.

"I feared you wouldn't come," Cole said.

"I told you I would." She was surprised when Cole joined her in the kitchen, Beast trailing behind.

"What can I help you with?" Cole asked.

"You want to help me make breakfast?" she asked, stunned.

"Yes. Is that okay?"

"Of course. Well, then, you could crack the eggs. Or mix something."

"Yeah, I'm not sure I'd be so good at cracking eggs," he said with a chuckle.

It felt so strange to have him in the kitchen, yet at the same time, it was comforting to be with him in such proximity. She found herself glancing at him as he hummed, mixing pancake batter. She could also feel his gaze on her, making her face heat up.

"I hope you're not bored working here. I mean, it can't be that exciting coming here every day and working for us. You arrive early and leave in the evening. You must have a social life. Friends?" Cole asked eagerly.

"Oh, stop it. I love working here. And yes, I have good friends in the community, but I'm definitely an introvert," Belle said. "I'd rather be alone reading a book than in a room full of people."

"I'm the same way." He paused and glanced at her. "Have you thought any more about working for the anti-sex trafficking organization?"

133

"Well, yes, I definitely have. It's just…" She paused while mixing the pancake batter. "It's just, I'm actually afraid that if I apply, I'll get the job."

"That's what you want, isn't it?"

"Of course. But if I get it, I'll have a huge decision to make. I'd be at a crossroads. I'd either have to turn it down or leave the community to take the job, as it includes working online," Belle said. "I haven't been baptized into the church yet, so I won't be shunned, but being Amish is all I've known. It would be hard to make such a life-changing transition. I might even have to travel. It would be a whole new world to me."

"It would be an adventure," Cole said with a smile.

"That's for sure."

"If it's what you really want, and if you think it's what you're meant to do, I think you should go for it. Although, I do admit I'd hate to lose you. You know, as a housekeeper. You do good work."

"Thanks." Belle looked away tucked a stray strand of hair into her *kapp*. She felt her cheeks burn. What had he really meant? Did he mean he'd miss her, or just miss her cooking and cleaning skills as his housekeeper? Maybe she was reading into it too much. "I'll still give it some more thought and prayer."

They worked in silence for a few minutes before Cole finally worked up the courage to ask the question he'd been wanting to ask for a while. "You told me that your family died. May I ask what happened to them?"

Belle froze, the knife hovering over the strawberries she'd been slicing. She hated talking about her family because it was a reminder of the past. However, she didn't want to push him away.

"I'm sorry. I didn't mean to pry." Cole shook his head. "It's none of my business. You don't have to answer."

134

Instead of remaining silent, Belle surprised herself when the words flowed out of her. "No, it's okay. It's time I talk about it. I did have siblings. I was the oldest of six." She took a deep breath and let it out. "One night, I heard the door open loudly. The others were playing board games in the living room, as we often did in the evenings, but I had gone to bed early with a headache. I woke up hearing voices I had never heard before. Loud and mean voices..." Her hands began to shake as she relived the horrible moment. She dropped the knife she'd been cutting strawberries with, and it clattered on the counter. "I still have terrible nightmares."

"It's okay, Belle, I understand," Cole said comfortingly as he took a step toward her.

Belle went on. "I just couldn't move. I was wondering who they were when I heard a gunshot. I was frozen to the spot, Cole. I heard my mother scream, calling out my father's name. I heard my siblings plead with those monsters, the younger ones crying. I heard another gunshot, then my mother stopped screaming. I was so scared. I was in shock, but I jumped out the window. I ran barefooted to the nearest phone shanty to call the police, even though my community didn't report crimes. I didn't care. I had to do it. But I was too late. By the time the police and I got back, they were all dead. The criminals were gone after ransacking the house. They'd taken the hidden cash and senselessly killed my family."

Tears slipped down her cheeks. She'd never forget the horrible sight to which she had returned with the police. She recalled herself screaming and shouting in pain upon seeing the bodies of her family.

"Marta was nineteen, Rachel was sixteen, Will was twelve, Daniel was ten, and little Rosaline was only seven years old..." A strangled sob escaped her, and she covered her face with her hands, remembering each one of them.

Cole's warm arms surrounded her, and she rested her head on his chest, soaking his shirt with tears.

"I'm so sorry, Belle. I'm so very sorry. I had no idea how much you've gone through. Losing a loved one isn't an easy thing. It has to be a

135

thousand times worse losing all your family in one night. Belle, you're a survivor. I wish I could do something. I'm sorry, Belle," Cole whispered.

"Sometimes I wonder if I did the right thing by running to get help. Maybe I should have stayed and tried to fight off the shooters," she admitted.

He held her at arm's length, looking at her intently. "No. There's no way. You would have been killed. They had weapons, and you were unarmed."

"I'm not sure if I ran to just get help, or if I was running because I was truly afraid for my own life." She looked down at the kitchen floor. "I've never said that to anyone. It's just been too painful to admit until now."

He touched her shoulder. "Belle, you did the right thing, and that's all that matters. We're all afraid sometimes. It's your body's natural reaction to danger, and it propelled you to get help. So what if you were afraid? You tried to save them by getting help. There wasn't anything more you could have done. You survived."

His words were comforting, but her pain was raw and came flooding back. For days after the shooting, she had remained in shock. She just could not believe that she had lost her parents and five siblings in one night. All of them were gone, without even a goodbye. One moment they had been relaxing after dinner, and the next they were gone. She'd never hold Rosaline in her arms again, or playfully pinch Daniel's cheeks. Thinking of them made her cry even more. She tried to act like she was past their loss, but she missed them every single day. What hurt most was that she was alone. They were all gone, leaving her behind.

"Belle, it's going to be okay. I promise you that it will be okay," Cole whispered.

She nodded. "This is why I read so much. Some turn to drugs or alcohol, but I turned to reading to escape. It's the only way I can forget about what happened, to get lost in a story and pretend I'm someone else." She remained in his arms as they stood in the kitchen for several moments. To be honest, she did feel better, and she had no idea why. She pulled away from him, flashing him an embarrassed smile.

"I wet your shirt." Belle sniffed.

"It's nothing, Belle. I'm really sorry about your loss. You're one of the strongest people I've ever met. You're hurting, but you take each day happily, looking on to the next. If that had happened to me, I think I would have blamed God and lost all my faith," Cole said, shaking his head slowly.

"Do you believe in God, Cole?" Belle asked.

"Yes, of course," Cole said. "My father and grandmother raised me to know and love God, and we used to go to church together. I had a good relationship with God. I used to enjoy reading the Bible and being close to Him. Even after my mother left, I found comfort in the pages of my Bible."

"I understand that," Belle said. "I've also found it comforting."

"Though, I must admit, I strayed away after everything that happened to me. I know that's no excuse. I haven't read my Bible in a long time."

"God doesn't drift away from us. We drift away from Him. But He always wants us to come back," Belle said. "Have you lost your faith?"

"No… It's not that. I don't blame God for what happened to me. It's more that I feel guilty for surviving the explosion when my comrades and Echo didn't make it," he said.

"I feel the same way with my family. It's not too late, Cole, for you to rebuild your relationship with God."

Cole paused, nodding in understanding. She was right.

They had a lot more in common than he would have imagined.

"Do you know why those monsters targeted your family?" Cole asked, anger flashing in his eyes.

"They were drunk and had stumbled across our house. They thought we were a wealthy family because of the large house, but many Amish families have large homes because the community builds them. They thought we'd have piles of cash hidden because they figured the Amish don't use banks. When all my parents gave them was the hidden cash that didn't amount to what they were expecting, the shooters killed them all."

"Please tell me they're behind bars now," Cole growled.

"It's the way of the Amish to forgive. We don't like to involve ourselves with the police. We prefer to forgive as the Lord forgives us. However, the killers had a trial and are in prison now, serving life sentences. I still haven't forgiven them," Belle admitted. She knew deep in her heart that God wanted her to forgive, but she just couldn't. "I know it's the Amish way to forgive, but I just can't bring myself to do it. They killed my family."

Cole said, "You have a kind heart, Belle. Life sentences are easy punishments for them. If I had my way, they would have received far worse."

A shudder ran through her body. She felt that if he had his way, he would make good on his words. She had never seen him this protective toward her.

Beast barked, and they pulled away from each other. She turned to the cutting board and continued slicing without a word. She hoped he wouldn't treat her differently now, like she was made of glass. Once they knew her story, people tended to treat her like she was a fragile being.

Above all, she hoped he wouldn't pity her like everyone else did, because that would be worse than keeping this secret to herself.

***

Loud voices boomed through the house, startling Belle awake.

She was back at her childhood home, in the old room that she shared with her sisters. Belle heard her sister Marta call for their father, crying out, "*Daed!*"

Throwing off the quilt, Belle rushed to her bedroom door and peeked out.

In the living room, she saw her siblings Marta, Rachel, Will, Daniel, and little Rosaline all huddled together along with her parents. Two tall gunmen dressed in black had invaded the house. One pointed a pistol at them while the other ransacked the house.

"Where do you keep it?" he demanded.

"Keep what?" *Daed* asked.

"All the cash, you idiot. I heard you Amish don't use banks, so you've got to have a pile of money hidden around here somewhere," the burglar said gruffly, searching in a closet.

"Actually, I don't know about other Amish communities, but here we do use banks, so we don't have a large amount of cash here. There's just a jar of cash hidden under that bottom step there. If you pull on it, the step comes loose," *Daed* explained. *Maam* gripped his arm, crying into his shoulder and holding the younger children close.

Belle's heart wrenched. She felt as though she should be there with them, with a gun pointed at her, too.

"We don't have a lot of money," *Maam* said. "Please, take the cash and leave us. We won't report you."

"This house is huge. You must be loaded."

"The community helped us build it. Please, we aren't wealthy. We don't have jewelry or expensive things. Take the money and go," *Daed* said.

"I don't believe that for a second," the other burglar said with a hiss. "What about these other bedrooms? What have you got stashed away

139

in there?" He walked down the hall. In the darkness, Belle backed away from the door, losing sight of what was happening.

A gunshot tore through the house. *Maam* screamed, calling out for *Daed*. Belle's brothers and sisters cried and screamed, their sobs ripping apart Belle's heart. Another gunshot sounded, then Belle's mother stopped screaming.

A sob escaped Belle, and she clamped a hand over her mouth. She had to run and get help. This was her only chance.

She scrambled toward the window, which she then opened and climbed out of. Fortunately, her bedroom was on the first floor. Barefoot, she ran across the yard and through the trees, which led to the lane where the nearest phone shanty was located. There, she could call the police for help.

Would they make it in time? Instead of watching her family in horror, she should have left immediately.

Rocks cut into her feet, but she didn't care. She sprinted faster and faster, leaping over fallen branches in the woods, her long nightdress trailing behind her.

Suddenly, she heard footsteps behind her. She glanced over her shoulder to see one of the gunmen racing toward her, his teeth glinting in the moonlight.

His pistol was aimed right at her.

"Come back here, little lady!" he called. "Stop!"

Belle ran faster, ignoring the burn in her lungs and the ache in her legs. She had to get to the phone shanty. She just had to.

"Stop, I said! Stop running or I'll shoot!"

But she couldn't stop or her family would die.

The sound of a gunshot tore through the air, and Belle tumbled to the ground, falling and falling…

Belle sat up in her bed, tears streaming down her face, her body soaked with sweat.

It had been a dream. Just a dream.

She looked around to see that she was at her aunt and uncle's house again. Trying to calm her pounding heart, she took several slow, deep breaths.

Over and over she had this dream, the memory of when her parents and siblings had been killed. Except she hadn't been shot herself. Instead, she had reached the phone shanty, but the police still hadn't made it in time. They'd been several minutes too late. Even if she'd left the house the moment the gunmen had entered, they wouldn't have made it in time.

Belle turned on the battery-operated lamp on her nightstand and reached for *Dynasty*, one of her favorite Tony Graham novels, which was about time travel. She flipped open to where she'd left off while reading it for the second time.

Fiona shook her head. "This is all my fault. If I had been on that boat, I would have sunk with the rest of the ship."

Garret touched her arm. "You were on the lifeboat, and you survived. You're alive, and that's all that matters."

"Don't you think I was a coward for getting on that lifeboat?"

"No. I know you feel guilty for surviving when so many others on the ship died, but you should be grateful you lived. You lit the distress signal. You tried to save them."

"No other ship came," Fiona told him in a strangled voice. "Not until later, after everyone had drowned. Then we were rescued. If only I had been at home in the twenty-first century, I would have probably had my cell phone on me. I could have called for help or posted on social media. Maybe, just maybe, if I had reception out there."

"That's true, possibly, if you had the right SIM card. But you were in the nineteenth century. There were no cell phones then."

141

Belle looked up from the pages.

Had she been a coward for running?

Even if she was afraid and ran for her life, she had run toward someone who might have been able to save her family.

But if her family hadn't been Amish, they would have had a phone. Then she wouldn't have had to run all the way to the phone shanty, and the police may have made it in time. She'd never thought of that before.

Shaking her head, Belle closed the book. *I'll never know,* she thought. *No sense in torturing myself with questions.*

Setting the book back on the nightstand, she reached instead for her Bible—the book that gave her the ultimate comfort—and opened it to *Psalms.*

***

Cole couldn't sleep. He was still in awe of Belle's strength. He couldn't believe what she had gone through. To have lost all her family in one day, and she still remained strong. He had always admired her, but now it had intensified.

He wished he could lay his hands on those monsters. When he was done with them, they would regret ever being born. To Cole, prison was a luxury for murderers. They deserved so much worse. But Belle, with her caring heart, was trying to forgive them, and he had to accept that.

He hated how lonely she was. She had tried to sugarcoat it, but from one loner to another, he knew how difficult it was to be understood. She had cried in his arms, and the sadness in her eyes still haunted him. How he wished to take it all away from her. He had thought the bomb and the scars were the worst that could happen, but Belle's story beat his. She was indeed a strong woman.

Though his comrades in the Marines were not biologically related to him, he had considered them family. He'd never had any siblings, so they were like brothers and sisters to him. Yes, he'd lost his parents, but not both in one day.

Belle had lost her entire family in one day and still lived life with optimism, kindness, and faith. If she could do that, maybe there was hope for him after all.

God, if Belle can continue living her life so joyfully after all she has lost, is there hope for me too? Cole prayed.

She had opened up a deep part of her life to him, and he was grateful for it. She had exposed her emotions to him, trusting him.

With her, he could no longer keep up those walls that had protected him for so long. He wasn't going to hide from her anymore. He had no idea where this was going to lead. He would probably be hurt in the end, but he was going to cherish his moments with Belle.

Cole spent most of the following day working in his office. Looking through what he'd written so far that day, he was impressed. It was the best progress he'd made since the writer's block began.

With Claire away, after Belle finished her work, she went to the library each evening before going home.

When Cole walked in, she was reading a book on her lap, with a notebook and pen on a stool next to her. She looked up as he walked in and smiled at him. "Hello, Cole, and you too, Beast," she said, smiling even wider as Beast wagged his tail in response. "Do you need anything?"

"No. I hope you don't mind my presence," he said, settling down into an armchair. It had been quite a while since he had sat in there comfortably.

"Of course not. This is your home," Belle said.

He nodded, and she returned her attention to the novel she was reading. The silence, although comforting, wasn't one he cherished. He wanted to hear her talk. "Which book are you reading?" he asked.

She flashed the book cover, and he recognized it as a mystery.

"That's a good one. I can't recall the details, but I've read it before. So, who's your favorite author?" he asked, very much curious.

"You probably don't know of him."

"Try me."

Belle grinned. "His name is Tony Graham. His books are amazing."

"Tony Graham?" Cole squeaked, his fingers digging into the armchair.

He was her favorite author?

"Yes, do you know of him?" Belle asked.

"Umm… You could say that. I mean, I've come across his books, but I don't think he's that good of an author," Cole managed to say, stunned by what she had just told him.

Belle glared at him in disapproval. "Tony Graham is an excellent writer. I feel such a connection to his books. There's something in his writing that speaks to having known tragedy and pain, something that makes me feel better, like I'm not the only one. Sometimes I read his books late at night when I wake up from the nightmares. They just make me feel better."

He stared at her, stunned. He felt the blood drain from his face.

Was this really happening? His books comforted her that deeply?

"They're wonderful. Sometimes I stay up well past midnight reading them, even though I have to wake up early. Have you read his book *Hidden Treasures*? *Dynasty*? *Sunset in Cabro*?" she persisted.

Well, technically he had read them, but he didn't tell Belle. He merely shrugged, and her glare intensified.

Cole desperately wanted to tell her that he was Tony Graham, but would she believe him? What if she laughed in his face and called him a liar?

"Then don't say Tony Graham isn't much of an author," Belle warned, waving a finger at him. "Although, I do admit his fifth book in the series, *Hallowed Ground*, was a disappointment."

"Oh?" he asked with curiosity.

"Yes." She furrowed her eyebrows. "All the other books I've ever read by him were so good, with intricate plots and detailed characters. This one was like he took all his other books and mixed them up. It just fell flat. It was like he ran out of good ideas." She shrugged. "I'm hoping his next ones are as good as his older ones."

His pride deflated. "Oh. Well, maybe he was just feeling uninspired but still had to meet the publisher's deadline."

If Cole told Belle that he was Tony Graham, would her admiration for her favorite author die?

It was true. He knew his last book wasn't good, but his publisher demanded a certain word count by the deadline listed in the contract, and he'd submitted what he knew was garbage, only because he couldn't come up with anything better. They'd edited it the best they could, but he knew it was terrible.

And yes, he hoped he'd have better ideas from now on.

"So, you've read all his books?" he asked.

"Yes, I think so. I could loan you a copy of one of his books to read. You know, if they helped me cope with my loss, I think they'd help you too. I think they'd give you hope."

Would she be disappointed in him, especially after his last book?

"I don't know about that. I don't think it would help me."

"Why not?"

"Well…" He looked at her, hesitating. "It seems silly to read something I wrote."

Belle stared at him, her nose scrunched up in confusion. "Something you wrote?"

"Yes." He stood up from the chair and took a step closer to her. "It's time you know the truth." He took a deep breath. "My pen name is Tony Graham. I'm the one who wrote those books. That's what I do in my office all day."

Not able to read her expression, he waited for the laughter to come, the mockery, or the angry outburst and accusations.

What would it be?

"You're…Tony Graham?" Belle echoed, eyeing him skeptically. "You're serious?"

"I'm one hundred percent telling the truth. I can take you to my computer and show you all my manuscripts on file and my emails with my agents. In my office, I have writing awards with my pen name on them. If you want, I can prove it to you. Do you want me to show you?"

"Well, yes, actually," Belle said slowly, as if stunned.

She followed him to his office.

"So this is your scary, forbidden office." She looked around, then rushed to the awards on the shelf. "This is amazing. You've won so many awards! And I've heard you've never collected any in person."

"That's true," Cole said, thumbs in his pockets as he rocked on his heels. He was surprised at how well she was taking this. He'd expected her to either jump up and down or hurl questions or accusations at him.

"Here. These are my manuscripts." He went to his computer and pulled up the files, opening them and scrolling through.

"The rough drafts of *Hidden Treasures, Dynasty, Caged Powers…* They're all here," Belle said in awe as she stared at the screen. "I can't

146

believe this." She stood up straight, turning to him. "You're Tony Graham, my favorite author, whose books have helped get me through the worst times in my life. Do you have any idea how many nights I stayed up until morning reading your books, how they've been an escape for me? How they comforted me in the middle of the night when I had nightmares? Do you know how many times I've hurried to get my chores done just so I'd have more time to read?" She eyed him intently, stepping toward him.

"No, but I'd like to," Cole said with a smile.

"I can't believe it's you. This is amazing!" Belle jumped forward and threw her arms around him. "I've dreamed for so long of meeting Tony Graham, getting just five minutes to ask my questions. Now my dreams have come true." She pulled away, red tinging her cheeks. "I'm sorry. You probably hate it when people fawn all over you."

Usually he hated it. Right now, he didn't mind at all, if it meant Belle hugging him. "It's okay."

She threw her hands up. "Ugh, I have so many questions! Where should I start?" She looked around the room as if searching her mind. "Do Fiona and Garrett end up together? Is Portia really Jane's biological mother? Does Ingrid develop powers and return to her century? And where do you get all the ideas for your books?"

"Whoa, slow down. That's a lot of questions." Cole raised an eyebrow, amused at her curiosity.

"I'm sorry. Really, what I want to know is if the next book will be as good as the earlier ones, because those truly are incredible."

"It depends on if I find inspiration. Lately, I've been completely uninspired and everything I've been writing is garbage. You're right. I ran out of good ideas."

"It can't be that bad."

"Really, it is. But I think I'll get past it and have good ideas again. I think every writer goes through this at some point, but I can't just sit

147

around waiting for inspiration to strike. I have a deadline. I write every day, whether inspiration strikes or not, because I want to be writing when it does hit," Cole explained. "I have to get it done before my publisher loses patience with me."

"I'm sure you will," Belle said.

"You know, my publisher wants me to go to this big authors' conference in New York City, where fans go to hear the authors speak. My agent wants me to be the featured speaker. Right now, they've made a big mystery out of who I really am. My photo is a question mark, and everyone wants to know my real identity. They want me to reveal myself to my fans," Cole explained.

"Really? Are you going to go?" she asked, her eyes wide as she leaned forward. "I'd love to go to something like that and hear authors speak."

Cole shook his head. "I don't think I can do it. First of all, I wouldn't be good at public speaking. I like my privacy. But it's not only that. I'm afraid they'll take one look at me and be disappointed...even disgusted," he admitted.

"These are your fans," Belle cried. "They won't care what you look like. They just want to meet you."

"You really think so?"

"Besides, haven't you ever heard that women like scars?" Belle said with a wry smile.

Cole chuckled. "Not scars like these."

"Cole, even with your scars, you're still very handsome. You'll have women at your feet in no time," Belle said, her cheeks turning pink.

Now it was Cole's turn to blush. "No, I don't think so."

"Well, I think you should go. This is a huge opportunity. Not only to sell more books but to get back out into the world again."

"I do want to live a normal life again, get out and do fun things and meet new people," he admitted. "I've just been too afraid of how people will react when they see me."

"Don't let fear hold you back. You should go. At least consider it."

"I will," he promised. "If I go, would you like to come with Claire and me?"

Her eyes lit up. "Truly? Go to New York City?" She sighed. "Oh, I've only dreamed of doing something like that. Now you have to go. You've gotten my hopes up."

Cole laughed, but his insides sank. What had he done? Had he just gotten her hopes up for nothing?

What if he couldn't do it and he disappointed her and Claire?

"So, in the next book, do Fiona and Garrett end up together? It really seemed like they had a connection," Belle asked.

"I'm not sure yet."

"Are you serious? You aren't sure yet?"

Was this how it was going to be now, with her constantly pestering him with questions? "I just don't know, Belle." He didn't mean for the annoyance to show through in his voice, but it had. When he saw her smile drop, regret twisted his insides. "I'm sorry. I didn't mean for it to come out like that. Of course, you can ask me questions."

"Well, I don't want to bug you. I guess I'll have to wait until the next book to find out along with everyone else." She paused, closing her eyes. "And I didn't mean for that to come out that way."

Cole raised his hands, palms up, as if making a peace offering. "How about you ask me your questions, but one at a time? If you've been wanting to ask Tony Graham questions, I want to grant your wish, Belle."

She grinned, her enthusiasm returning. She pulled up a chair next to his at his desk. "Let's get comfortable. I have a lot of questions to ask. We might be here a while."

Chapter Eleven

A laugh spurted out of Belle's lips at the silly sight of Cole covered with flour. Beast ran around in circles and barked playfully.

The evening before, they'd spent hours discussing Belle's questions about past and future books, and truthfully, they'd both enjoyed it. It had given Cole many new ideas for the book he was working on. At the end of their discussion, he'd given her a heartfelt thank you. Her questions had been good practice for Cole, as his fans would probably ask him plenty of questions at the conference.

She'd arrived home late that evening, and her aunt had asked questions, but Belle had assured her everything was fine and she'd just had to work late. She'd been eager to return to work the next morning, and now they were making breakfast.

"Very funny. Continue laughing and you'll be covered in flour as well," Cole threatened.

"You wouldn't!" she cried, but she couldn't stop laughing.

"You've enraged the beast!" Cole cried in mock anger, taking a handful of flour and hurling it at her. It covered her face and prayer *kapp*, and she laughed even harder, then began to cough.

"Oh, Belle, I'm sorry," Cole said, coming closer. "Did you get some in your mouth?"

She nodded but smiled. After filling a glass of water, she took several sips. It reminded her of the night she had first shown up there and helped herself to a glass of water. Cole had been so different then.

A small smile crept upon her lips.

"What? Why are you smiling like that?" he asked, cocking his head to the side.

"I'm just remembering the night I barged in here to use your phone and get a drink of water. You were so…ornery. Cranky. It was like you couldn't wait to get me out of here. But now…"

"What? I'm what?"

"You're not so ornery anymore. You've changed since that night, Cole." She smiled at him and watched his face soften.

"That's all because of you, Belle."

"What?" Her heart tripped. What did he mean by that?

He took another step closer. "I think Claire has mentioned it to you, too. You've brought joy back into my life. For so long, I lived in darkness, but I don't want to be that way anymore. I haven't played the piano in years, and you've inspired me to play again. I got upset with you for trying to play it that day. Not only did I realize how wrong I was but you showed me that my father would want me to play. You've changed me, Belle, in so many ways." He reached out, gently wiping flour from her cheek.

So that was why he had started to play the piano again after so long. He was so close to her, she could smell the pine tree scent of his aftershave. She took in a deep breath, savoring the aroma and the moment.

"And I have to thank you again for giving me so many new inspiring ideas for my book last evening."

"It was my pleasure. I enjoyed talking to you about your books," she said.

"Me too," he said, his voice barely above a whisper. "A lot more than I thought I would."

If her relatives knew about this, she'd be in deep trouble. She backed away.

"I should clean up the mess," Belle said, looking away from him.

"Let me help," Cole said, reaching for the vacuum. "It was my fault, after all." He shot her a playful glare, and she was relieved that the awkward moment had passed.

"I really wanted Claire to be proud of me when she returned. I wanted to learn to bake a cake, not wear flour," he said.

"She would have been speechless."

"Yes, for once in her life," Cole said with a laugh.

Using another bag of flour, Belle was able to make pancakes for them, with Cole watching carefully and promising that his pancakes would taste better than hers when he had perfected his skill.

Beast sat underneath the table, eating his own breakfast quietly.

I'm going to miss this.

The thought suddenly occurred to Belle, dulling her mood. She couldn't work here forever, could she? Eventually, Claire would pass away. After that, would Cole still need her to work here? And besides, one day, she would most likely marry a nice Amish man and stop working when she had children.

Belle thought of Gilbert, then tried not to squirm.

"What's wrong?" Cole asked, dropping his fork.

"Nothing," Belle said with a shrug.

He slid his hand to hers, covering it. She didn't pull away from him, with his touch giving her comfort. "I know something is upsetting you. I'm your friend, right?" Cole asked.

"Well, yes. Why?"

"Aren't you supposed to share with a friend what's troubling you?" Cole asked.

Belle sighed, pulling her hand from him. "Well, there's this man who wants to court me—"

She observed Cole's change in mood. His body froze and his eyes hardened. "Go on," he urged.

"My aunt and uncle have encouraged me to accept his proposal. Gilbert is a good Amish man, he works hard, and he's kind—"

"What do you want? Do you want to marry this Gilbert?" Cole asked. Her brows furrowed, and he added calmly, "Do you love this man?"

Belle shook her head. "No. I feel nothing but friendship for him. I don't love him. But my aunt and uncle are getting older, and they're worried about me. They promised my parents they'd take care of me, and I think they believe that includes finding me a husband before they die. I know they want what's best for me, but..." She sighed. "I don't want to disappoint them, but I don't want to marry someone I don't love."

"You shouldn't be with someone you don't love. You'll find someone better. Someone who will love and understand you. A man who will help you fulfill your dreams. You deserve so much more."

She doubted that. Where in the community could she find such a man? "Thank you for saying that, Cole."

He scowled. "I'll always be here when you need me. Understand?"

Belle nodded, smiling gratefully.

"In fact, I have an idea. Do you still want to work for the anti-sex trafficking organization?"

"More than anything."

"Let's send them your application." Cole's eyes were lit with rare enthusiasm.

Belle almost choked on her pancakes. "What? Seriously?"

"Yes. I'm sure they have online applications. We can fill it out today, or you can email them your resume."

"I don't have an email account."

He waved his hand. "We can make one for you. It's easy. Then we can check it later to see if they've responded, and if they need a phone number, you can leave mine."

Belle hesitated, staring at her plate. Was this a bad idea? What if her aunt and uncle found out?

And what if she got the job? What would she do?

"Belle, come on. You're always encouraging me to step outside my comfort zone. Now it's your turn. Will you take this leap of faith if you truly believe it's what you're meant to do?" Cole prodded.

Belle nodded with finality. "You're right. Let's do it today."

A sound from the front door reached them and they shared a look. Who could that be? Cole's eyes narrowed, then a key slid into the door.

"Claire!" Belle said, hurrying over to the older woman. She wrapped her arms around her in a hug. She had been so lost in her conversation with Cole that she hadn't heard the car pull up.

"You came home early! It's good to have you back, Grandma," Cole said, joining them.

"You look different," Belle observed. Claire was supposed to have gone on a vacation to relax, but she looked tired, with bags under her eyes. Was it just her, or did the woman look paler and thinner? Was that why she had come home so early?

"Seeing so many friends and traveling can be tiring, my dear," Claire said, handing her bag to Belle, who took it.

"Do you feel okay? Is that why you came back early?" Cole asked with concern, staring down at his grandmother.

155

Claire laughed. "Pish posh. I'm fine. I think I had too much fun this time around. I certainly won't be going back any time soon. A few days' rest and I'll be back to normal. I missed both of you so much, and I knew I had to come home."

"You should have called so we could prepare for you," Cole said with disapproval.

Waving a hand, Claire said, "Why, so you can make a big fuss over me? So, how have the two of you been in my absence?"

"Fine," they said in unison, sharing a smile.

"Still the same then," Belle heard Claire mumble as she walked past them.

Although Belle was glad that Claire had returned home, she couldn't help but worry about her relationship with Cole. Claire's absence had made them closer. Now that she was back, would they return to the way it had been? She hoped not.

After Claire was settled in, Cole turned to Belle. "Now, Belle. Let's go fill out that job application," Cole said.

"What job application? Are you leaving us?" Claire's hand flew to her heart.

"No, no. It's a marketing job for an organization that rescues children from sex slavery," Belle explained.

Claire's eyes widened. "What on earth? Sex slavery? How is that possible, especially for children? Isn't it illegal?"

"Sadly, many people have no idea millions of children around the world, even in America, are trapped in sex slavery. Yes, it's despicable, and it needs to be stopped."

"Indeed. I've never seen anything like that on the news."

"For some reason, I've heard the news doesn't report on it much. I wouldn't know. I don't watch TV."

"It's true that they don't report it. But they should," Cole added.

"I want to work for them by raising money and awareness for them. The work might be mostly online, or I might have to travel. Either way, I have no idea what's going to happen, but I do want to know if they'd be interested in hiring me. Working for them, helping children be rescued from slavery, is my dream."

"Do they take donations?" Cole asked.

"Yes, do they?" Claire asked.

"I'm sure they do. Let's check the website."

***

Cole eagerly helped Belle fill out her application, then added himself as a reference. Yes, he wanted to help her fulfill her dreams and get the job, even if it might take her away from him.

He sighed, watching as Belle and Claire left the room, with Claire asking Belle never-ending questions about sex trafficking.

Bittersweet feelings filled him. He didn't want her to leave, but he would never hold her back from pursuing her passion.

"God, I'm going to trust You on this. If her new job takes Belle away from me, I trust You'll somehow bring her back to me if we're meant to be together. Your will be done," he prayed as he clicked the button to donate a large sum of money that he would never tell Belle about.

***

After work, Belle didn't head straight for home. Instead, she biked to Gilbert's house.

He was sawing a plank of wood when she walked in, and he stopped at the sight of her, a broad smile on his face.

"Belle. Your visit is a surprise," Gilbert said, dusting sawdust off his clothes.

157

"Gilbert, I'm sorry to interrupt your work," Belle said.

"It's no bother, Belle. Your presence is highly welcome," Gilbert said. "Do you need anything? Water? Tea?"

"No, Gilbert. My visit here will be quick," Belle said, not willing to take any more of his time.

There was a bit of silence with both of them staring at each other, then she said, "I've thought over your proposal."

"And?" Gilbert asked excitedly, his eyes wide.

"I'm sorry, Gilbert, but I'm turning it down. You're an amazing man, Gilbert, and the woman you marry will be blessed to be your wife, but I'm not that woman. When the time is right, the Lord will reveal her to you."

The excitement in his eyes quickly vanished, and his shoulders slumped with disappointment. "Belle, why? Have I done something to upset you?" Gilbert asked with worry. "I know maybe we didn't get off on the right foot…"

"No, it isn't you, Gilbert. It's me. I just don't…" She had no idea what to say so as not to hurt him. "I just don't love you. I can't marry someone I don't love. I'm sorry. You deserve someone who's in love with you. I see you as a friend."

Looking into her eyes, Gilbert asked, "Is there someone else? Someone who has your affection?"

She looked away. She didn't want to hurt his feelings more than her refusal must have done.

"You're in love with someone else," Gilbert said at her silence.

"I…" She couldn't deny her feelings for Cole. She realized, in that moment, that her curiosity about him had turned to friendship and now…something more. It scared and excited her at the same time.

158

"Who is he? Is it Timothy? I heard he tried courting you in the past, and he's quite close to your family. Or is it Amos? I've been hearing rumors that he'll soon be married. I know it's none of my business, but I'd just like to know who the lucky man is," Gilbert pleaded.

Sighing, Belle said, "Gilbert, it's none of those men. Just let things be. I'm grateful if I can still have you as a friend. I have to go home now." She quickly headed home on her bike, relieved.

As she rode away, she felt free.

"Belle?" Damaris called as she walked down the lane.

"Hi, Damaris," Belle replied to her friend.

"Wow. Are you okay? You look…" Damaris cocked her head to one side. "You look really happy, actually."

"I am," Belle cried. "I'm relieved. I just went to Gilbert's house and turned down his proposal."

"What?" Damaris cried, shock all over her face. "Why? Why turn down someone like Gilbert?"

"I don't love him. He deserves someone who loves him. He's a very nice man, but not the one for me."

"He's so sweet and funny once you get to know him. I know you only just moved here, but he's probably the kindest man I've ever met. A bit awkward sometimes, but he's a hard worker, and when he smiles, he has this little dimple on his cheek…" Damaris' sentence trailed off as she stared into the distance, a dreamy look on her face.

"Damaris!" Belle said, gasping. "You're in love with him, aren't you?"

Her friend's face turned red, and she stammered. "Well… I mean…"

"Why didn't you ever tell me?" Belle asked. "You knew he was pursuing me but that I didn't feel the same about him."

159

"I didn't want to interfere. Besides, he's in love with you. You're so beautiful. Why would he care about me?" Damaris looked at the ground and kicked a pebble. "We grew up together, so he probably sees me as a sister. But I've been in love with him for years."

"You're beautiful and kind, Damaris, and a wonderful person. You should tell him how you feel. Maybe he has been in love with you for years but didn't want to make your friendship awkward. Who knows?"

"Really? You think so?"

"Of course. I can't believe you never told me! Don't waste any more time. You've got to tell him."

Damaris' eyes lit up. "You're right. Maybe one day I'll work up the courage to tell him. One day."

Belle laughed. "Don't wait too long. Seriously. You should tell him before he tries to court someone else."

"I will. Thanks, Belle." Damaris gave her a hug.

"You're such a good friend, Damaris. Any man would be blessed to have you."

"The same goes for you."

The friends parted ways, and Belle made her way home, a grin on her face.

Chapter Twelve

When Belle knocked on the mansion door the next morning, Cole answered. He let her inside, then took one look at her smiling face and asked, "What is it?"

"I turned him down. I told Gilbert I won't marry him," Belle told him.

Cole threw his arms around her, holding her close. She took in as deep of a breath as she could with him holding her so tightly, inhaling his woodsy, clean scent. Savoring the warmth that flooded through her and the way his strong arms felt around her, she closed her eyes.

Finally, he pulled away. "Did you tell your family yet?"

"No. I haven't had the courage to tell them. I'll tell them later today."

"Well, still, this is a reason to celebrate. Now," he said, shooing her away. "Go to the library and don't come out until I say so."

"What? Why?"

"Because…" He grinned at her like a mischievous child. "I have a surprise for you. You'll just have to wait and see."

***

The noise downstairs infuriated Belle. She knew that if she went out the library door, Claire would be standing guard and drive her back into the library. They were planning some sort of surprise for her.

It wasn't just the whispers from grandma to grandson. It had more to do with the stranger in the house. Watching from the window, she had seen a vehicle arrive, with the person quickly whisked in.

Who had been invited to the house? What were Claire and Cole up to? Belle had been on the same page in her book for so long and had no interest in going further. If they didn't tell her what was going on, she would—

The door opened and Claire stepped in with a smile. Belle glared at her in return, making the woman smile broader.

"Can I come out now? I need to start cooking lunch," Belle said, glancing at the clock above the mantle.

"Oh, you don't have to worry about that. Why don't you come with me?" Claire asked.

Suspiciously, Belle followed the other woman, needing to find out what was going on.

"It's time," Claire said.

"Time for what?" Belle asked.

Refusing to answer her question, and taking her hand, Claire led her downstairs, out to the greenhouse.

Belle gasped. The garden still wasn't finished, but Belle noticed that so much more of the overgrowth had been pruned to make it neater than it had been before. Belle and Claire been working on it but hadn't been able to tend to all the plants on their own yet. It had been a larger job than Belle had anticipated.

What really grabbed her attention was the table next to the now budding rosebush in the center of the garden.

The table was set for two with fine china and candles.

"How…?" Belle asked, wondering how the greenhouse had improved so quickly.

"Cole and I worked on the plants with the help of a professional," Claire said, clearly proud of the results. "We wanted to surprise you. Just wait until you see this place in the spring."

"It will be spectacular," Belle said, looking around. "I can just imagine it."

Spread on the table were white cloth napkins with gold threading. Also on it were empty plates, glasses, and cutlery for two with a trolley beside it.

"What's happening?" Belle turned around to ask. Claire was gone, the back door closed. Why had the woman left her?

Cole walked into the greenhouse, and Belle stifled a gasp. He looked different—even more handsome than usual.

He was wearing an elegant black suit and tie. His eyes were pinned on her as he approached. Her heart began to race in excitement. What on earth was going on? Why was Cole wearing something other than his usual jeans and long-sleeved shirt? Why was a table set in the garden, with aromas drifting from the trolley? And why was he looking at her in that way that made her heart race?

He bowed dramatically and she laughed, full of joy at seeing him happy to be in this greenhouse again. He beamed, clearly pleased with her reaction.

"This place looks miraculous," she said. "I'm so glad you decided to work on it."

"Well, Claire and I wanted to surprise you. So, Belle, will you be my date for lunch?" Cole asked, smiling down at her. He bent to pluck a small rosebud from the rosebush and handed it to her.

She took it and tucked it into the hair under her prayer *kapp,* above her ear.

He smiled. "Beautiful."

She stared up at him in surprise. Was he referring to the rosebud or to her?

"So, will you be my date for lunch, Belle?" he repeated.

His date? Was he serious?

"Yes," Belle said with assurance.

163

Taking her hand in his, he led her to the table, pulled out a chair for her, and helped her sit, then went to the other chair. They stared at each other. She wondered where all of this was going. Why had he asked her out to a formal meal? She wouldn't have minded having lunch in the living room.

"You look so handsome, Cole," Belle said shyly, barely getting out the words.

He waved his hand, his face reddening. "Thanks, Belle. It's just my old suit."

"Is Claire not joining us?" she asked.

"No, this is just for us," Cole said.

She was lost for words again and merely nodded. The back door opened and the stranger she had seen from earlier walked toward them. He was dressed in a chef's uniform.

"Good afternoon, sir, ma'am." The chef bowed. "I'm Andrew, and I am your chef and server for today."

He handed them two plates of salad and garlic bread, followed by chicken parmesan a few minutes later. After serving their meal with a bottle of sparkling water, Andrew left.

"Is he a real chef?" Belle asked.

Cole chuckled. "Yes, he is. Before I was injured, I used to frequent his restaurant. He was surprised to receive my call, but he dropped everything on his day off to come here and make lunch. I'm sure you'll enjoy the meal."

He was right. The meal was amazing. Two bites in and she had fallen in love. She looked up to see Cole watching her, and questions struck her. What exactly was she doing with Cole out here? Were they here as friends? Or was it more? Had he really meant this as a real date, or was this just a lunch between a boss and an employee?

The door opened and Andrew returned to take away their empty plates. He replaced them with dessert, serving it with coffee and tea. She moaned at the first taste of the melting strawberry cake. It was perfect. She had to ask Andrew for the recipe.

"He's not going to share the recipe," Cole said, as if reading her thoughts.

"We could swap recipes," Belle suggested.

"No chance. Professional chefs don't give away their secrets."

Belle smiled. She loved talking to Cole. He was so comfortable to be with and had a listening ear.

"Have you thought any more about the conference?" Belle asked, finishing her cake.

"Well, yes. But I haven't decided yet."

"I'm sure Claire wants you to go."

"Oh, yes. She's been encouraging me to go and do the things I used to do."

"Have you ever been to New York City?" Belle asked, leaning forward.

"Oh, yes, many times."

"What's it like?"

"There are so many restaurants with so many different types of food. There are people from all over the world, from all different walks of life. There are horse-drawn carriage rides, and Central Park, and street performers. The subways go so fast, you have to hold on to something or you might tip over."

Belle chuckled, then put her elbow on the table, resting her face on her palm like a schoolgirl. "It all sounds incredible. Where else have you traveled?"

"My father took me to so many places. He loved to travel. We've been to Paris, Rome, Chicago, Australia, New Zealand, the Bahamas, and Hawaii. I'm sure there are more places, if I think way back."

"Oh, wow!" Belle cried, sitting up. "I wish I could travel. I've only been to places in Ohio and here. We've visited relatives in other states, but we're allowed to travel only by bus or train. We don't ride in airplanes, so I've never left the country."

"Really? You mentioned that before, that it's against the rules. So, the Amish aren't allowed to fly in airplanes?"

"Not the Amish here. But I've always dreamed of flying on a plane to another country," Belle admitted wistfully, looking up at the sky through the top of the greenhouse.

"Maybe when you get that job, you will," Cole offered.

"*If* I get it."

"Don't sell yourself short."

"And even if I do get it, I have no idea if I'd be brave enough to take it."

Belle's stomach was full when Andrew cleared the table. The chef smiled as she sang his praises.

They continued talking, and Cole told her all about the places he'd traveled. Belle listened intently.

"Thanks for lunch. I really needed this," Belle said. Though she had hardly traveled, it was as if Cole had just taken her on a long trip through their meal and conversation, just like a good book would also allow her to travel in her imagination.

"I'm glad you enjoyed it. Are you up for a walk?" Cole asked.

She nodded. Before she could stand, he was right behind her, pulling out her chair and helping her up. He took her hand in his, and they walked side by side.

166

They put on their jackets and went out to the back yard, where no one could see them. The yard was surrounded by trees, perfectly secluded.

Cole and Belle took a path she had never seen before. Although the greenery was thicker, a neat path was in the middle, leading into the woods. It was quiet and peaceful. She didn't say a word, fearing it would ruin the atmosphere. They reached a clearing inside the woods, with trees shading the area. She could tell instantly that this was a special place. Unlike the garden, it was well maintained, and tall trees arched over the clearing like an umbrella. Then she spotted it—a family cemetery.

"Where are we?" Belle asked.

"This is where my grandfather is buried. He passed this house down to my father, and he passed it down to me. This is also where my father is buried," Cole said brokenly, his shoulders slumping. He let go of her arm, moving ahead until he stopped in front of one of the headstones. She went to him and read the inscription on the headstone: *George Henderson, loving son and father.*

Where had she seen that name before? Why did it seem familiar?

"He died when I was in Afghanistan. I didn't even know he was dead until a week later because I was on a mission and I couldn't be reached. I wasn't there to say goodbye to him. I couldn't come home to see him before he died. I was completely shattered, Belle. I was lost and couldn't function for weeks. I loved that man so much, but when he needed me, I wasn't there."

"It is not your fault," Belle said, ignoring how the name tugged at her memory. Right now, Cole was revealing something so deep to her, and she didn't want to seem distracted. "You were serving your country. If you could, you would have been with him."

He shook his head. "It isn't just that. When Dad died, we weren't on speaking terms. We had a serious quarrel before I left for Afghanistan. He wanted me to leave the Marines, give up my dream of writing, and come home to join the family business. But I didn't want to run the family business."

167

"Why not? What type of business was it?"

"It was a logging company that had been owned by the family and passed down for three generations. In my opinion, it was just stripping the environment and wasn't even very profitable anymore. I wanted to reforest the land and give it time to regenerate. But when I told him I wanted to write novels and had even gotten published, my father scoffed and told me I'd need a 'real business' or 'real job' because I wouldn't make any money writing novels. He took my wanting to sell the logging company as a slap in the face because it had been in the family for so long. He accused me of living off the success of my ancestors and being a spoiled rich kid, not wanting to work."

"I'm sorry, Cole. That must have hurt to not have his support."

"Well, he said that in the heat of the moment. I know he didn't mean it. The reason he wanted me to take over the logging company was that he wanted to retire and try to get back with my mother after seeing her at an event. I was having none of it. I yelled at him and called him an idiot who had refused to accept that she didn't love him or me. I mean, she left me when I was just a child, like she didn't even care about me. She never even tried to contact me." He threw his hands up. "How can a mother do that? I told him I was never going to leave the Marines and join his business. I told him if he went after her, he no longer had a son."

Her heart winced in pain at the tears filling his eyes. He was so heartbroken. She knew he must regret not having been on good terms with his father before he died.

"I was a coward, Belle. I was furious. I was disappointed. I left that night for my tour. I refused to settle my dispute with him. I told myself he was being a fool. I told myself there would still be time for us to reunite. I was proud and couldn't apologize. But I was wrong. I was never going to see him again. After my mother cheated on him and broke his heart again while I was in Afghanistan, I wasn't there to comfort and support him. He died from a heart attack. I never got to tell him how sorry I was. I never got to tell him that I loved him so much." He covered his face with his hands and leaned into her.

Belle held him in her arms as he wept. She didn't say a word, feeling how much he was hurting. She now understood him more. He had gone through so much in life and was drowning in guilt.

Cole pulled away, wiping away his tears. "He tried to call me, tried to reach out to me when I was in Afghanistan, but I refused to listen to him. I was just so stubborn and unwilling to hear him out. If only I had. Before he died, he was staying with my mom, so Grandma didn't get to talk to him either. So she doesn't even know what his final feelings toward me were. She kept assuring me he forgave me, but I'll never know for sure. If only I'd given him a chance to talk to me…"

"He knew you loved him, Cole. He was your father and had to have understood you. Sometimes we don't understand our parents. We feel they're too overprotective. We feel they're not making the right decisions. But we love them, and they love us back. Cole, please don't do this to yourself. You've allowed this guilt to seep into your being, making you sad and alone. You can't continue this way. I'm sure wherever your dad is, he loves you so much and is proud of the man you've become. I'm sure he forgave you. He probably did a long time ago," Belle said.

Henderson. Where on earth had she seen that name before, and why was it nagging at her so much?

"You know the worst part of it? He wrote to me before his death. He wrote me a letter that I never opened. I was so angry at him that I didn't even bother. Even Grandma doesn't know what it said. I lost it, and now I'll never know what his last words to me were."

Belle's heart raced. Sweat broke out on her forehead. *Could it be possible?*

"Yes. I should have read the letter the moment I received it in Afghanistan, but I couldn't bring myself to open it. Then I got injured in the explosion and came home, and it went missing. I looked for it but never found it. Now I wish I'd read his last words to me. I wish I had a part of him with me."

"You still don't know where the letter is?" Belle asked, her throat going dry.

Was this the same letter she'd found in the Tony Graham book from the bookshop? What were the odds of that?

He shook his head. "I don't. I tried everything I could after he died, but it was too late. It must have gotten lost in Afghanistan. I just wish I got to say goodbye. I wish I could talk to him one last time and ask him what was in that letter. I'd let him know how sorry I am and how much I love him."

She looked at the gravestone where the name was written, then felt the blood drain from her face. *Hender* had been on the letter, with the rest smudged. Had it originally said *Henderson*? Cole and Claire had not been forthcoming with their last name until very recently, probably because Cole was so private. He trusted her now, so she had only just found out.

Her ears were ringing as she held onto Cole's arm.

"Cole, your father forgave you. I think I have proof."

Cole's eyebrows shot up as he pulled away and stared at her. "What do you mean?"

Belle explained how she'd found the book at the bookshop with the letter inside. "The name on it is smudged, and I didn't know your last name, so I had no idea it was from your father. At least, I think it's from your father. If I had known, I would have given it to you sooner."

"Where is it? Do you have it?" Cole asked eagerly.

"It's at my uncle's house, in the pages of *Hidden Treasures*, under my bed," she said. "I can go get it."

Cole hesitated. "Go all the way back home? Are you sure? You can just bring it tomorrow if you want."

"No. I want to go now. I know how much this means to you, and how long you've waited to know how your father felt. I'll go get it on my bike and come right back."

"No. Let me take you in my car," Cole offered.

"Are you sure? You want to go to my community?"

Cole nodded with determination. "Yes. This is important to me. It's time for me to step outside my comfort zone."

Belle smiled. "Let's go."

Cole led her to his garage and opened the door to reveal a shiny black car that looked quite expensive. Her eyes widened.

"It seems silly to even have this when I never use it," Cole said. "I bought it before…" He gestured to his face. "I used to drive it all the time. Now I keep it only for emergencies."

They got in. Belle couldn't deny that she was impressed with the clean, modern interior.

"You look like you've never been in a car in your life," he said.

"We aren't allowed to own cars, but we can ride in other people's cars. Like on the night I first came here, I rode in our driver's car, and I've ridden in my *Englisher* friends' cars back in Ohio. But I've never been in a car nearly as nice as this."

Cole chuckled. "Hopefully, it still runs." He turned it on and the engine roared to life.

They drove to her community. When they passed people walking on the lane, she ducked in her seat, not wanting to spark rumors.

"I'm sorry," she said apologetically. "People know I work for you, but I just don't want them to get the wrong idea about us."

"Of course. I understand," he said as he drove slowly down the dirt lane.

When they reached Uncle Josiah's farm, Belle went inside the house and grabbed the book with the letter inside. Then they returned to the manor. Fortunately, her aunt and uncle weren't home, so she didn't have to answer any of their questions.

Belle got back in the car and showed Cole the letter. "Do you want to read it now? Or maybe drive down the street a bit, then pull over and read it?"

Cole shook his head. "No. I want to wait until I get back to my father's grave, where I feel closest to him. This is important. I want to do it right."

They returned to the house and Belle handed Cole the letter. "Your father loved you very much. He would have wanted you to be happy. He would have wanted you to continue living and not hold on to regret."

"I know, Belle. I know." He looked away, then, with a sigh, looked back at her. "Thank you so much for this."

She watched as he opened *Hidden Treasures* and found the letter inside.

"It's opened," he realized out loud.

"I'm so sorry, Cole. I'm the one who opened it. I couldn't read the smudged names on the front, so I was hoping the names would be on the inside. That way, I could return it. I'm so sorry for reading it," Belle said, touching Cole's arm.

"Don't worry, Belle. It's okay. You got it to me, and that's all that matters. It's his name on the return address. It's his handwriting."

She watched as tears welled up in his eyes. Suddenly, she felt like an intruder.

"I should give you some privacy while you go to the gravesite," she said. "I'll make some tea in the kitchen."

***

Cole nodded. "Thank you." Yes, he needed to do this by himself, and he was glad she could see that.

After he walked out to his father's grave, Cole's heart pounded and his breath hitched in his throat as he gingerly opened the worn and smudged envelope. With shaking fingers, he unfolded the letter, his eyes devouring the words.

Dear Son,

I don't even know where to begin. I am so sorry for those hurtful things I said to you. I was so wrong. I also forgive you for everything. I do realize now that selling the logging company was the right choice.

You have the right to choose your career, and now that I've read your first book, I can see that you are remarkably talented, Son. Once I read your book, especially the part about the father and son who have a terrible argument but finally make amends, it all became clear to me.

I can see now you wrote that about us, and now I understand all the things you probably wanted to say but maybe you were afraid of how I'd react. I understand what you wanted to say now because of the story. The story pays tribute to our family history.

I understand you, and I am proud of you for serving your country, following your dream, and being a wonderful son.

I will always love you,

Dad

Tears now coursed freely down Cole's cheeks. His father had forgiven him! Oh, what a joyous day this was. The weight he'd been carrying around all this time had finally lifted.

"I'm so sorry, Dad, and I forgive you too," Cole said to his father's grave. "I also said horrible things to you. I should have been more understanding. I do think selling the logging company was the right choice, though I'm sorry it upset you. You were the best father I could have ever asked for, and I miss you so much." Cole bent his head and knelt in front of the tombstone. "Please forgive me. God, I hope You forgive me too."

Peace washed over Cole, and he smiled through his tears. The wind blew through the trees, rustling dead leaves and sending them spiraling to the ground. He felt a good, calming presence around him.

He knew, in that moment, that he felt the presence of God, and that he was forgiven.

Now Cole knew there was something else he had to come to terms with.

"God, You know I haven't prayed much since Afghanistan. Ever since the explosion, I've felt guilty for surviving when so many of my comrades didn't. Why was I in the back? And Echo," his voice choked on emotion. "She tried to save me and the others, but I lost her too. For so long I haven't understood why You spared me and not them. Why?"

Again, the breeze ran through the trees, sending flurries of snow flying. Cole sighed.

My ways are higher than your ways, he heard a small voice say in his heart. Where had that come from? Was it God speaking to him?

Cole trembled as he prayed, "I may never know why, but that's okay. I don't need to understand why things happen the way You want them to. I just need to have faith. Whatever the reason, Lord, I accept it. I've realized that what's been missing in my life is You, and I vow to grow closer to You again. Now I'm committing to living my life fully instead of wasting it."

The sun emerged through the clouds, shining warmth down on Cole. He closed his eyes, even more peace washing over him. Never in his life had he felt the presence of God more.

Have faith, the small voice said to him.

Now he was sure of it. That was the voice of God, speaking to his heart. He was filled with joy, and it overflowed out of him in the form of tears coursing down his face.

"Thank You, God. Now, please show me what you want me to do." He stood up, then saw Belle hesitantly walking toward him, with Beast following her. He motioned for her to come, and she ran to him.

***

"Are you all right?" Belle asked. Cole's eyes were red as if he'd been crying. She pulled her jacket around her more tightly, trying to ward off the winter cold.

He grabbed her hand, and they sat back down on the bench in the cemetery. Cole covered his face with his hands, a sob escaping him. She rubbed his back gently.

"Belle, I've never been better. You were right. My father forgave me. God forgave me. Now I have peace." His shoulders shook. "I can't wait to tell Grandma. This means so much to me, Belle. More than you could ever know. I guess I tucked the letter away in *Hidden Treasures*, planning to read it later. I was still so angry at him and didn't realize he was asking for forgiveness. Then I went on the covert mission. The book and letter must have been accidentally donated after I came home from the hospital. You found it and brought it to me. This was destiny."

Belle grinned. "I'm so glad, Cole."

"Also, I've finally decided to come to terms with the fact that I survived the explosion when so many of my comrades were killed, including Echo. I've accepted it as part of God's plan for my life." He gently took her hand. "This is all because of you."

"No, Cole. This is because of God," she told him. He smiled.

Something tugged at her heart. She knew it was God telling her she also had grudges and guilt that she had to let go of.

No. I don't want to, she thought stubbornly and looked away. *It's just too hard.*

"What is it?" Cole asked.

175

"You've talked to God about your survivor's guilt and you've forgiven your father and asked for forgiveness, but I haven't been able to bring myself to let go of my own survivor's guilt and forgive my family's killers," Belle admitted. "Now I feel like I can't move on with my life until I do."

Cole nodded with understanding. "That's exactly what you have to do, then. Afterward, there's something I need to talk to you about." His eyes twinkled, and her heart raced, wondering what he had to say to her. "First, I'll give you some time here alone."

Belle nodded. "Thank you."

As Cole walked back to the house, Belle took a deep breath and gazed around at her surroundings.

"God, you know I haven't talked to you as much as I should since my family died. I don't blame You for taking them. I know man has free will, and those burglars were heartless. I blame myself, God, for not being able to save them."

Her heart wrenched, and a few snowflakes fell around her. She pulled her jacket around her tighter, though the cold out there was nothing compared to the winter in her heart.

"I've been hateful toward those men, God. I can't forgive them on my own, I know that. I need Your help. I need You to thaw my heart and help me forgive them. Only then will I be able to move on with my life, to move on with Cole."

An overwhelming peace filled her, covering her like the blanket of snow on the ground.

Forgive them, Belle, a small voice whispered.

"I can't! It's too hard!" Belle cried out, tears slipping down her cheeks, almost freezing in the frigid air, but she didn't care.

Forgive them as I have forgiven you.

176

A strangled cry escaped her. "I forgive them, Lord. I want to forgive. Help me have faith. I forgive the men who killed my family."

As sobs overtook her, she felt as though the hardness that had overtaken her heart was flowing out of her, falling in drops to the snow on the ground.

Gone. The hate was gone.

"And God, I ask that You take away my guilt for being the only survivor. I don't know why I was in my room that night, or why You allowed me to get away. I still don't understand why You didn't allow the police to get there in time," Belle prayed.

My ways are higher than your ways, whispered a voice surrounding her. *Have faith.*

"I want to have faith, God!" Belle cried. "And I want to let go of this guilt. Please, God, take away my guilt. I should have asked You so long ago instead of carrying it around, letting it weigh me down."

Like the breeze that lifted flurries of snow from the ground, her guilt was also lifted from her, leaving behind that peaceful feeling and a heart full of joy.

"Thank You," she choked out. "I miss them, God."

I am with you always.

She nodded, sending up a wordless prayer. She didn't have the words, but she knew God knew her heart.

As she stood and looked around, it was as if she was seeing the world in a new light. The colors seemed brighter, the white of the snow seemed to glow.

Cole slowly walked toward her and she waved to him. He then hurried to meet her, and they sat on the bench again.

"How do you feel?" he asked.

"I feel like a weight has been lifted off of me," Belle said breathlessly. "I've never felt so close to God."

"Me too. I felt the exact same way." Cole took her hand.

"I'm so glad we were both finally able to do this," Belle said, wiping away her tears. "I felt as though it was holding me back from my life, all that guilt and the hate in my heart I had for those murderers."

"I think it was holding us back, but we're past all of that now. Now, it's time for us to begin our lives anew. Belle, I believe God brought you to me. I believe all of this happened for a reason. I've realized something that I should have told you a while ago," Cole said, squeezing her hands and leaning toward her. Joy and excitement shone in his eyes, as if he could barely contain his emotions.

"What are you saying?" Belle asked, raising one eyebrow. Her heart raced. Was he about to say what she wished he'd say?

"That I love you, Belle," Cole said quietly.

She looked up at him. All she saw in his eyes was sincerity. A few snowflakes fell from the sky. "You… You love me?"

"Yes, Belle. I know I was a jerk to you when we first met. I had no confidence in myself. I thought you'd be repulsed at the sight of me, but you weren't. You're an inspiration. I wanted to build a wall around myself, but you weakened my resolve, and then I got to know you more. I got to hear you laugh. I got to see how beautiful you are inside and out."

So many thoughts swirled through her mind like the snowflakes that flurried around them. What about her aunt and uncle? What about her community?

"I don't want to get you in trouble, Belle. But I can't keep my feelings a secret anymore. Not when I could lose you to someone else. I understand if you don't love me, but I just had to tell you," Cole confessed.

Belle admitted, "I want to be with you, Cole, and I love you, too. I love you so much, it hurts when I'm not with you. But we're from two different worlds. I'm Amish, and you're not."

"I know that. I'll do whatever it takes to be with you. I'll join the Amish if you want me to. I'll give up this manor and this life to be with you," Cole promised.

The honesty radiated from him. As much as she wanted to be with him, she couldn't let him make such a sacrifice, which he could regret later on. "No, Cole. I can't let you do that. Why don't we give this some time and some serious thought?"

"For me, there's nothing to think about, Belle. My feelings won't change. You made me live again. You make me happy. You've made me a changed man, and I don't want to stop feeling this way, ever."

When he reached for her, pulling her into a hug, she went to him, her head resting on his chest. She felt so safe in his arms.

He leaned his face down, and when Belle realized what was about to happen, her heart leaped. She smiled, looking up at him, slowly closing her eyes as he lowered his lips to hers.

Before their lips could meet, something shook a bush nearby. Belle jumped, jolted out of the perfect moment as Beast ran to the bush, barking loudly.

"What was that?" she whispered, her pulse racing.

"Probably a squirrel," Cole murmured. "There are lots of animals out here." He pulled her to his chest again, and she happily let him, but the moment had passed.

She felt right at home, even if she knew it was wrong. She wished she could be in his arms forever. Even if it was for the moment, she could imagine a life with this man whom she was scared to love.

Chapter Thirteen

Belle went home with a smile. It was certainly one of the best days of her life. So much was going through her mind. Cole had confided a lot in her, which had unraveled mysteries about himself. It still seemed so surreal that the letter in the book belonged to him.

Gilbert's buggy was outside her uncle's house.

Groaning inwardly, she thought, *What is he doing here?*

When she stepped into the house, she could feel the tension. Gilbert got up from a chair at the kitchen table, unable to meet her eyes. Her aunt was crying, and her uncle was pacing.

"I'm sorry, Belle, but I had to tell them. They need to know," Gilbert said.

Belle's eyes narrowed in confusion. "What are you talking about? How I turned down your proposal?"

Aunt Greta gasped softly. "Belle, is this true?"

"I was going to tell you today," Belle said. "It happened only yesterday."

"Well, that isn't the only thing I came here to tell you, Greta and Josiah." Gilbert turned to Belle. "I saw you come home in a dark car with a stranger this afternoon, then leave again. I thought it was odd, and I was worried about you, so I followed you to work, to the manor. I saw you with him."

The blood drained from her face. What exactly had he seen? Was it when they had held hands outside, or hugged, or…almost kissed? Her heart raced.

"Well, yes. I work there. Everyone knows that," Belle said, trying to act calm.

"I'm worried about you, Belle. You can't be with him. He's not Amish," Gilbert said with concern. "You deserve better."

Anger coursed through her veins. "You don't know what's best for me, Gilbert!"

"Belle," her aunt whispered harshly.

"I saw you kiss him," Gilbert blurted.

Aunt Greta and Uncle Josiah gasped.

Belle's blood was infused with angry fire. "That's a lie. We almost kissed, but we didn't actually kiss. You were in the bushes, weren't you? I heard you. Clearly, you couldn't see us well and your vision was obstructed by the leaves. How dare you follow me and spy on me?"

"But...but..." he stammered.

"You should leave," Belle said quietly to Gilbert.

Aunt Greta gasped in horror.

"I'm sorry, Belle," Gilbert said with his head lowered, walking past her. "I just want the best for you."

"And you deserve someone better for you, Gilbert. Why, there's a young woman you know well who's in love with you, but you can't even see it."

Confusion clouded Gilbert's face. "Who?"

"She hasn't told you yet?" Belle asked. She shook her head. "It's not my place. She'll tell you when she's ready."

Gilbert glanced around awkwardly, then backed toward the door. "I'm sorry," he muttered. "I should go." He fumbled with the door and walked out.

Silence shrouded the living room and Uncle Josiah stopped pacing. When he looked at her, his eyes conveyed his disappointment. "You're romantically involved with an *Englisher*?" he spat. "Be honest. Did you kiss him?"

"No!" Belle retorted. "Gilbert was lying. We didn't actually kiss. We were talking."

"You almost did," Aunt Greta added, shaking her head. "Is he Amish? Is he one of us? Does he know our ways? Of course, he doesn't. Otherwise, he wouldn't have held you close to him. If he was one of us, he would know not to kiss you."

"He didn't kiss me!" Belle shouted, throwing her hands up in frustration.

"We're so afraid of losing you to this *Englisher*. We promised your parents to take care of you, but how can we do that if you're living somewhere else, married to an *Englisher*?" Uncle Josiah asked.

"Hold on a minute. No one said anything about me marrying him." Belle put her hands on her hips.

"Where do you think this is heading? He's not one of us, Belle. Why are you doing this to yourself? Why are you trying to ruin your life? You're a young woman who should be thinking of joining the Amish church and starting her own family with a nice Amish man, not some *Englisher* who doesn't know our ways." Aunt Greta crossed her arms.

Uncle Josiah stepped forward and put a hand on his wife's shoulder to calm her. He took a deep breath. This time, when he stared at Belle, there was sadness in his eyes.

"I know how much you're hurting from the loss of your family. I miss them every day as well, Belle, but this isn't what they would have wanted for you. You have a future, and it's not with that man," he said.

"Do you feel a connection with him because you've both been through a tragedy?" Aunt Greta asked. "I've heard he has burn scars, so something terrible must have happened to him."

"Yes, something terrible did happen to him," Belle said, sitting at the table with her aunt. "And yes, I do feel a connection to him, but that's not all of it."

"What if you only feed each other's misery?" Aunt Greta asked.

Belle shook her head. "It's not like that with him."

"Is this because you don't feel at home here? Does living the Amish life remind you of your family?" Uncle Josiah asked. "Is that why you haven't been baptized into the church?"

"It's about none of that!" Belle said, slamming her hand on the table. "I love him. He's a kind, good, honorable man. That's why I want to be with him."

Uncle Josiah and Aunt Greta looked at each other. Then Uncle Josiah sat at the table beside Aunt Greta and across from Belle.

"Gilbert came to us with his concerns. He won't tell anyone what he saw—or says he supposedly saw. But you must put an end to it. Your home is here, and you must cut all ties with that man. You will no longer work there, Belle. It all ends now," he said. "Before things get out of control. Don't go back there."

He got up and walked away before she could say a word. How could she possibly not go back there again?

Belle turned to her aunt in desperation. "Aunt Greta, please, talk to him. I know he's concerned about me, but there's nothing wrong with Cole. He's a kind man, and I adore his grandmother. I'm her companion. He—"

"How is this going to end, Belle? What future do you have with someone like that? Someone who's not one of us? Do you think he'll understand our ways? You cannot serve two masters, Belle. You cannot be here and be there. You belong here, Belle. We've tried to make this a home for you, and we apologize if we have ever erred. Maybe we've failed you."

183

"No. You haven't failed me. You've done your best, and I'm grateful," Belle said, grabbing her aunt's hand.

"Your uncle is right. It has to end now, before you ruin your life. Your uncle is just trying to ensure you have a good future. You should listen to him. If you continue to work there, we can no longer let you live here, and we'll go to the elders about your situation so that you can be corrected by the church. I'm sorry. We can't risk bringing shame upon our household."

With tears stinging her eyes, Belle ran up to her room.

Hours later, Belle was sitting on her bed, her eyes aching from crying, unable to sleep. She wanted to honor her aunt and uncle and not be taken before the elders of the church, but what they were asking her to do was difficult—seemingly impossible. How could she give up working for Cole, never go back there again? She had come to care for Cole and Claire deeply.

If she continued working there, where would she live?

Today had started as the happiest day of her life, and now it was a disaster. Her happiness had been snatched from her. Their time together in the cemetery played over and over in her mind. If she left, Cole would be cut deeply and attribute incorrect motivations to her absence. She had seen love in his eyes. He truly cared for her. If she left, he would retreat once again into his shell. Could she do that to him?

God, I asked for a way out. Please, don't make me go before the elders. That would be so embarrassing. Please help me make a decision that will not hurt those I love. Please God, help me find my way. Help me emerge from this a victor. And please be with Cole now and comfort him.

She kept praying, over and over, before drifting into a dreamless sleep.

The next day, Belle stayed home. As much as she wanted to go to the manor and tell Cole and Claire what had happened, she needed to try to talk to her aunt and uncle.

"What do you want me to say, Belle? You're under my care. I'm worried about you. I won't allow my niece to walk down a path of destruction. No. I won't!" Uncle Josiah said when she talked to him again. "If you go back there, you are no longer welcome in this house, and we will take you to the elders to be reprimanded."

"I have to go back to quit, at least," Belle protested.

"No," Uncle Josiah said with a wave of his hand. "I can't allow that. He'll just try to talk you out of it."

"They'll worry about me," Belle said, giving her aunt a pleading look.

Aunt Greta shook her head. Her aunt refused to budge as well. She knew they were only trying to protect her in the way they could. They couldn't understand why she wanted to be with an outsider. It went against everything they believed in.

By the end of the day, she knew that there was no way her uncle and aunt would allow her to work at the manor anymore.

For the next three days, she didn't go to the manor because her aunt and uncle kept an eye on her. She was heartbroken. She wondered what Cole thought of her. He must have thought she was repulsed about his feelings for her. After all, she had stopped showing up the day after.

On the fifth day, Belle couldn't take it anymore. She needed to be with Cole. Uncle Josiah left for a meeting, and Aunt Greta went to see a friend who had just given birth. Belle left, her heart heavy on the bicycle ride to the manor.

She was just walking up to the door when it flew open. Claire hurried over to her.

"Belle. Are you okay? Are you hurt?" Claire asked with concern, hugging her tightly.

"I'm fine, Claire," Belle said.

"Where have you been? We've been so worried about you, Belle. If you didn't come today, Cole was going to go look for you. He has been

185

unable to sleep or function. He has been devastated. I've never seen him this way," Claire said. "He thinks it's because of everything he said to you the last day you were here. Or that you were sick, possibly."

"No, it's none of those things. Where is he?" Belle asked.

"In his office."

She didn't have to go to his office. He was now coming down the stairs. In a moment, his arms were wrapped tightly around her. She realized she had missed him so much, and she pushed back the tears. She didn't need them now.

"I've missed you so much, Belle. What happened? Were you sick? Was it something I said?" Cole asked, refusing to let her go.

Belle shook her head. "I wasn't sick, and it wasn't anything you said. Something has happened."

He led her to a couch and sat next to her while Claire sat opposite them. Was it her imagination or had Claire gotten paler?

"Are you okay, Claire?" Belle asked.

"Of course, I am, young lady. Now, what's wrong?" Claire asked, dismissing her concern.

Belle told them everything that had happened the evening she had returned home after her amazing lunch with Cole. When she was done, she could feel Cole's temper rising.

"They can't do this to you," Cole said, standing.

"Please, Cole. You need to consider where her people are coming from and their customs," Claire said. "You two being together is against their ways. They're trying to look out for her."

Cole took a deep breath. "I know your family cares about you, Belle, but so do I. I want us to start our lives together, if that's what you want."

She wanted the same as well, but so much was going on, and she had no idea how to handle the situation.

"I'm not supposed to be here, and I can't just up and leave the Amish." Belle stood, backing away.

"I'll join the Amish to be with you, if that's what it takes," Cole pleaded. "Please, Belle, I'll do anything."

"No, I can't ask that of you. I think you'd regret it later. I have to go. If my aunt and uncle return home and I'm not there, I'll be in huge trouble. I'm sorry." Belle turned and hurried out the door. As she got on her bicycle and rode away, her heart clenched.

The wind rushed past her face, drying the tears on her cheeks.

What now, God? Show me what to do. What is the right thing to do?

Chapter Fourteen

He hated the house so much with Belle gone.

It had always been his sanctuary, but not anymore. Not without Belle. He felt worse than he had before Belle walked into his life.

In the greenhouse, Cole watered the plants, carefully tending to the budding rosebush. With Claire not feeling as energetic lately, and with Belle gone, he felt responsible for taking care of the plants and reviving this place.

It was a shame that Belle was not here to see the rosebush's new rosebuds, which were starting to open.

Cole shook his head, chiding himself. He was doing just what his father had done—keeping this greenhouse alive for a woman, hoping that if he made it beautiful enough, she'd come back. He'd promised himself he wouldn't do such a thing, and here he was.

He'd promised himself he'd be stronger than that.

Cole's stomach rumbled in hunger, but he didn't do anything about it. Ever since she'd left, he hadn't eaten much. All he could see was the pain in her eyes.

Beast was also missing Belle. The puppy waited by the door every morning for her, and when she didn't come, he let out a sad howl.

Cole found Claire in the living room, reading. She glanced at him with a frown, then turned her attention back to the book. He frowned. Claire was getting thinner. There were bags under her eyes, as if she hadn't been getting enough sleep.

"Are you okay, Grandma?" he asked with concern.

"Of course. Why do you ask?"

"Because I care, and because you look pale," Cole said.

Claire sighed. "This issue you have with Belle has me under the weather. I was rooting so much for both of you. I thought you'd give me great-grandchildren. Seeing you sad has me down, and I know Belle must feel the same way, even worse."

Cole sighed. "I think we should employ a new housekeeper."

"No," Claire said vehemently. "We're not hiring a new housekeeper. I don't want anyone but Belle. We can manage on our own."

He knew how to cook now, thanks to Belle, but Claire would get lonely. What about the greenhouse? "Eventually, we'll have to hire someone else, Grandma."

"I know. But your priority right now should be getting Belle back. You need her. We need her!" Claire insisted, her face reddening.

"Grandma, why are you so angry?" Cole asked, taken aback by her rare outburst.

"Because you let her slip away! You didn't even fight for her. You should have gotten down on one knee and proposed to her. She would have left the Amish for you, I know it. If she was worried about what her family would do, you should have gone to them and spoken to them until they listened to you. You should have fought for her, Cole, if you truly love her." Claire stomped her foot, glaring at him.

Cole looked away, knowing she was right. "I'm a coward, Grandma."

"Yes, you are. But you don't have to be. You can make this right. It's not too late."

It wasn't as if she had a cell phone. The only way he could get across to her was by leaving his home and going to her house in the Amish community, coming face to face with her aunt and uncle and whoever else happened to see him.

A blast of cold ran through him at the thought. He hadn't faced anyone new—let alone a village of people—in so long.

Cole had lost Belle because of his insecurities. He deserved this. He deserved to have his love wrenched away from him. Besides, he couldn't take her away from her family and the Amish community. What if she resented him later on for it?

No. If she wanted to leave, it had to be on her own terms. She knew he loved her.

He had tried to survive after the explosion but Belle had shown him love, how to truly live. She had made him believe in a future. She had given him a glimpse of the life he could have, and now it was gone.

***

It was a warm day for winter, and Belle was out with Damaris, running errands in town. Damaris was saying something, but Belle couldn't grasp the words. Her mind was elsewhere.

"Are you even listening to me?" Damaris asked.

"Huh? Yes, of course," Belle said.

"Then what was the last thing I said?"

"Umm…"

"I knew it. Belle, is everything all right? Or am I just boring?" Damaris asked.

She was about to say something when she saw Gilbert walk by with a friend. Before Belle could stop her, Damaris waved him over.

Belle groaned, rolling her eyes.

"What?" Damaris asked, shrugging. "I want to say hi."

Before Belle could answer, Gilbert said, "Hello, ladies. How are you today?"

"Well, Gilbert, and how have you been?" Damaris asked with a broad smile.

"I'm fine, Damaris. We thank God," Gilbert said, smiling back.

"Are you going to the Singing this weekend?" Damaris asked eagerly. "I'd love to see you there."

"Yes, I am," Gilbert said, oblivious to Damaris' hint. His gaze, filled with concern, rested on Belle. Softly, he said, "How have you been, Belle?"

"Good," was her reply.

After an awkward silence, Damaris shot Belle a questioning look. Gilbert shifted his feet uncomfortably.

"Well, I'll see you around," Gilbert said before walking off.

Damaris stared after him, a forlorn look on her face. Belle touched her friend's hand, sorry to see Gilbert so oblivious to the fact that Damaris cared for him.

"You still haven't told him you love him yet, have you?" Belle asked.

"That's beside the point." Damaris turned to Belle. "What on earth was that?" she asked, throwing her hands up. "Is everything okay between you and Gilbert? I mean, I know you turned down his proposal, but that was the most awkward thing I've ever seen. Is there something else you aren't telling me?"

Belle sighed. She'd been holding this in for over a week, and it was hurting her. She just needed to share her sadness with someone. She couldn't talk about this with her relatives. They wouldn't understand.

"Can we go for a walk?" Belle asked. "I'll tell you about it."

The women walked quietly down the street for a while before Belle began to open up. First, she made Damaris promise not to tell anyone what she was about to say.

"I promise, Belle. You're my best friend, and your words are safe with me," Damaris said.

"I hate to tell you this about Gilbert, because I know how you feel about him, but it's only right that you know." So, Belle told Damaris about how Gilbert had spied on Belle and Cole and had told her aunt and uncle that he'd seen her kiss Cole.

"He outright lied to them, Damaris. He told them we kissed when we didn't actually kiss."

"Wow. I can't believe all this has been happening and you're just now telling me." Damaris scolded her. "If he was hiding in the bushes, do you think he just thought he saw you kiss?"

"I don't know. It's possible. Either way, he thought he was doing the right thing. I'm sorry, Damaris. I know you love him. Maybe he'd tell you the truth."

"This is so complicated, Belle. But yes, I'll have to ask him about it. I do hope he didn't outright lie. I can't believe you've been going through all of this alone. You and Cole are from two different worlds even though he lives down the street, but that doesn't mean that can't change."

Belle let out a mirthless laugh.

"Maybe your home isn't with the Amish. Though, if Cole really loved you, he would have asked you to marry him. Why didn't you accept Cole's offer to join the Amish?" Damaris asked.

"I can't ask him to do that. Especially with his grandmother. What would happen to her? I don't think she'd want to come here at her age," Belle answered.

"I don't think that's why. It's not because you don't think Cole would fit in, or because you don't think they belong together, or because of his grandmother. It's because you know you belong together *out there*, where you can be yourself and do what you dream about. Maybe God wouldn't have brought you both together if He didn't mean for you to be together. You haven't officially been baptized into the church yet, so if you leave, you wouldn't be shunned. Why not go for it, Belle?

What do you have to lose besides the love of your life?" Damaris urged.

Stunned, Belle stared at her friend, in awe at her advice. She hadn't expected that.

Belle had prayed to God to help her navigate this. Was this the way out? God knew what was best for her. She closed her eyes and took a deep breath.

She knew it would take a while to heal from the death of her family, if she ever did heal. However, she hadn't come this far to not move on and live her life the way she wanted.

"What about my dream of helping those children?" she asked quietly. Many times before, Belle had told Damaris about her passion for helping the organization that rescued children from sex slavery.

"I think if you don't work with the anti-sex trafficking organization, you may regret it later. You should go for it, Belle. That's all I can say. The Lord will never forsake us. He will never give us a problem that we can't handle," Damaris said.

Her friend's words warmed her heart. Belle wasn't going to give up on her dream. She had no idea where it would take her, but whatever the course, she would follow.

After hugging Damaris, Belle returned home. Her uncle and aunt had become more overprotective since Gilbert told them about Cole. They monitored her closely, and she had to tell them where she was going before she left the house. She knew they were worried about her. They didn't want her to bring shame and ruin to herself and the family. Gilbert had been kind enough and hadn't told anyone about her and Cole, and she was grateful to him. She knew how such news could ruin her and her family.

When she stepped into the house, the aroma of apple pie hit her, making her hungry for one of her favorite desserts. Cole came to mind. He loved apple pie as well. The last time she had made apple pie, he had eaten almost all of it, until Claire finally took the pie away from him. Tears itched in her eyes. How she missed them! She missed Cole and his mysteriousness. How he could make her laugh with just a simple word. Being around him had always given her peace.

But if he really loved her, he would have proposed to her or would have come to speak to her relatives. He would have taken her away from here.

She wondered what Claire was doing at the moment. Belle had come to care for her like she was family. She knew Claire must be upset about her absence.

Belle tried to push away the pain, but she couldn't. It would take a while for her to get over the brokenness she felt. She was going to hold even tighter to her faith in God to help her through this trying time.

Right now, He was the One who could give her the strength she needed.

Chapter Fifteen

Although she had forgiven him a little, Claire was still angry with Cole.

"Grandma?" Cole called, knocking on Claire's door. He got no reply. He called to her again. This time he heard a faint mumbling, like someone was in pain. After flinging open the door, he hurried over to his grandmother, who lay on the floor, struggling to get up.

"Grandma, what's wrong? Are you okay?" Cole asked.

"I'm fine, Cole. I just had a fall, that's all," Claire said as he helped her up.

There were bags under her eyes, and she looked even paler.

"What's wrong, Grandma?" he asked firmly.

"I told you, I fell," Claire mumbled, looking everywhere but at him.

Then he noticed it: the bottles of pills in the open drawer of her bedside table. He hurried to them, lifting one of the bottles to read the label. His heart began to race, and he turned to his grandmother. "You're sick? You've been hiding this from me?" he whispered, loud enough for her to hear.

"It's nothing serious," Claire said dismissively.

Nothing serious? Then why had she hidden so many bottles of pills in her drawer? Why did she look so tired? From what he knew, she ate well and rested well. It was more than that. He could tell from the guilty look on her face.

"Please, don't lie to me. What's wrong with you?" Cole asked. "Here, let me help you sit."

Cole helped her up, then helped her sit on the bed. She patted the spot next to her, motioning for him to join her. Weakly, he sat next to her.

"I've been sick for a while, Cole," Claire said.

"You've been sick and you didn't tell me? Why? Why would you do such a thing?" Cole asked as anger began building up inside him. He knew so much was happening in his life, but that didn't mean she should keep such a thing from him. "How long has this been going on?"

"My heart is growing weaker. I've been taking pills, but now it has gotten worse," Claire said.

Her heart? She had kept this from him for so long, infuriating him even more. But this wasn't the time to scold her. This woman mattered a lot to him. He loved her with all of his being. "How bad are we talking about?" he asked, not wanting to know her answer.

"I may have just a few months to live," Claire said. "It could even be a few weeks."

His chest clenched as pain overwhelmed him. Then tears began to well in his eyes. "No. Grandma, no!"

"On my last visit to town, I saw my doctors, and they told me my heart has gotten worse. They don't know when it will stop, but they gave me an estimate."

Then it clicked. All the times she had left on vacations. When she had been going to see her "friends," had she really been seeing her doctors?

"Why didn't you tell me, Grandma? Why? When were you going to tell me? When?" he snapped as he got up.

"I'm sorry, Cole. I know I should have told you, but you've been going through so much. You live like a recluse. I knew if I'd told you, you would have put yourself on the line to ensure that I was all right. That means going out of your comfort zone. Besides, I thought I was doing better. But then I began getting weak. Headaches. Dizziness."

He was such an idiot to not have seen what was right before him. He shook his head, refusing to accept defeat. "There has to be something we can do. We'll get you new doctors. We'll fly in the best doctors.

196

We'll arrange for a heart transplant for you. I can't lose you, Grandma. I can't." Tears spilled down his cheeks. "You're all I have left in this world."

Weakly, she got up. He opened his arms, welcoming her in for a hug as she rested her head on his chest. "My body is too weak to take a new heart, Cole, and I don't want to do that. You may not realize it, but I'm old. Besides, it would take years for me to get a heart on the waiting list. I know you have the money to push me up the list, but there are people out there who need a heart more than I do. Young and vibrant people who deserve a shot at living. I can't take that from someone else. I've accepted my fate."

"You deserve to live," Cole disagreed. He couldn't imagine a life without Claire. He just couldn't.

"I know, but I've lived a great life, Cole. I've lived to pursue my dreams. I've lived to be a wife, a mother, and a grandmother. I'm proud of how I raised you. Sadly, I may not live to be a great-grandmother because you let the woman you love slip away," Claire said with tears in her eyes.

Now he understood why she had been so insistent that he fight for Belle. She didn't want him to be alone when she left.

"I don't think I was ever going to tell you about my heart, Cole. You've been hurt too much. Your mother was never right for my son. She hurt my son so badly, but it was you she hurt the most. Then you lost your father and all who were closest to you, and you could never forgive yourself. You've gone through so much, Cole, and then with Belle. I didn't want you to worry about me. All I want is for you to be happy."

"I was happy with Belle," Cole said sadly. Belle had changed him. She had made him leave his shell, and he had become a better person.

"Yes, you were," Claire said, patting his face. "I knew from the moment you employed her that there was something different about her. My Cole wouldn't just hire someone on the spot. Then, when I saw her, I had a feeling I was about to witness a change in you. I watched it bloom. I watched how you changed from my grumpy

197

grandson to the happy man I once knew. Belle is an amazing woman, and I have come to care so much for her. You love that woman, Cole, and I know she loves you. The moment you let her leave that day instead of proposing, she must have concluded that you weren't meant to be together. But I do have hope. I don't want you to be alone when I'm gone."

"Don't talk like that. I can't bear the thought." Cole refused the truth. His eyes pricked with tears as sorrow welled up within him. "You're all I have left, Grandma."

"I'm old, Cole. It will happen to every one of us, and my time is near. I know so much has happened to you, but I want you to be happy. Someday, you'll find someone. I don't want you to remain trapped in here for the rest of your life. My life may end soon, but I'll always be grateful for the choices I've made. I loved and I was hurt when my husband and then my son died, but I continued to live. You have so much potential, but you underestimate yourself. You're scared of failing. Life is all about failing. We fall, and we rise again. That's the beauty of life."

"I don't want to lose you, Grandma. I can't... I can't imagine life without you. You've been there for me all my life. I know I must have been a pain, but you always stood by me. I can't lose you. There has to be some other way." He didn't stop the tears as they spilled. He couldn't lose Claire. They had become so much closer after the explosion. She was the only one he had allowed into his life. The only one he had allowed to look after him. The only one he had loved until Belle came into his life.

What would life be like without her? It would be empty. Claire was the only link connecting him to sanity. He'd lost everyone he had cared for. His mother. His father. Echo. His friends. Belle. And now his grandmother?

Cole would never recover.

It dawned on him that he was going to be lonely. Was he going to stay here alone? Whom was he going to talk to? Whom would he laugh with? Whom would he share his memories with? All he would have left was Beast, and he reminded Cole of Belle.

Claire tried to comfort him. "It's going to be all right, Cole."

He hugged her tightly, refusing to let go as devastation filled him. He wanted her to remain in his arms. He wished he had the power to heal her. He had money, lots of it, so why couldn't it save her? He closed his eyes. He wasn't going to be defeated. He'd do all he could to make sure he didn't lose Claire.

"Now, whatever comes for me, I'm happy to accept it. Perhaps it's time I go to be with your grandfather," Claire said with a sad smile.

He didn't like her talking like this. Grandpa could wait. Cole needed her more.

"I know what I'm saying, Cole. I don't want to see different doctors. I don't want to change my medications. I've accepted my fate. I've lived a fulfilled life, and wherever the wind takes me, I'll go. My body is tired of it all."

He understood what she was saying. He wanted to save her, but she didn't want to be saved. She had accepted her fate.

"I love you, Grandma. I love you so much," Cole said, blinking back tears.

"And I love you, Cole. I remember holding you in my arms when you were born. You were such a little thing, and I knew I was going to love you forever. We'll be all right, Cole. That I'm sure of," Claire said.

He didn't know whether to believe her. Life had treated him cruelly. Taken away everything he had loved, and now Claire was part of that loss. Did life have anything good in store for him? He was beginning to doubt that.

Cole heard a sound at the bedroom door. He smiled when he saw Beast scurrying over to Claire. Cole bent down and picked up the dog, then handed him to Claire. She held him in her arms, smiling contentedly and the puppy snuggled her.

Dogs certainly were perceptive. It was as if he knew she needed comforting.

Claire had made her decision and as much as it hurt him, Cole would live by it. However, he was going to make her last days memorable. He had been so selfish. He had been so focused on his own problems that he hadn't realized what was going on in Claire's life.

Never again. She needed him now more than ever. He was going to be there for her. He was going to make her fight, even if she didn't realize it. Whatever the outcome, if she did leave him, she would leave with the knowledge that he loved her so much.

"What will you do when I'm gone?" Claire asked.

He looked at her, stunned. "What do you mean?" he asked.

"You heard me, Cole. When I'm gone, what will you do with yourself? You'll have this big house and Beast. Will you continue to be a recluse until you die? Will you continue to hide your identity from the world?"

"I don't know, Grandma. When the time comes, I'll think of what to do."

She grabbed his wrist with surprising strength. "No, Cole. I know you so well. When I leave, you'll bury yourself in misery." Claire shook her head. "I can't leave you that way. I refuse to die leaving you like this. Promise me you're not going to be a coward."

"Grandma," Cole protested.

"Will you do something for me?" Claire asked, tears welling in her eyes as her grip on him loosened. He knelt before her, sitting at her feet, just as he did when he was a little boy and she told him stories.

"You know I can't refuse you." Cole would do anything for her.

"I want you to reveal your identity to your fans at that conference," Claire said.

"What?"

200

"Yes, Cole. The authors' conference is coming up. I want you to be there. Please, do this for me. Please, don't hide yourself anymore. I know I'm asking for a lot. I know I'm asking for you to pull off your mask and face the public's eyes, but I want this from you. You may not realize it now, but you need this. Please, Cole, do this for me," Claire said.

He looked away, his heart racing. He could always deny her this, couldn't he? He could ask her to make another wish. But he knew how important this was to her. It was going to cost him a lot. His privacy. His security.

"On one condition. You have to be there with me. I don't think I can do this on my own," Cole confessed.

She patted his hair with a smile. "I'll be by your side, Cole. Even if it's the last thing I do. Literally. Now. There's one more thing I ask of you," Claire said softly.

"Anything, Grandma."

"Go get Belle. Get her back."

***

Every day when Belle woke up, it seemed like a wave of sadness descended upon her. Even in her dreams, she wasn't safe from heartbreak. She had thought time would heal the damage Cole had caused, but time only made it worse. With every day that passed, she missed him more.

She tried to act like things were okay. That she didn't yearn for more outside the community, but deep inside, she was hurting badly. Perhaps what hurt the most was that there was no future for her and Cole. They were worlds apart. She belonged in her community, where she wore a mask, and he would stay in his manor, where he wore a mask of his own.

When she was done mending her uncle's clothes, she went to her room and pulled out her box of books from under the bed. She stared at the red and black cover of one of Tony's works. No, Cole's works. The author she had admired had ended up being the man she had fallen in love with. She was glad he was Tony. Writing must have given him the solace he needed when he had given up on the world.

Now maybe it was time to let all these Tony Graham books go. Maybe tomorrow she'd donate them to the local bookshop. Truthfully, she'd been avoiding the book shop, afraid it might cause painful memories of Cole to come rushing in.

No. She just couldn't bring herself to go. Not yet.

Placing her hand on the cover, she knew in her heart that these would only remind her of Cole if she kept them, causing her more pain.

There was a knock on the door downstairs.

"I'm coming!" Belle called as she hid her collection back under her bed. When she opened the door, she saw Damaris, and she hugged her friend. Belle had become closer to Damaris ever since the situation with Cole.

"I'm glad to see you," Belle said.

"I knew if I didn't come around, you'd be locked away in your room all week, reading. You need some fresh air, Belle. You look so tired. Have you been sleeping?" Damaris asked with concern.

"Well... I try to," Belle said. "Most nights I think about Cole and Claire. I hope they're doing well."

Had they gotten a new housekeeper and forgotten all about her? Hadn't she been more than a housekeeper to them? Was she the only one hurting?

"Do you mind going out?" Damaris asked.

"Umm... I guess there's no harm in that," Belle said. She had been stuck indoors for way too long. She called out her goodbyes to Aunt Greta, who was in the kitchen, telling her she was going for a walk with Damaris. Then the two women bundled themselves up and went outside.

"So, honestly, how have you been?" Damaris asked when they had walked a good distance from the house. "Have you thought more about what we talked about?"

"I'm fine. But, yes, I've been thinking about it constantly. I'm so torn about what I should do. My life is here, but my heart is with Cole. I'm just afraid to up and leave everything I know."

Damaris sighed. "You look so distant, Belle. Your body may be here, but certainly not your mind...or your heart."

"I'll be okay eventually, Damaris. Heartbreak is difficult to recover from. In time, I should be back to normal." However, even as she said the words, she knew she was lying. She doubted she would ever recover from her experience with Cole. There were some things one never recovered from. Perhaps time would heal her wounds.

"I'll be praying for you," Damaris said with a kind smile. "I'm not sure what else to say."

Belle nodded, staring at the ground. Yes, she'd experienced complete heartbreak when her family had been shot and killed, and that had nearly crippled her. She was still nowhere near recovered from it, and she knew she wouldn't be for a long time, if ever.

"Have you spoken to Gilbert since?" Damaris asked as they made the walk back home.

"Actually, he came to the house to apologize. He admitted that he lied about me kissing Cole to my aunt and uncle, and I've forgiven him. My aunt and uncle were also there to see him admit it, but they're still keeping a close eye on me. What about you? Have you told him you love him yet?"

"Actually, yes. He did also tell me he lied to your aunt and uncle. He admitted it was wrong, and I've forgiven him too. We're going on a date next week. He'll be taking me to the Singing." Elation covered

Damaris' face. "I can't believe it. After all this time, I'm finally going to go on a date with him."

"I'm so happy for you," Belle said, pulling her into a hug. "He really is a good man. I know you'll be great for each other. Truly, I wish you the best."

"Thank you, Belle. I'm so glad everything worked out."

"Me too." Belle smiled at her friend. "You were so brave to tell him how you felt, to take action like that."

"You know, you could be brave too. You're moping around here, waiting for Cole to fix everything, when you could fix the problem yourself. I know you want to be with Cole, so why don't you take the leap of faith we both know you're meant to take and go be with him?"

"You mean...leave the Amish for good?"

Damaris nodded slowly. "I think we both know this life isn't meant for you. You want to do so much more, and if you stay here, you won't be able to."

Belle turned when a dark car came down the lane. They rarely saw cars in their community, and when they did, most of them belonged to passersby or curious outsiders who wanted to get a glimpse of their lives.

Her blood froze when she realized it was Cole's car. He'd left the manor—faced his fears—for her.

"Who's that?" Damaris whispered.

"It's Cole," Belle whispered back, stunned.

The car slowed and then stopped beside them. "Belle," Cole said from the driver's seat, rolling down the window.

They stared at each other. The first thing she noticed was how tired he looked.

"What are you doing here?" Belle asked, walking up to the window. "Is Claire okay?" she asked with worry.

Cole said, "She's dying, Belle. Her heart is failing. She just told me she has only a few months to live, maybe even a few weeks. She begged me to come get you."

"Oh, Claire!" Belle cried out, her hand covering her heart. The poor lady. She must feel so alone.

"Please, Belle. Get in the car," Cole pleaded. "Let me take you to see her."

She looked to Damaris questioningly, as if silently asking her opinion.

"Go, Belle." Damaris smiled and playfully shooed her away. "I'll cover for you."

"Thanks." With that, Belle said her goodbyes to Damaris, who had dozens of questions in her eyes. She hurried to the other side of the car and got in, looking around. Had anyone seen her? Had anyone besides Damaris seen Cole? News spread fast here.

The drive to Cole's was quiet. Belle noticed Cole glancing at her as he drove, but she ignored him. Yet her heart raced in excitement. It had taken all her self-control to not lunge at him for a hug. She had missed him so much.

Just as the silence was getting unbearable, they took the bend that led to the driveway of the manor, and the car stopped. Belle stepped out and Cole joined her as she walked into the house.

Beast came bounding toward her and licked her ankles, pawing at her.

"I missed you too, buddy." Belle knelt beside him and scratched behind his ear. He jumped up excitedly, right into her arms, licking her face. Giggling, Belle rubbed his back and tummy.

"He's really happy to see you," Cole said quietly.

With Beast in her arms, she got up and faced Cole, then froze when she saw the emotion in his eyes.

"Let's go see Claire," Cole said, suddenly turning and leading her up the stairs.

When they reached Claire's room, Cole gently knocked on the door. "Grandma? Belle is here."

"Come in," Claire said.

Cole opened the door. Claire sat in a chair by the window and smiled at Belle.

"Claire," Belle said, rushing past Cole. "I'm so sorry. I wish I'd come sooner. I would have if I'd known."

Claire shook her head. "You have your own life to live. I don't want you worrying about me. I'm not dying yet, dear. Right now, I can still walk around and live as I've been living. I still have some time, but my condition may deteriorate fast."

"I'm so sorry, Claire." Sorrow choked Belle's voice.

"I'll give you two a minute." Cole shut the door and left.

"I'm worried about him, Belle. He's worse off than before," Claire told her. "I'm so afraid he'll be alone after I'm gone."

Belle put a hand on her heart, guilt tearing a hole through her. "Claire—"

"Look, I know I can't ask that of you, so I'm not. All I'm saying is, if one or both of you are being stubborn or too afraid, you shouldn't let that get in the way of the two of you being happy together, if you truly love each other. If you're going to be together, don't do it for me. Do it for yourselves."

Belle stared at the floor, tears stinging her eyes. "I'm the one who's afraid, not him."

"You're afraid to leave the Amish?"

"It's all I've ever known."

"Would you be shunned if you left?"

"No, because I haven't joined the church yet."

"So, what's stopping you? You could live here with Cole, be happily married, and visit your community whenever you'd like." Claire's eyes twinkled at the prospect. "And you could pursue your dream of working for that organization that rescues children from slavery."

It all sounded too good to be true.

"If I'm going to leave the Amish, it should be because I want to leave for myself, not to be with someone," Belle said.

"Of course! So, why don't you? What's really stopping you, Belle?" Claire urged, leaning forward in her chair.

Belle shrugged. "Fear of the unknown, if I'm honest."

"Sometimes you have to give up something good to get something great."

"You are a wise woman." Belle took Claire's hand.

"No, I'm an old woman who has seen and lived through a lot. When I see two people in love, I know it."

Belle chuckled. "I'd better get going, but I'll visit you again soon. I promise. Even if I have to sneak away."

"I'll hold you to that." Claire grinned. "Now, go talk to my grandson."

Belle stepped out of the room and went downstairs to find Cole waiting for her.

"I'm so sorry about Claire," Belle said, then stopped when emotion clogged her throat.

Cole pulled her close to him. When he hugged her, she didn't pull away. Instead, she rested her head on his chest. She felt more at peace than she had in a long time.

Would he propose to her? Right here, right now, where they'd first met?

Oh, how she wished he would. She knew she'd be happier being married to Cole as an *Englisher* than remaining Amish, but she had to do it for the right reasons.

Then she pulled away and shook her head. "I shouldn't be doing this."

"We can make things work. We can. I promise you. I'll do anything," Cole pleaded. "I'll join the Amish so I can be with you. Then we can be together."

She couldn't make him do something that he would eventually regret, and she knew in her heart she wouldn't be happy that way. Belle's heart was not at home with the Amish. "No. I can't ask you to join the Amish."

"Why not? I'd do it, Belle. I don't want to ask you to leave for me. I'd never ask that of you. I don't want you to resent me later because of it."

"If I do leave the Amish, I'll do it only for myself, because I want to leave. Then, after that, I'll see what happens."

"Belle, I wholeheartedly agree. There's something I have to show you." Cole walked to the coffee table, picked up a paper, and handed it to her. "This is the email from the anti-sex slavery organization. They want to interview you in person at their headquarters in New York City."

Belle gasped, grabbing the paper from him. "Really?" Tears pricked her eyes. "But how would I get there?"

"I could take you."

"Really? You'd do that for me?"

"Of course. You know, if you're going to leave the Amish, it truly should be for yourself. For this. For helping children escape slavery. That's your passion, your calling." Cole gestured to the printed-out email.

Belle nodded slowly. "I need some time to think about this."

"I understand."

"Thank you for bringing me to see Claire. I'm going to walk home so I have some time to think." Belle's heart wrenched as she turned and walked away. A tear escaped down her cheek.

As she left, she glanced over her shoulder to see Cole standing in the doorway to the manor. The anguish in his eyes made more tears course down her cheeks.

But she also saw something else in his eyes: hope.

Chapter Sixteen

Cole sat in the dark of his office, his eyes glancing at his phone once again. Still, he was stopping himself from making the call to Simeon.

He continued staring at the phone. With a groan, he finally grabbed it.

Simeon sounded surprised. "Are you okay, Cole? How's Claire? How is she holding up?" he asked.

After he had found out about Claire's heart, Cole had called Simeon, the only one he could think of calling. His agent had told him everything would be all right and had even suggested a couple of doctors.

"Claire is fine. She's sleeping now," Cole said.

"Oh good." Simeon sighed in relief. "Do you have something for me? Please tell me the book is ready. The publisher is getting impatient."

"It's not ready yet," Cole admitted.

Simeon groaned. "You've got to be kidding."

"Sorry."

"Okay, look. I have to make one last-ditch effort at this. Will you please, please reconsider coming to speak at the conference? Just imagine what it would do for your career. I know you're scared, but it'll be worth it, I promise. We can do a whole promo on your big reveal. Right now, everyone knows your identity is a mystery, and that's part of what makes you so popular."

Cole was about to say no, but then he paused. He didn't really care about what it would do for his career, and he knew Claire wanted him to take this step, but that wasn't why he suddenly realized he had to do this.

He was the one who had told Belle that if she was going to leave the Amish, she had to do it for herself first and foremost. Not for him or anyone else.

And what a hypocrite he was.

Cole knew he had to reveal who he was at the conference, and he had to do it for himself. Not for Claire, not for his fans, not even for Belle, but for himself.

"I want to go, Simeon. I'll go speak at the conference. It's about time I tell my fans who I am."

There was total silence at the other end.

"You're not fooling around with me, are you? I don't think I can recover if this is a joke," Simeon finally said.

"I'm not joking, Simeon. It's time I do this," Cole said.

"Are you sure? This will bring you out of your comfort zone," Simeon warned.

"What, are you trying to change my mind?"

"No, of course not. Thank you, Cole," Simeon said excitedly. "Women will be swooning and falling at your feet. Tell your grandmother you'll be married in no time."

Cole rolled his eyes. He didn't want anyone but Belle.

However, Cole was beginning to question his decision. Simeon was right. He had millions of fans all over the world. Wouldn't they be disappointed in him or disgusted by him? Reading his fan mail, he knew some of his fans had created an illusion of him. They expected him to be some good-looking man, or at least a normal-looking man, when he was actually the complete opposite.

There was no going back now.

"I'll email you the details," Simeon said, then thanked him again and ended the call.

Trying to push away the daunting thoughts in his mind, Cole reached for his laptop and powered it on. He thought about Belle, and the memories of their time together flooded his mind.

She was his inspiration.

A few minutes later, he stared at the written words on the screen, and his fingers began to type away without hesitation.

Chapter Seventeen

A few days later, Belle took a trip to the bookshop with Damaris. First, they made some stops in town, running errands given to them by Aunt Greta and Damaris' mother, then they stopped by a small café to have lunch.

"Let's go. It's just down the street," Belle said as they left the café. She drove the buggy to the bookshop.

When they entered, Damaris immediately started browsing the titles.

"Good morning," Belle said to Mr. O'Malley.

"Good morning. Where have you been, Belle? I was worried, but I hoped for the best," Mr. O'Malley said.

"I had some personal issues," Belle said. It had been quite a long time since she'd bought books, and she couldn't wait to return home with exciting new titles.

"Well, it's great to have you back here. Many books have been donated and new shipments have arrived since you last came," Mr. O'Malley said.

There was only one writer she was concerned about. Tony Graham. Cole. Even if the store did have a new book from him, she wasn't sure she could bring herself to read it, though she was still curious. "Do you have any new Tony Graham books? Maybe some of his older books?" Belle asked, her heart racing.

Mr. O'Malley shook his head. "No, dear. I'm sorry."

Her shoulders slumped. Although she read other writers' works, she had been curious to see if she could find more of Cole's books here. She guessed she'd have to go home with some other books.

"This looks interesting," Damaris said, pointing at a book on a shelf.

Belle recognized the author's name, Kimberly Jones. She was a well-known Christian romance author. "You should go for it," Belle said.

With a smile, Damaris took it from the shelf. While she conversed with Mr. O'Malley, Belle went about the shelves, looking for books she would take home. She chose three books from different authors and joined her friend at the counter. Mr. O'Malley placed the books in brown paper bags.

"So, when will I be seeing you next?" the elderly man asked.

Belle shrugged. "I really don't know. I was looking forward to finding another book by Cole... I mean Graham, but I should be back when I'm done with these books."

With excitement in his eyes, Mr. O'Malley said, "Before I forget, there's going to be a big authors' conference in New York City where readers can go to hear their favorite authors speak. Tony Graham is going to be there. He's going to be the featured speaker."

Belle went pale. Her fingers dug into the brown bag. She shook her head. The Cole she knew wouldn't do such a thing. He loved his privacy too much to leave his home and go to New York. "It can't be," she whispered.

"I just found out. The writing industry has been buzzing with excitement since the news was made known by his manager. It has been all over social media the past few days. I wish I could go, but I'm too old to go traipsing down to New York City."

Cole was going to be in New York? Impossible. Belle turned to Damaris with surprise in her eyes. Her friend flashed her a comforting smile.

How had this happened? Cole was scared of what the world thought of him. But then, he had changed in the time she had known him. What if something had pushed him to change his mind?

If Cole could summon the courage to reveal his identity to his fans at the conference, then she could overcome her own fears and go to the conference to support him.

"Are you sure about this, Mr. O'Malley? Tony Graham has remained anonymous for years," Belle said.

"Yes. Hold on. I'll be right back," Mr. O'Malley said, hurrying into the back room.

Belle exchanged a look with Damaris. Her friend knew all about Cole being Belle's favorite writer. Thankfully, not many people had seen him the day he'd come to the community, and she had been saved from the numerous questions that would have been asked otherwise.

"Here it is. I printed out the email I got about the conference," Mr. O'Malley said, handing it to her. "Take it."

Belle took the paper from him. Shaking, she stared at the email. Mr. O'Malley was right. Tony Graham was listed as one of the authors who would be present at the conference. While every other author had a photo, Tony Graham had only a big question mark near his name instead of a photo.

"I know how passionate you are about Graham. I'm sure you would go if you could," Mr. O'Malley said.

"I can keep this?" she asked.

"Sure, you can," Mr. O'Malley replied.

"Thank you. Bye." She ran to the buggy, her heart racing in excitement, as Damaris followed closely behind.

"Belle!" Damaris cried. "You have to go."

Cole was going to be at the authors' conference. He was facing his fears, finally.

"This is incredible. Cole is going to New York. He's going to come out as Tony Graham. This is…" Belle said excitedly. She was so happy for him. She was glad he was going to take a leap. He deserved to be recognized for his works instead of hiding in the dark.

"Yes, it is," Damaris said. "And you need to be there for him."

"I can't do that." Belle wished she could be there. She wished she could be right beside him as he made one of the most important moves in his life. She wished she could hold his hand and tell him he could do it. Whether or not the public liked him, she was going to be there for him.

She was going to love him no matter what.

Tears spilled down Belle's face.

"What's wrong? Why are you crying?" Damaris asked, hugging her.

"I want to be with him, Damaris, forever. You have no idea how much I want to be with him," Belle sobbed. She missed Cole so much that it hurt.

"Then go be with him," Damaris said quietly. "I'm serious."

With tears in her eyes, she looked at her friend. "You really think I should go? And leave everything behind for him?"

"If you love him, then yes."

"What? Leave the community? My family? You?"

"Yes!" Damaris threw her hands up. "Come on, Belle. We both know you want more than this simple life. Ever since your family…" Damaris paused out of respect. "I know it has never been the same, and you've told me you feel like you don't fit in the community here."

"That's true…"

"You've become a shadow of yourself," Damaris continued. "I've seen you crawl into a shell. You smile, but it isn't real. There's so much sadness in your eyes, Belle. I don't want you to be this way. I don't

216

want you to be miserable. If Cole is the one you want to be with, if he's going to make you happy, then go be with him."

"But… I can't leave the community. My family. You…"

"Stop saying that. Don't worry about us. We'll survive, Belle. We'll miss you so much, but your happiness is what matters. Don't let the community hold you back from your dreams…and Cole. What do you want?"

"I want to be with Cole," Belle said with finality. "To go to the conference, interview for that job, and leave the Amish." She laughed as she finally said the words out loud. "That's what I want."

"You need to do what you think is best. Well, what are you standing around here for?" Damaris cried out with a laugh, making a shooing motion with her hands. "Go see him now. I can drive the buggy to your uncle's house, and you can go straight to his house if you want. You could call a driver to pick you up."

"It's not that far from here. I'll walk."

"You'd better get going then." Damaris playfully shoved her, and Belle laughed.

"Wait," Belle said, stopping and turning to her friend. "I don't know what's going to happen after this. I might not see you again for a long time. Things might not be the same."

"We have no way of knowing what will happen," Damaris said, taking Belle's hand. "No matter what happens, we'll always be friends. Right?"

"Of course." Belle's eyes stung with tears at her friend's loyalty. "You're the best friend I could ever ask for. I'm going to miss you." Belle gave her friend a tight hug.

"I'll miss you more. You'll be in my prayers, and when you can, please contact me. Be safe, Belle. I wish you the best," Damaris said, trying not to cry.

Belle dabbed at her face as she watched her friend drive away in the buggy. She turned and started walking toward the manor, anxiety overwhelming her. She had a lot ahead of her. It would be filled with ups and downs, but she would do it. She was, after all, a fighter.

She finally arrived at the mansion and ran up the driveway, her heart racing. Was she really going to do this?

Tears welled in her eyes. She was going to miss her family, she was going to miss her friends, and she was going to miss the community, but it was time to spread her wings and fly.

She walked up to the manor door and knocked, waiting impatiently.

The door opened.

"Belle?"

She looked up to the face of a stunned Claire, who quickly hugged her. The woman refused to let go of her for some time. When she did, Belle saw tears in her eyes.

"You're here, Belle. You're here. Tell me I'm not hallucinating," Claire said.

"No, this is me," Belle said. "You look tired. Shouldn't you be resting?" There was no way she could miss Claire's pale complexion, the bags under her eyes, or how frail she looked.

"I'll rest when I'm dead," Claire joked, but Belle frowned. Claire waved her hand. "Oh, Belle. I've missed you so much." She hugged Belle again. Claire laughed heartily, happy tears rolling from her eyes. "Cole will be so happy to see you. This will mean the world to him."

"I heard he'll be revealing who he is at the conference in New York. I can't believe he's going to do this."

"Yes, but he's still not himself, not the way he was when you were here," Claire said with a faraway look. "You know, I just don't want him to be alone."

Her throat constricted at Claire's words. "I'm so sorry, Claire. If he'll have me, I'll make sure that won't happen."

Placing her hand over Belle's, Claire said, "Thank you, Belle. I don't have much time left, but during the time I do have, I want my grandson to be happy. Now that you're here, I know my wish has been granted. Now, don't cry, I've lived my life. It's left for you youngsters to do the rest."

Belle fought back her. She didn't want to lose this woman, but with the stubbornness in her voice, she could tell that Claire had accepted her fate.

"I'm going to miss you, Claire," Belle said.

"I know, Belle, but I take solace in the fact that you and Cole will have each other."

They turned when they heard the sound of footsteps coming down the stairs.

"Belle?" Cole asked, then hurried toward her.

"Cole."

He rushed to her, pulling her into his arms. All that mattered was that he was holding her. She didn't think about her relatives, or the consequences, even if she should have been. All she could focus on was the feeling of his strong arms around her.

"I'm sorry, Belle, I should have fought for us. But you're here now. It's not too late for us," Cole said into her *kapp*.

"I was just scared and confused," Belle said. "I needed time anyway."

"I can't believe you're here. It feels like a dream. One I don't want to wake up from," Cole said.

"I've decided to leave the Amish for good, Cole. I need to pursue my career, and I want to be here with you. I love you. I've just been afraid to take this leap of faith."

"That makes me so happy. I love you too, Belle," Cole whispered.

"You make me happy. You inspire me. You make me want more. You make me want to live. I'm ready for whatever comes our way as long as we're together," Belle told him.

Claire clapped, making Cole and Belle turn to her.

"Finally!" Claire cried, laughing. "You two are the most stubborn people I've ever met."

"You're one to talk," Cole said to his grandmother, laughing. He turned to Belle. "When we go to New York City, I can take you to your interview. I already spoke with them, and we can schedule it during the time when we'll be there for the conference. What do you say?" Cole watched her expectantly.

"Really? They still want to interview me? Then yes!" Belle grinned and hugged him again.

Then she stepped back, a shadow crossing her face.

"What's wrong?" Cole asked.

"Now I have to face my aunt and uncle." Her stomach sank. What would they say? What would they think of her? "They may never want to see me again, even though I won't be shunned. I have no idea how they'll react. I think Aunt Greta will be very upset, though."

Cole took her hand. "Let me go with you. Let's do this together."

"Are you sure? You want to go into the community?"

"Of course. I'm ready to face my fears. I don't want you to do this alone."

Belle smiled. With him, she could do anything.

"First, I want to show you something in the greenhouse," Cole said.

"What is it?" Belle asked. "Is it the rosebush?"

"Yes. It's blooming." Cole beamed with delight like a child on Christmas morning.

The three of them went to the greenhouse, and Belle gasped when she saw the now thriving red blooms gracing the rosebush. "It's beautiful!" she cried.

"Cole has been taking care of it, since I haven't been feeling so well," Claire said, clearly proud of his work.

Belle turned to Cole and smiled. "Thank you, Cole. It's wonderful. It's a wonderful miracle."

"Well, you two are the ones who took care of it and never gave up hope that it would bloom again, even when I was convinced it was a lost cause and ordered you to leave it alone. I was a stubborn fool, but you both never gave up faith, just like you didn't lose faith with me," Cole said, tears reddening his eyes.

Belle felt her own eyes sting with oncoming tears. She reached out and held his hand, at a loss for words.

"Well, are you two going to stand around here or go talk to Belle's relatives?" Claire asked, breaking the silence.

Belle nodded. "Let's get this over with."

As they drove in Cole's car to Belle's uncle's house, so many thoughts somersaulted through Belle's brain. She could hardly breathe.

"I know you're worried about telling them, but you need to live your own life, Belle. Your parents wouldn't want you to be unhappy just so you could please your aunt and uncle, would they?" Cole asked.

"No. My parents always encouraged us to pursue our dreams, and they always told us they would support us, even if we decided to leave the Amish. They were wonderful parents. I know they'd be happy that I'm following my heart."

"Well, good. Remember that when we see your aunt and uncle."

As they drove up to the house, Belle's heart tripped. There was no going back now, and for that she was thankful.

Cole squeezed her hand, smiling at her, then they got out of the car. They walked up to the front door and knocked. Though Belle had been living there, it felt odd to just walk in now.

Aunt Greta opened the door. "Belle," she said, then her face scrunched up when she saw Cole, as if she'd smelled a skunk. "Who is this?"

"This is Cole."

Realization came over her aunt's face. "Josiah!" Aunt Greta called without taking her eyes off of Cole.

Uncle Josiah came to the door, looking as startled as his wife.

"We're here to talk to you," Belle said. "May we come in?"

Wordlessly, her relatives ushered them inside. After Cole and Belle removed their jackets and shoes, they all sat at the table.

"I think we know why you're here," Uncle Josiah said.

Aunt Greta's eyes filled with tears, and she looked away. Belle's heart clenched.

"I'll just come out and say it then. I'm leaving the Amish. I want to pursue a career with an organization that rescues children from sex slavery, if they'll have me, and I can't do that if I'm here. I want to travel and see the world. I'm in love with Cole." She glanced at him, and his small smile gave her the strength she needed to go on. "I'll keep my faith in God, but I can no longer call myself Amish. I'm sorry. I know this must be upsetting to you. But I do believe my parents would have supported my decision."

Aunt Greta let out a sob, covering her face. Uncle Josiah patted her shoulder.

"You haven't yet been baptized into the church, so you won't be shunned. I had a feeling you were hesitating because you were thinking of leaving," he said. "It seems as though since your family's death, you've been restless as an Amish person."

Belle nodded.

"I want you to know I love Belle with all my heart," Cole told them. "In fact, I want to make my intentions known. I want to ask Belle to marry me. We won't be living together until we're married. We can find her another place to live until then. Anyway, I'd love to have your blessing." Cole beamed as he glanced at Belle. Joy sparked within her and warmth filled her heart.

He wanted to propose? When would he do it? How would he do it? A thousand questions flitted through her mind, but she turned to Uncle Josiah when he spoke.

"We also support your decision," her uncle said. "There's nothing we can do to stop you, so we might as well give you our blessing." He smiled. "Truly, I'm happy for you both."

"What?" Aunt Greta cried, throwing her hands up, her face reddening. "Josiah, how can you say that? We promised her parents we'd look after her and do what's best for her."

"This is what's best for her," Uncle Josiah replied. "This is where her heart is leading her. If she believes it is God's will for her life, we need to support her decision. We've been fighting it, but now I see this is what makes Belle happy."

"I do believe it is God's will," Belle agreed.

Aunt Greta looked at each of them, at a rare loss for words. "But... How..."

"Belle, we pray God blesses your lives together. You are both welcome back here to visit any time," Uncle Josiah said. He extended his hand to Cole. "Please, take care of her."

Cole shook his hand firmly, looking him in the eye. "I will, sir."

"Cole is a good man," Belle told her aunt and uncle. "You don't have to worry about me."

Aunt Greta was still watching them, but her expression was softening. "Belle, this is what you truly want? Are you sure?"

Belle nodded. "With all my heart. I've never felt more at peace."

Uncle Josiah turned to his wife. "Greta, this is what Belle wants. She has made her decision. Let's support her in this. Let's not argue about this anymore. Agreed?" He raised his eyebrows at Aunt Greta, and her face softened in understanding as she slowly turned to Belle.

Aunt Greta stood. "I told your mother I'd do what is best for you. I suppose that now means that I'll be praying for you while you begin your new life." Tears fell down her cheeks, and Belle hoped that now they had been transformed into tears of joy. "I'm happy for you, Belle."

Tears escaped Belle's own eyes as she ran to her aunt. "Thank you, Aunt Greta. Thank you for everything. Thank you both for taking care of me."

"It was our pleasure," Uncle Josiah said.

"It truly was," Aunt Greta said, pulling away. "My heart wasn't in the right place at first, and I'm sorry about that. I'm glad we got to spend this short time with you here."

Belle nodded, knowing that if she spoke, her voice would fail her.

"Now, I know you must have people you want to go talk with here," Aunt Greta said. "Your friends."

"For now, I want to speak with Damaris most of all," Belle said, knowing her friend would be so happy for her. She didn't want to ask Cole to meet all of her friends. Not yet. He had shown courage by coming here, but she didn't want to ask him to meet several new people in one day. Maybe in the near future, they would come back and he could meet them then, when he was ready.

224

"I'm looking forward to officially meeting her," Cole said.

"You have our blessing," her aunt said, her eyes still glimmering with tears. "Now go and live your lives and may God watch over you wherever you go."

"Thank you both," Cole said.

Belle smiled at them. After gathering Belle's belongings from her room, they left the farm and went to Damaris' house.

As they drove there, Belle looked around, trying to capture everything around her. She didn't know when she would return, but she wanted to have a piece of home wherever she went.

***

"How many siblings does Damaris have?" Cole asked as he drove. Anxiety knotted his stomach at the thought of meeting more new people, but he had to do this to show his love for Belle. He wanted to meet the people she cared about most.

"Well, six. But her older brother Dominic got married to my friend Adriana and moved out, so five of her younger siblings still live at home with Damaris and their mother. Damaris and her younger siblings will be so happy to meet the person who's taking care of Beast," Belle told Cole as they drove. "They were quite fond of him."

Cole was silent, staring at the road ahead.

"Are you okay?" Belle asked.

He gripped the steering wheel with white knuckles as if squeezing it would ease the tension within him. "Yes... It's just that I haven't met anyone new in so long. Now I'm about to meet a whole family. You know the children and teens around here sometimes call me the beast."

"No, no. They're kind. You'll see. They'll love you. The only Beast around here is the little puppy you adopted from them." She smiled.

225

He remained silent until they arrived a minute later. When they pulled into the driveway, Cole got out of the car immediately, probably before he could talk himself out of it. Belle scrambled to keep up with him.

They walked up to the front door and Belle knocked. A few seconds later, Damaris opened the door.

"Belle!" Damaris cried, flinging the door open and throwing her arms around Belle. She then turned to Cole. "And you must be Cole. We haven't officially met." She stuck out her hand and, after hesitating for only a brief moment, Cole shook it. Damaris didn't even flinch at the way his warped skin must have felt. He appreciated that.

"So, Belle," Damaris said, a smile playing at the corner of her mouth. "You've made your decision, then? Are you leaving?"

"Yes, Damaris. I just told my aunt and uncle."

"We plan on getting married," Cole put in, then felt his face heat. "I haven't officially asked her yet." He glanced at Belle mischievously. "I have plans for that you don't need to know about."

Belle grinned.

"Well, I'm so glad for both of you!" Damaris said with a squeal.

Just then, five younger children clamored into the entryway and out the door, running straight past them and toward the barn like a whirlwind.

"Whoa. What was that?" Cole asked with a laugh.

"My younger siblings," Damaris said.

"Damaris, who are you talking to?" a woman's voice asked from inside the house. An older woman stepped into the entryway. "Oh, Belle. How nice to see you." The woman glanced at Cole but didn't step back or flinch. In fact, she just smiled at him.

"Hello, Constance. This is Cole," Belle said, beaming.

"Nice to meet you, Cole," Constance said, and also shook his hand kindly. Cole smiled, encouraged by their friendliness. "Well, I've got to get back inside. I've got a casserole in the oven." With that, she hurried back into the house.

"Do you want to go meet Coco, Beast's mother? Belle told me she gave Beast to you as a Christmas gift," Damaris said.

"Yes, she did, and he was the most wonderful Christmas gift I've ever received," Cole said. "I'd love to."

Cole, Damaris, and Belle made their way out to the barn. The kids were running around and laughing in the yard, playing what looked like tag. A German shepherd barked playfully, darting around the children. Tears pricked Cole's eyes when he saw the dog. She looked so much like Echo, it made his heart ache. Yes, Beast looked like a miniature version of Echo, but this dog looked much more like her. Oh, how he missed her.

When Damaris' siblings saw the three of them coming, they gradually stopped playing to stop and look at them.

"Cole, these are my siblings." Damaris pointed to each child as she said their names. "Dean, Delphine, Daisy, Danny, and Desmond. Hey, guys, this is Cole. He adopted Beast. Remember Beast?" Damaris asked.

At first, they were all silent, just staring at him. He felt his face burn, feeling their eyes on the scars covering half his face and his hands.

"How is Beast doing?" Dean asked suddenly, then sneezed loudly into his elbow.

"He's just a dog, Dean," Danny said, rolling his eyes. "Who cares?" The boy put on a tough act, but Cole could see the curiosity in his eyes.

"Does he love it at the manor?" Daisy asked, clapping her hands. "With all that room to run around, he must be so happy!"

Delphine walked slowly over to Damaris and hid behind her skirt, peeking out at Cole.

227

Desmond just yawned and rubbed his eyes.

"Well, yes, Beast is doing very well. He's very happy living at my house," Cole explained. He gestured to the German shepherd. "So, this is Coco, his mother?"

"Yes!" Daisy explained. "Come here, Coco!"

The dog scampered over, wagging her tail. Cole tentatively bent down. When the dog sniffed his hand and then rubbed her head against him, he couldn't stop the tears from falling. He wiped his eyes, memories of his canine companion rushing back to him, from how he'd played catch with her to the day she saved his life.

"What's wrong, Cole?" Daisy asked.

"Nothing," Cole said and sniffed. "It's just that Coco reminds me of a dog I used to have. She looks just like her. Beast is still just a puppy, but this dog really reminds me of the dog I had a long time ago. That dog saved my life."

"Is that why you have scars all over you? You were in an accident?" Daisy asked.

"Daisy!" Damaris chided.

"It's okay, Damaris," Cole said, putting up his hand. He told Daisy, "Yes. That's why I have these scars. I was in an explosion and my dog Echo pulled me out and saved my life. This dog reminds me of her." Cole turned to Coco. "And she was sweet, just like you, Coco."

Cole's eyes stung again, and he quickly wiped away another tear. How wrong he'd been, to think these children had malicious intentions when they'd named his puppy Beast. He could see now that he had been a fool to think that.

Just then, little Delphine came out from behind Damaris's skirt and slowly made her way toward Cole. He looked at her questioningly, wondering what she was about to do.

228

Delphine threw her arms around Cole's neck as he remained kneeling beside Coco. The girl hugged him tightly, making his heart melt. His eyebrows shot up at her sudden display of kindness, and he gingerly lifted his arms to hug her back.

All the other children rushed over to Cole and hugged him also, except for Desmond, who just watched. But after a moment, he joined them.

Cole couldn't contain his emotion as tears spilled from his eyes, rolled down his face, and landed on the dirt. He lost his balance and laughed as he fell over. All the children began laughing too. He rolled over and got up, dusting himself off.

"Thank you for letting me meet Coco," he said, clearing his throat, trying to get rid of the lump that had formed there.

"Why are you crying now, sir?" Delphine asked quietly.

"Well, Delphine, I haven't met anyone new in a long time. To be honest, I was scared to meet you today, but you've shown me love and kindness, and I'm thankful for that." Cole glanced over at Belle, who was smiling and also crying, along with Damaris.

As they left the farm, Cole was still stunned at what had just happened. He had no idea people could be so welcoming, so nonjudgmental.

"You've just got to give people a chance, Cole," Belle told him. "And that's what you're going to do at the conference. You'll find that people are a lot more accepting than you think. You might be surprised."

"I think you're right. I know I can do anything as long as I have you."

Hand in hand, ready for whatever life would throw at them, they headed toward their new life.

Together.

Chapter Eighteen

The crowd was vast, and as Belle peeked at the auditorium from behind the stage curtain, it seemed as if it went on forever. Thousands of people had gathered here for the conference. She'd never seen so many people in one place.

In the lobby, she had been captivated by the dozens of book stands she'd seen. She had also seen a couple of writers whom she recognized.

Ever since they'd arrived in New York City, Belle had been swept up in the bustling atmosphere. The day before, Cole had taken Belle to her interview, and it had gone well. Any day now they'd be calling her with an answer about whether they'd be hiring her. She tried not to worry and just kept praying about it, knowing it was in God's hands.

As she waited backstage with Cole and Claire, she rested a hand on Cole's arm.

"They're all here for you," she murmured. "Are you okay?"

"I'll admit it. I'm nervous." He tapped his foot anxiously, staring at the curtain, then glanced at her and smiled. "I'd be a wreck if both of you weren't here." Cole smiled at Belle and Claire.

"Well, we all know that no one could have stopped me from coming," Claire said with a chuckle.

Cole put his arm around his grandmother appreciatively. "Of course not."

"I'm just so glad to be here," Belle said. Gone was her prayer *kapp* and Amish dress. Instead, she wore a modest, semi-formal red dress. Her long, dark hair hung past her waist in curls.

"Have I told you how beautiful you look?" Cole asked, pulling her closer to him.

Belle's cheeks burned.

"I think that was the eighth time today," Claire said with a chuckle. She smiled at him contentedly.

"And Grandma, I wouldn't be here if it wasn't for your persistence," Cole said.

Claire nodded. "That's probably true."

"Seriously. I'm glad you both encouraged me to do this, not only for my fans but for myself. Thank you."

"Your father would be proud, Cole." Claire beamed at him.

Belle squeezed Cole's arm. She was also proud of him.

Unable to resist the urge to look out at the audience one last time, she was surprised to see that even more people had crowded the room. She spotted some people with "I love Tony Graham" T-shirts, while others waved signs or his books. They were all here for the man she loved, and her heart swelled. She hoped his fans remained just as enthusiastic when he revealed himself.

***

What Cole wanted to do was hide away from the world. He could still do that. He could leave here, go back to his hotel room, and get away from the crowd and the excitement.

But he couldn't disappoint his grandma, his fans who were out there. Most of all, he couldn't disappoint himself. He had come this far and would continue, even if it meant being laughed at or insulted.

"So, are you ready? Everyone's excited out there. They all want to see you. Bets are going on that you're going to be some stud." Simeon laughed as he joined Belle and Cole backstage.

"Sorry to disappoint them." Cole shook his head, amused.

"Oh, come on, Cole. You're a great-looking dude. Even with the…" Simeon waved his hand around his face.

"I have to agree with that," Belle said with a grin, putting her arm around Cole.

"Thanks." Cole laughed and looked away, blushing.

Simeon said, "You underestimate yourself, Cole. I'm happy that at last you've emerged from your cave." He turned to Belle. "I'm guessing you had some influence in this. Nice job. I've been trying to get him to leave that house for years."

Belle smiled.

"Let's do this and get it over with," Cole said gruffly. He was wearing a black suit but had turned down the tie his grandmother and Simeon had tried to force on him. He would have rather worn a T-shirt and jeans, but his grandmother had gone even paler at the idea.

"Let's go," Simeon said.

Simon walked onto the stage. Cole heard him say, "I present to you the reason why you're all here. Known as Tony Graham, this man has wormed his way into our hearts, leaving us obsessed with his books. He's too modest to say this, but he's a military hero who pulled eight of his comrades out of the rubble and flames when they were hit with explosives in Afghanistan."

Pride and confusion radiated on Belle's face. "Cole…" she said, looking as though she was full of questions. He had told her he'd pulled as many of his comrades from the explosion as he could, but hadn't told her how many.

Simeon went on, "The explosion along with his heroic actions injured him terribly and almost killed him. While saving his comrades from the fire, he was burned himself. Today, he reveals himself to us for the first time. I present to you Cole Henderson, also known as Tony Graham."

Belle squeezed his hand and smiled at him, giving him the courage he needed.

The crowd went wild with applause as Cole walked on stage. The light was so bright that it startled him for a moment. His palms were sweaty as he walked to the podium, his heart pounding. He could feel hundreds of eyes on him. He could hear the whispers, and he imagined what they were saying. Here on the stage, there was no hiding who he was. His scars were obvious, illuminated by the lights. He was afraid to lift his eyes, to see the contempt on their faces. Then it began.

"Cole! Cole! Cole!"

The chant began from the front seats and traveled all over the hall.

With tears in his eyes as they used his real name, Cole looked up at the crowd that had turned up for him. He didn't see disgust. He didn't see contempt. All he saw was excitement about seeing him. They didn't hate him. They didn't loathe him. They had come here for him, and he realized that with or without the scars, he mattered to them.

"Hello, everyone," Cole said, his voice halting the chants.

"I love you, Tony Graham!" cried a woman in the front, making everyone laugh.

This calmed Cole, who chuckled. He felt more relaxed now. "I must confess that coming here today took a lot of guts for me. I'm not the most handsome man here," Cole said, earning a round of laughter. "It's really exciting being here with you all. I have to appreciate you all for being with me over the years. For being patient. For reading my books. Without you all, there would be no me. After I was injured in Afghanistan, I was ashamed of how I looked, so I isolated myself from the world. Now I realize I was doing more harm than good. Your love and support have pushed me on, giving me something to cling to and believe in. Thank you." He paused, waiting for the applause to die down.

"I'd like to read a chapter or two from my new book that hasn't been published yet. In fact, I'm still writing it."

Belle was watching him from behind the curtain, on the side of the stage, beside his grandmother. She smiled in that beautiful way of hers and waved at him.

Happiness was an understatement for what Cole felt. Belle was here for him. In fact, she had left her home to be here for him. This was the best gift ever. Strong will and confidence overwhelmed him. With Belle here, he could take on anything.

He flipped open the manuscript and began to read.

The night we first met, she came to my door, standing in the rain with a cut on her arm. I bandaged her arm, but she healed my heart. I had no idea how much she would turn my life upside down...

He read several pages. When he finished, a huge round of applause followed his last words. There were tears in many people's eyes. There was sadness, but there was also hope. He looked at the woman who mattered the most. Belle was crying, her eyes on him. He had written this story for her. He had written the story for them, the sequel to *Hallowed Ground,* and it contained a love story. His love for her had kept him going, and now hope gleamed in his heart.

"I wrote this book for the love of my life, Belle, who's here today. Can you come up? Please, Belle?" he said without using the microphone, his eyes on her as she peeked out from behind the stage curtain.

"Come on, Belle," he persisted, and she took a tentative step onto the stage.

The crowd applauded. He went to her, escorting her to the podium. Shyly, she walked to the center of the stage with him.

"Your story is so beautiful, Cole. It's the best work you've written," Belle said once the audience quieted.

He chuckled. "Thanks. Even though it's sci-fi, the story is really about us. It's about you, Belle. But there's one scene in the book that hasn't actually happened yet in real life."

Belle looked at him with confusion, then he got down on one knee. The crowd went silent.

"Belle, I love you with all my heart. You broke the spell, led me out of darkness, thawed my frozen heart, and brought me back to life. Will you marry me?" Cole asked, taking a small box from his pocket and opening it to reveal a diamond ring that sparkled in the stage lights.

Behind the curtain, Claire gasped, tears streaming down her face. She clasped her hands in front of her heart.

Belle's heart filled with joy, overflowing in the form of tears in her eyes. "Yes!" she cried and threw her arms around Cole as he stood.

The crowd roared with applause. Cole pulled away just long enough for him to slip the ring on her finger. The Amish didn't allow jewelry or rings, so Belle had never imagined she'd wear an engagement ring, but she loved the way it looked on her finger.

He knew she had fears, but he was going to make a great future for them. They were going to pursue her dreams together, as he could write anywhere. With her by his side, they were going to strive for greatness. He was going to make sure she was happy. She deserved to be happy.

"I love you, Belle," Cole said.

"I love you, Cole," Belle said. Her fingers caressed his scars, ones he had loathed but that had always been beautiful to her.

"Kiss her already!" shouted someone in the audience.

His body rumbled in laughter and his hands wrapped around her waist as he pulled her to him. His lips met hers and he kissed her deeply, with applause erupting around them. He held on to Belle.

With her, he felt alive and brave.

Epilogue

"Settle down, kids. Mom is playing the piano." Cole wagged a finger at their children and turned to Belle. "I don't know how you can focus through all that racket." He chuckled.

Belle smiled, pausing the song she was playing. Cole had taught her how to play after they started dating, and seven years later, she was still playing every day and continuing to improve. "No, it's all right. Let them play. Kids are loud and there's nothing you can do about it."

Their seven children ran around the piano room with Beast, chasing each other as the dog barked playfully. Four of the children were adopted, and three were their biological children. Each was beautiful and unique in their own way.

"You're right." Cole raised his hands, imitating claws. "Especially when the hungry beast is chasing them. I'm gonna get you!" He growled loudly, and Beast barked again, wagging his tail. All the children shrieked, scattering. Some dashed out of the room, some hid under the piano.

Belle laughed out loud, resting a hand on her seven-months-pregnant belly. She'd always known she wanted many children, and her prayers had been answered. While working with the anti-sex trafficking organization, she'd met hundreds of children who had been rescued from sex slavery. She'd wanted to take each and every one of them home with her.

Four of them were running around her piano room now.

She glanced at the photo of Claire on the piano and sighed. "Oh, Claire. You would love this," Belle whispered. Claire had lived long enough to see Belle and Cole get married, but had died shortly after and hadn't been able to meet their children.

Belle took a sip of tea from the old, chipped tea cup that Claire had given to Belle shortly before she died. When they were at home, Belle refused to drink tea from anything else, as it reminded her of Claire's

236

love and wisdom, and the fact that value remained even in what seemed broken and damaged.

Belle and Damaris were still best friends, taking turns visiting each other.

Belle still visited the Amish community, usually at least once a week when she wasn't traveling for work. She was still in good standing with the entire Amish community, including her aunt and uncle.

As for the greenhouse, it was flourishing during these summer months, especially the vibrant red rosebush. It continually reminded Cole and Belle of how the bush once seemed dead but was given new life, thanks to the tender care of Belle and Claire. It showed him how new life can be restored, even when it seems impossible, just like the new life God gives to those who believe in him.

Though she traveled often, Belle always made time to tend to the roses and other plants in the greenhouse year-round.

While working with the organization, Belle had traveled all over the country to churches, raising money and finding sponsors for the organization. The more money they raised, the more rescue missions they could perform both in the United States and abroad.

Her phone buzzed in her pocket and she jumped. It was the anti-sex trafficking organization emailing her.

As she checked her email, she grinned at the scene before her, of her husband rolling on the floor with their children. Oh, how she wanted even more of them. If she could, she'd fill this entire manor with children, both adopted and biological.

"They wore me out," Cole said, plopping down on the piano bench beside her. "I don't know how you take care of them every day, especially while you're pregnant."

"It can be tiring, but I wouldn't have it any other way." Belle smiled at the children who were still tackling each other, squealing with laughter, as Beast yapped and playfully nipped at them.

Cole wrapped his arms around his wife. "I love our life, Belle. I love you."

"I love you too." She held him tightly, wishing the moment wouldn't end, though she knew all too well how fast time went. "I love our life, too. All my dreams have come true."

No matter where her job took her, no matter what happened, she knew she'd be all right as long as she had Cole.

His arms were her home.

About the Author

Ashley Emma knew she wanted to be a novelist for as long as she can remember. She was home-schooled and was blessed with the opportunity to spend her time focusing on reading and writing. She began writing books for fun at a young age, completing her first novella at age 12 and writing her first novel at age 14, then publishing it at age 16.

She went on to write 8 more manuscripts before age 25 when she also became a multi-bestselling author.

She owns Fearless Publishing House where she helps other aspiring authors achieve their dreams of publishing their own books.

Ashley lives in Maine with her husband and children and plans on releasing several more books in the near future.

Visit her at ashleyemmaauthor.com or email her at:

ashley@ashleyemmaauthor.com. She loves to hear from her readers!

If you enjoyed this book, would you consider leaving a review? Reviews tremendously help authors because they help other customers decide whether or not they want to buy the book or not.

Here is the link:
https://www.amazon.com/gp/product/B089PR9ML1

Thank you!!

Download free printable checklists at www.AshleyEmmaAuthor.com!

Looking for something new to read? Check out my other books!

Click here to check out other books by Ashley Emma

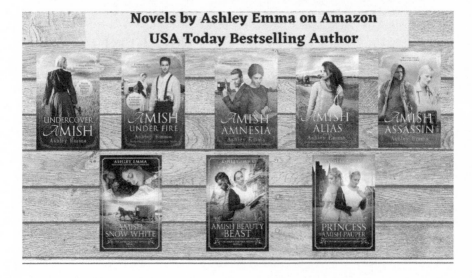

GET 4 OF ASHLEY EMMA'S AMISH EBOOKS FOR FREE

www.AshleyEmmaAuthor.com

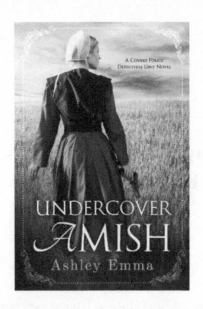

(This series can be read out of order or as standalone novels.)

Detective Olivia Mast would rather run through gunfire than return to her former Amish community in Unity, Maine, where she killed her abusive husband in self-defense.

Olivia covertly investigates a murder there while protecting the man she dated as a teen: Isaac Troyer, a potential target.

When Olivia tells Isaac she is a detective, will he be willing to break Amish rules to help her arrest the killer?

Undercover Amish was a finalist in Maine Romance Writers Strut Your Stuff Competition 2015 where it received 26 out of 27 points and has 455+ Amazon reviews!

Buy here: https://www.amazon.com/Undercover-Amish-Covert-Police- Detectives-ebook/dp/B01L6JE49G

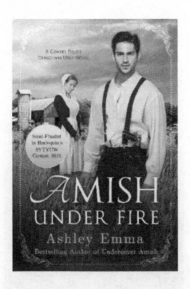

After Maria Mast's abusive ex-boyfriend is arrested for being involved in sex trafficking and modern-day slavery, she thinks that she and her son Carter can safely return to her Amish community.

But the danger has only just begun.

Someone begins stalking her, and they want blood and revenge.

Agent Derek Turner of Covert Police Detectives Unit is assigned as her bodyguard and goes with her to her Amish community in Unity, Maine.

Maria's secretive eyes, painful past, and cautious demeanor intrigue him.

As the human trafficking ring begins to target the Amish community, Derek wonders if the distraction of her will cost him his career...and Maria's life.

Buy on Amazon: http://a.co/fT6D7sM

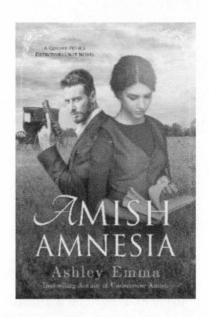

When Officer Jefferson Martin witnesses a young woman being hit by a car near his campsite, all thoughts of vacation vanish as the car speeds off.

When the malnourished, battered woman wakes up, she can't remember anything before the accident. They don't know her name, so they call her Jane.

When someone breaks into her hospital room and tries to kill her before getting away, Jefferson volunteers to protect Jane around the clock. He takes her back to their Kennebunkport beach house along with his upbeat sister Estella and his friend who served with him overseas in the Marine Corps, Ben Banks.

At first, Jane's stalker leaves strange notes, but then his attacks become bolder and more dangerous.

Buy on Amazon:
https://www.amazon.com/gp/product/B07SDSFV3J

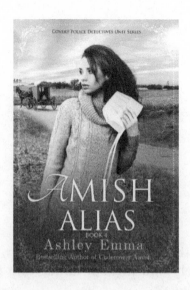

Threatened. Orphaned. On the run.

With no one else to turn to, these two terrified sisters can only hope their Amish aunt will take them in. But the quaint Amish community of Unity, Maine, is not as safe as it seems.

After Charlotte Cooper's parents die and her abusive ex-fiancé threatens her, the only way to protect her younger sister Zoe is by faking their deaths and leaving town.

The sisters' only hope of a safe haven lies with their estranged Amish aunt in Unity, Maine, where their mother grew up before she left the Amish.

Elijah Hochstettler, the family's handsome farmhand, grows closer to Charlotte as she digs up dark family secrets that her mother kept from her.

Buy on Amazon here: https://www.amazon.com/Amish-Alias-Romantic-Suspense-Detectives/dp/1734610808

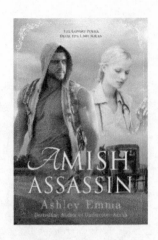

When nurse Anna Hershberger finds a man with a bullet wound who begs her to help him without taking him to the hospital, she has a choice to make.

Going against his wishes, she takes him to the hospital to help him after he passes out. She thinks she made the right decision...until an assassin storms in with a gun. Anna has no choice but to go on the run with her patient.

This handsome stranger, who says his name is Connor, insists that they can't contact the police for help because there are moles leaking information. His mission is to shut down a local sex trafficking ring targeting Anna's former Amish community in Unity, Maine, and he needs her help most of all.

Since Anna was kidnapped by sex traffickers in her Amish community, she would love nothing more than to get justice and help put the criminals behind bars.

But can she trust Connor to not get her killed? And is he really who he says he is?

Buy on Amazon:
https://www.amazon.com/gp/product/B084R9V4CN

Ever wondered what it would be like to live in an Amish community? Now you can find out in this true story with photos.

Buy on Amazon: https://www.amazon.com/Ashleys-Amish-Adventures-Outsider-community-ebook/dp/B01N5714WE

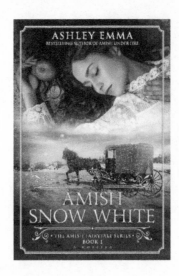

An heiress on the run.

A heartbroken Amish man, sleep-walking through life.

Can true love's kiss break the spell?

After his wife dies and he returns to his Amish community, Dominic feels numb and frozen, like he's under a spell.

When he rescues a woman from a car wreck in a snowstorm, he brings her home to his mother and six younger siblings. They care for her while she sleeps for several days, and when she wakes up in a panic, she pretends to have amnesia.

But waking up is only the beginning of Snow's story.

Buy on Amazon: https://www.amazon.com/Amish-Snow-White-Standalone-Fairytale-ebook/dp/B089NHH7D4

She's an Amish beauty with a love of reading, hiding a painful secret.

He's a reclusive, scarred military hero who won't let anyone in.

Can true love really be enough?

On her way home from the bookstore, Belle's buggy crashes in front of the old mansion that everyone else avoids, of all places.

Though she just moved to Unity, Maine, she's already heard the rumors of the vicious beast of a man who lives there, tormented by tragedies of his past.

But Belle's not afraid of monsters.

What she finds inside the mansion is not a monster, but a man. Scarred both physiologically and physically by the horrors of military combat, Cole's burned and disfigured face tells the story of all he lost to the war in a devastating explosion.

He's been hiding from the world ever since.

After Cole ends up hiring her as his housekeeper and caretaker for his firecracker of a grandmother, Belle can't help her curiosity as she wonders what exactly Cole does in his office all day.

251

Why is Cole's office so off-limits to Belle? What is he hiding in there?

Buy on Amazon: https://www.amazon.com/gp/product/B089PR9ML1

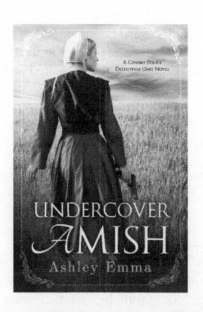

Chapter One

"Did you find everything you were looking for?" Jake asked.

Olivia Sullivan looked up to see her husband staring at her with furrowed brows and narrowed eyes. The anger flickering in them would soon grow into a hungry flame. He wouldn't yell at her here in the grocery store, but she should hurry to avoid a lecture later at home.

For a moment, she pondered his question. Had she found everything she was looking for?

No.

This was not the life she had signed up for when she had made her vows to Jake Sullivan.

"Olivia? Did you hear me?" His voice, low and menacing, came through clenched teeth.

"Sorry. I just need to find some toothpaste. I'll be right back."

"Hurry up. I'm hungry and want to go home."

Liv scurried with her basket toward the other end of the store, her long purple dress flapping on her legs. She tugged on the thin ribbons of her white prayer *kapp* to make sure it wasn't crooked and almost ran into her neighbor, Isaac Troyer.

She halted so fast, her basket tipped and her groceries clattered to the floor. "Hi, Isaac. I'm so sorry! I almost ran you over."

"It's all right, Liv. Don't worry about it!" He grinned, green eyes sparkling reassuringly. Then the smile slid from his face and concern shadowed his expression.

Fear swelled within her. Did he know?

She squirmed and avoided his gaze. "I'm so clumsy. I really should watch where I'm going." She shook her head, clearing her thoughts as she dropped to the floor to pick up her groceries. Isaac hurried to help her.

"Really, everyone does these things. So how are you, Liv?" he asked in all seriousness, using the nickname he used to call her when they had dated as teens. They had been so in love back then—until Jake came along and stole her heart with his cheap lies. Isaac was an old friend now and nothing more. The piece of her she had given to him when they had dated died the day she married Jake.

She told herself to act normal, even if he did suspect something. "I'm well. How are you?" She reached for a fallen box of cereal. Her purple sleeve rode up her arm, revealing a dark bruise. She took in a quick, sharp breath and yanked her sleeve down, turning away in shame.

Had he seen it?

Isaac rested his fingers on her arm. "Liv, be honest. Is Jake hurting you? Or did you 'walk into a door' again? You know I don't believe that nonsense. I've known Jake since we were children, and I know how angry he can get. And I know you might be silly sometimes, but you aren't that clumsy."

She sure wasn't silly anymore. Her silliness had also died the day she

254

married Jake.

Olivia stared at Isaac wide-eyed, unable to breathe. He *did* know the truth about Jake. Her pulse quickened as the grocery store seemed to shrink around her, closing her in. Who else knew?

"You don't deserve this, Liv."

What would Jake do to her if he found out Isaac knew?

"Isaac… Promise me you won't say anything. If you do, he will hurt me terribly. Maybe even—"

"Olivia! Are you okay?" Jake strode over to them. He helped her up in what seemed like a loving way, and no one else noticed his clenching grip on her arm.

Except Isaac. His eyes grew cold as his jaw tightened.

He knew.

Oh, God, please don't let him say anything.

No one would believe him, even if he did. Jake was known for being a polite, helpful person. He was the kind of man who would help anyone at any time, even in the middle of the night or in a storm. No one would ever suspect him of hitting his wife.

He hid that side of himself skillfully, with his mask of deceptive charm that had made her fall in love with him so quickly.

Jake finished piling the groceries into the basket as Isaac stood.

"Good to see you, Isaac." Jake nodded to his former childhood friend.

"Likewise. Take care." Isaac offered a big smile as though nothing had happened.

When Liv glanced over her shoulder at him as she and Jake walked away, Isaac stared back at her, concern lining every feature of his face.

Most of the buggy ride home was nerve-wracking silence. They passed the green fields of summer in Unity, Maine. Horses and cows grazed in the sunlight, and Amish children played in the front yards. Normally she would have enjoyed watching them, but Olivia squeezed her eyes shut. She mentally braced herself for whatever storm raged in Jake's mind that he would soon unleash onto her.

"Want to tell me what happened back there?"

Jake's voice was not loud, but she could tell by his tone that he was infuriated. Who knew what awaited her at home?

"I bumped into Isaac and spilled my groceries. He was just helping me pick them up," she answered in a cool, calm voice. She clasped her hands together in her lap to stop them from shaking, acting as though everything was fine. Their buggy jostled along the side of the road as cars passed.

Did he know what had really happened?

"I was watching from a distance. I saw him touch your arm. I saw the way he smiled at you. And I saw the way you stared at him. You never look at me like that."

Here we go. She sucked in a deep breath, preparing for battle. At least he hadn't heard what Isaac had asked her. Jake was always accusing her of being interested in other men, but it was never true. He was paranoid and insecure.

"You know I love you, Jake."

"I know. But did you ever truly let go of Isaac before you married me? Does part of you still miss him?"

"No, of course not! You have all my love."

"Then why don't you act like it?" His knuckles turned white as he clenched his fists tighter around the reins. "Why don't you ever look at me like that?"

How could he expect her to shower him with love? She tried, but it was so hard to endure his rampages and live up to his impossible standards. Yes, she had married him and would stay true to her vows. She would remain by his side as his wife until death.

However soon that may be. Every time he had one of his rampages, she feared for her life more and more.

She had given up on romance a long time ago. Now she just tried to survive.

If only her parents were still alive… but they had been killed along with the rest of her family in a fire when she had been a teenager. How many times had Liv wished that she could confide in her mother about Jake? She would have known what to do.

"I'm sorry, Jake. I'll try to do better." She told him what he wanted to hear.

"Good." Smugness covered his face as he glanced at her and sat up a bit taller.

When they arrived home, he helped her unload the groceries without saying a word. She knew what was coming. He internalized all his anger, and one small thing would send him over the edge once they were behind closed doors.

When everything was put away, he stalked off to the living room to wait as she prepared dinner. She began chopping vegetables, and not even ten minutes had passed when he stomped into the kitchen. As he startled her, the knife fell on the counter top.

Jake snarled through clenched teeth, crossing the room in three long strides. "You love him, don't you?"

"No, Jake! I told you I don't love him. I love you." She struggled to keep her voice steady. They had had this fight more than once.

"Are you secretly seeing each other?"

She spun around to face him. "No! I would never do that." She might wonder sometimes what her life would have been like if she had married Isaac, but that didn't mean she loved him or had feelings for him, and it certainly didn't mean she would have an affair with him. Happy or not, she was a married Amish woman and would never be unfaithful to her husband.

"I can see it all over your face. It's true. You are seeing him." He lunged toward her, pinning her against the counter top.

She tried to shield her face with her hands. The familiar feeling of overwhelming panic filled her. Her heart pounded as she anticipated what was coming. "No, that's not true!"

"After everything I've given you!" His eyes burned with an angry fire stronger than she had ever seen before. He raised his clenched fist and swung.

Pain exploded in her skull. Her head snapped back from the impact. Before she could recover, he wrapped his hands around her neck, squeezing harder and harder until her feet lifted off the floor.

She clawed at his hands, but he only clenched tighter. Her lungs and throat burned; her body screamed for oxygen.

This was it. She was going to die. She was sure of it.

A strange calm settled over her, and her eyes fluttered shut. It was better this way.

Her eyes snapped open.

No. Not today. For the first time in her life, she had to fight back.

She tried to punch him, but it was as if he didn't feel a thing. She tried to scream for help, but her vocal chords were being crushed. She reached behind her for anything to use to hit him in the head. Her fingers fumbled with something sharp, and it cut her hand. But she ignored the pain.

The knife.

She gripped the handle. Before she could reconsider, she thrust the knife as hard as she could into the side of his neck.

Blood spurted from the wound as his grip loosened. His eyes widened in shock, and his knees gave out as he crumpled to the floor.

"What have I done?" She inhaled shaky breaths, struggling to get air back into her lungs. Tears stung her eyes. Bile crept up her throat, and she clamped a hand over her mouth. Panic and fear washed over her and settled in her gut.

She had stabbed her own husband.

A sob shook her chest. "Oh, dear Lord! Please be with me."

There was so much blood. Her stomach churned, and her ears rang. Her head was weightless, and her vision tunneled into blackness. She slid against the handmade wooden cabinets to sit on the floor.

She should run to the phone shanty and call an ambulance, but she couldn't move. There was no way she could run or even walk all the way to the shanty without passing out. She would have gone next door to her uncle's house, but her relatives were out of town.

As her vision tunneled, she wasn't sure if she was possibly losing consciousness or dying from being choked.

Either way, she was free.

If you enjoyed this sample, view it here on Amazon:
https://www.amazon.com/Undercover-Amish-Covert-Police-Detectives-ebook/dp/B01L6JE49G

Made in United States
North Haven, CT
29 December 2023

46781580R00161